DOPPELGÄNGER

STUART JAMES

Doppelgänger was edited by Abigail Fenton.

For my wonderful family who I love more than life.
Thank you for all the support.
Tara, Oli and Ava.
The three most incredible people in this world.
Also, to my beautiful mother and father, Jimmy and Kathleen,
and sister Catherine who I'm certain looks down from above.

NEWSLETTER

Sign up to my newsletter and receive a free short story called Seance.

You'll also be able to keep up to date with all my future plans and get an insight into my life as an author.

Here's the link.

https://dl.bookfunnel.com/es984sqtnz

FOREWORD

They say we all have a double. A doppelgänger. Some say they live a similar life in a parallel universe. Many believe that once you see it, your fate is already sealed.

1

Saturday Morning

In the distance, Connor could see the Ashford train edge around a bend towards the station. A muffled voice announced its arrival with a warning about people's belongings.

A train going in the other direction startled him as it whizzed past without stopping. The sharp force pushed the wind hard against his face.

His phone rang in his pocket as the train pulled next to the platform, and Connor grabbed it, seeing Liv, his girl-friend's name appear on the screen. Jabbing the answer button, he held the phone in front of his face. 'Hey. You're up early.'

'Yeah. I want to get on with some work. So, all set for the big meeting?' she asked, the screen jumping as he saw her fill the kettle with water and flick on the switch. Her brown eyes opened wide, and her smile expanded as if to express her excitement.

Once the doors beeped open, Connor stepped into the train carriage. With the mobile phone held in front of his face, he watched as Liv made tea and sat on a chair in the kitchen. He took a seat by the train window, the carriage empty around him.

'Miriam is so talented,' he said. 'We've been after her for a while. It's great that she wants to showcase her paintings with us.'

'Make sure we're exclusive,' Liv instructed, placing her lips on the rim of the cup, the hot tea causing her to wince.

'I'll try. I need to negotiate the commission as well. I don't have a clue how much she'll want.'

Liv and Connor had been dating for just over a year and had met at work. They were employed full-time at an art gallery in Rye. Connor was responsible for exhibiting local artists' work and negotiating the best rates. When another colleague left, he'd interviewed Liv. After he'd recommended her for the position, they'd hit it off immediately, and then he'd mustered the courage to ask her out. She was from Hastings, a half-hour drive from Rye. Recently, Liv had been a full-time carer for her mother until she'd passed away quietly in her sleep, suffering from Motor Neurone disease. Her father had left, unable to cope with seeing his wife suffer, and Liv hadn't heard from him in over a year. Needing a fresh start, she'd only been in Rye a week before landing the job. After studying art in sixth form, it was a perfect opportunity for Liv to showcase her paintings one day with the dream of them both setting up a business together. Mr Humphries, the gallery owner, was nearing retirement age, but he'd recently suffered from a heart condition, and his health was slowly deteriorating. If forced into retirement, he'd promised he'd give Liv and Connor first refusal.

The train rattled on the track as it ramped up speed, the fields, lakes, and greenery blurry in his peripheral vision, and the smell of damp earth wafting through an open window.

'It paves the way for us in the future,' Liv continued. 'Getting our own business, I mean. Meeting potential clients and working out rates is great experience.'

'Yeah. Definitely. Can you imagine one day having our own gallery and showcasing your work?'

'I'm nowhere near good enough yet.'

'Liv. You are. You have an incredible talent. Don't think like that.' For a moment, her face froze as the reception dipped in and out. It looked like her eyes were shut, her mouth ajar as though in pain. 'Liv. Can you hear me?'

The picture returned after a few seconds. Liv was now standing by the fridge with the door open, swigging from a bottle of sparkling water. She must have leaned her phone against the pile of books that always sat on their kitchen table, surmised Connor.

'Yeah. I'm here!' She returned the bottle to the fridge, closed the door, and sat back down. 'I don't know why I'm so thirsty. So, what time are you meeting Miriam?'

'Ten thirty in Kings Cross. Starbucks.'

'Oh,' Liv said, 'you know how to spoil a woman.'

'Only the best with me.' Connor laughed, stretching his legs out under the table. 'So, what are you working on today?'

After sipping her tea, Liv placed the cup on the table

and with a deep sigh stated, 'I'm contacting a few local galleries about exhibiting my art. The pep talk you gave me last night has given me inspiration. I have to motivate myself.'

'That's great news. It's about time you believed in—' His sentence was cut short as a shadow darted across the hallway behind his girlfriend. Connor frowned. Rubbed his eyes.

'What's wrong?' Liv said, pausing. 'You look like you've seen a ghost.'

'I... I thought I saw someone behind you.'

'Stop! I'm on my own. Don't try to freak me out.'

'I'm serious, Liv. Go and check the flat is empty.' Listening to the chair scrape along the floor, he watched as his girlfriend stood, her breaths hard and intense as she turned.

'What did you see?' she asked, her voice low and husky.

'A shadow. It rushed along the hallway. Only for a split second, but I'm certain I saw something.'

Her body was still as though the screen had paused. Only her whispers alerted Connor to the live feed.

'What should I do?'

'Can you hear anything?' Connor asked, holding the phone screen closer to his face.

'Nothing. Hang on.' Picking up the phone, she reversed the screen and walked across the kitchen to the hallway. 'Here?' she said. 'You saw something here?'

'Yes. It might have been a glitch with the reception.' Connor could hear her soft footsteps as she walked along the hallway and opened the bedroom door. Flicking on the light switch, she scanned the phone around the room.

'Hello? No one's in here.'

'Under the bed. Check under the bed.'

Turning, she left the bedroom, closing the door. 'I'm not checking under the bed,' she whispered. Further along the hall, she opened the bathroom. Connor could see the white toilet with a reed diffuser, a decorative container filled with scented oil, placed on the cistern. Watching as she stretched her arm out and pulled back the shower curtain reminded him of the film *Psycho*.

Turning, she continued with the live feed, pointing the phone to the basin, and the hot tap leaking from a broken washer.

Drip. Drip. Drip.

'You must be imagining things. There's no one here.' Liv left the bathroom, closing the door, and crept back to the kitchen, again sitting on the chair and pulling it closer to the table.

'My bad. Sorry if I freaked you out.' He watched as Liv reversed the screen. Her short brown hair rested on her shoulders, and her eyes were bloodshot.

'Right. I have to do some work. I'll never sell paintings if I don't pull my finger—'

'What's wrong?'

With her forefinger pressed to her lips as if to order silence, she mouthed, '*Did you hear that?*'

'No. What was it?'

'It sounded like... like something dropping along the hall.'

'Liv. Get out of the flat. Go!'

Again, she pushed the chair back and stood. 'I need to check.'

'Get out of the flat. Please, Liv. I can cancel the meeting and come back.'

'Wait a second.' Placing the phone down, Liv left the kitchen. The silence was overbearing. Connor felt his stomach almost turn over as his fingers tapped on the table. A train passed in the opposite direction, causing the windows to vibrate, and his body swayed as the track veered to the left.

Watching the kitchen ceiling, the anticipation crippling him, his phone pinged to indicate a low battery. 'Shit! Liv, what's happening? Liv?' Shifting on the seat, he felt a rash develop on his chest, and his skin tighten. 'Liv.'

'Here. I'm here.'

The screen became blurry momentarily and then suddenly focused on Liv's face.

'What was the noise?' Connor asked.

'The weirdest thing. The lamp in our bedroom toppled over. How that happened, I'll never know.'

'Is the window open?'

'No.'

Visions of someone hiding under the bed raced through his mind. Someone crawling out and knocking the lamp over. His eyes focused on the hallway behind his girlfriend. 'My phone's about to die. I think the charger must be broken.'

'Don't worry,' Liv assured him. 'You know where you're meeting Miriam. I'll see you in a few hours. I'm going to get on with contacting a few galleries. Good luck.'

As Liv finished her sentence, Connor clearly saw a man standing in the hallway. Hair cut short, stubble on his chin.

Connor froze. *What?* His mind couldn't compute what he was seeing.

'Connor?' Liv asked, concern in her voice. 'Are you okay? You've gone—'

'Liv!' he finally shouted. 'Run! Someone's behind you!'

As she turned, the figure raced towards her. Liv's screams penetrated through his mobile as the call ended.

Connor shouted as his fingers fumbled with his phone, desperately trying to redial.

Someone was in their flat with Liv. And then Connor's mind caught up with the nightmare. A stranger was in their home, and he looked exactly like Connor.

2

*S*aturday Morning

Desperate for someone to help, Connor turned, his heart pumping hard in his chest, scanning the empty carriage. As he rushed along the aisle, the train's movement throwing his body against the seats, he dialled Liv's number, but it went straight to her voicemail.

'You're through to Liv. I'm not available at present. Please leave a message, and I'll call you back as soon as I can.' Her voice was calm and soothing.

'Liv. Oh shit! Please answer.' After ending the call, he dialled again. A sharp bend caused him to stumble as her voicemail kicked in, and he listened to the same message. 'Liv. Please call me!' It felt like his skin was on fire. Loosening his tie, he opened a shirt button, feeling his damp chest. Again, he dialled. Sweat dripped from his forehead onto his nose, causing his nostrils to itch. The carriage became blurry as his eyes watered. After listening to the message a third time, he went to say something. It felt as though his tongue was stuck to the roof of his mouth as he stuttered, 'I... I don't... er... I'm... fuck... please answer the phone. Liv!' The screen went blank as the phone powered off. 'No. Don't do this now. Oh, fuck.'

A woman's voice resonated through the tannoy speakers.

'We will shortly be approaching Appledore. The next station is Appledore. Thank you for choosing Southern Railway, and we hope to see you again shortly. Have a safe onward trip.'

Stumbling along the aisle as the train shifted on the tracks, Connor stood by the door, watching the platform, the large signs indicating Appledore, and a few commuters standing and waiting patiently for the train to stop.

His mind was plagued with the visions of the man standing behind Liv, rushing towards her, and the FaceTime call ending. The man who looked just like him. It was like a horrible nightmare, and he hoped that any second now, he'd wake in his comfortable bed next to Liv. *Who the hell was he?* Connor thought. The person in their flat was his double. A doppelgänger of Connor. Although he wore dark glasses, the cropped hair and thick stubble were an exact replica. *How? How is it possible? Am I fucking imagining this?* Scenarios played out of Liv running around the kitchen table, desperate to escape and screaming for help.

The beeping sounds dragged him from his chilling thoughts as the doors opened. Connor pushed through, barging against a young couple holding hands.

'Watch it!' the young guy shouted.

Across the tracks, a train returning to Rye arrived at the platform. Charging across the concourse, Connor reached the train, his body vibrating with pure panic. The carriage was a quarter full with families, couples, and a group of friends.

He stood in the aisle, checking his mobile phone, hoping it would miraculously come back to life. He jabbed the side button, but the screen remained blank. With the back of his hand, he wiped his brow, paranoid that people were staring at him. His cheeks burned, his ears felt hot, and the sun blazing through the window made him uncomfortable.

Through the glass, the fields seemed to drift by in slow motion. Cows and sheep grazed as far as the eye could see. Their world was tranquil and calm. Connor's had turned upside down in a matter of seconds, and it felt like he'd explode.

Please be okay, he thought. Beside him, a group of friends passed a phone around, and laughed at something. One of them tapped the screen, and they bunched together for a selfie.

'Hey,' Connor shouted. 'Can... Can I use your phone? It's an emergency.'

'Sorry,' one of the girls said. 'I haven't got much battery.'

'Anyone? Please, it's an emergency,' he repeated.

The girls ignored him and proceeded to take more selfies.

The minutes felt like hours, as though time was standing still. The world around him was oblivious to his situation, unaware of his desperation. The scene played over and over in his mind. Liv sat at the table. The figure charging towards her. Her screams as the call ended. *Who was at the flat?*

'No,' he shouted as his body shook, aware of the eyes suddenly piercing him. Scrutinising him. The group of friends eyed each other with nervous giggles and then took another selfie.

Again, the woman's voice over the speakers. Calm. Serene.

'We will shortly be approaching Rye. The next station is Rye. Thank you for choosing Southern Railway, and we hope to see you again shortly. Have a safe onward trip.'

Pushing his phone into his jeans pocket, he ran towards the doors, urging the train to stop. Shuffling from one leg to the other, head resting against the cold glass, he felt the doors shift open, and he charged along the platform and out of the station. As he rushed along the road, Connor checked his phone, seeing the blank screen, urging it to turn on. With his finger pressed against the side button, he held it for a few seconds and returned the phone to his pocket.

The flat was a ten-minute walk from Rye station. He could run it in around five. He dodged the many tourists outside coffee shops and cafes offering meal deals and announcing their specials. Above, a flock of seagulls squawked as they hunted for food. The screech of tyres and the sound of a horn bellowed around him as he ran in front of a car, holding his hand up to apologise. Although it was sunny, the cold morning air whipped against his face, causing his eyes to stream.

When he arrived at the three-storey building, almost stumbling into the trimmed bushes planted at the front, he took the steps two at a time, jabbed the trades button, and pushed the door back, hearing it pound against the wall. They rented on the ground floor. Flat number two. As he reached their front door, he saw it was slightly ajar. With a deep breath, bracing himself, he edged the door back and stepped into the dark hallway.

'Liv? Liv? Are you here?' Creeping past the bedroom, he noticed the lamp was standing and in its usual position. After a quick scan around the room, he backed out, stepping into the bathroom. The shower curtain was still pulled back. Turning, he walked back out to the hallway and made towards the kitchen. It felt as though his heart was in his throat, and he couldn't stop trembling. 'Liv,' he called again. 'Where are you?' Entering the kitchen, he saw Liv's phone still resting on the table with her half-full cup of tea.

But Liv wasn't there: the flat was empty.

Connor stopped by the table and placed his hands on the back of the chair she'd been sitting in only thirty minutes before. He screwed his eyes shut. *Think, think, think.* His phone, he needed to charge his phone and call the police. And that was when he saw something.

On the fridge door was a yellow Post-it note.

Written in black felt-tip pen were the words:

It will come for you, too.

3

Saturday Morning

Pacing the kitchen floor, Connor pressed the tips of his fingers against his forehead. On the side unit, his mobile phone was charging but hadn't yet come on. The note rested on the table. Connor picked it up, again reading the message.

It will come for you, too.

Seeing felt-tip marks seeping through the Post-it note, he turned it around. On the back were the words, "*Call the police, and Liv dies.*"

It felt as though his stomach dropped through his body, like a lift crashing to the ground.

His phone beeped, and Connor rushed over, holding it to his face to unlock it, and searched for the name Liam Anderson – his best friend who'd left Rye a few months ago. As he heard the dial tone, Connor eyed Liv's phone, the cup with her tea still slightly warm inside. Wiping the tears from his eyes, he pulled at the skin of his cheeks and inhaled deeply to release the stress.

'Hi, Connor. You okay?' Liam's voice was rough, as though he'd just woken up.

'You need to come back to Rye,' Connor said, his voice harsh.

'I am back.'

Placing the phone on loudspeaker, with an urgent tone, Connor asked, 'What? When did you come back?'

'I... Mum and Dad have gone away for a month or so. I'm covering Dad's plumbing jobs while they're on holiday. They asked me to look after the house. Some place in—'

'Why didn't you call me?' he interrupted, raising his voice.

'I've only been back a matter of hours. Chill out.'

Eyeing the note on the table, Connor sat, bracing himself for the conversation he was about to have. 'Liv's... I found... She's—'

'What's going on, Connor?'

'Liv's gone missing.' The words caused Connor to jolt as they left his mouth.

'Gone missing. What are you talking about?'

He went on to explain how he'd been on the train, talking to Liv on FaceTime, how he'd seen a shadow behind her and the figure charging through the kitchen, followed by him arriving home and finding the note. As it went silent, Connor thought he'd lost connection. 'Liam, are you there?'

'I'm... I'm here,' he answered, his voice turning to a mere whisper.

'What am I going to do?'

'Have you called the police?'

'No! They've written on the back that they'll kill her. Fuck,' he shouted, aware how loud he was. 'This can't be happening.'

'You've checked over the flat?'

'Yes. She's not here.' After a brief pause, Connor said, 'Liam.'

'Yeah.'

'He... He looked like me.'

'How do you mean?'

'I mean' – Connor turned around, looking to the hall-way, triggered by what he'd seen on the FaceTime call – 'he had cropped hair and heavy stubble. Roughly the same height and build. It was like looking at my twin.'

'This doesn't make any sense.'

'You're telling me! I have to find her. I love her so fucking much.'

'Have you called Ella?' Liam asked.

'No. Ella has nothing to do with it. This... This double of me, a... a doppelgänger, raced at Liv. The call ended. Now she's gone. Why would I call Ella? I haven't spoken to her for ages.'

'Maybe you should?'

'You're not helping.' The mobile phone began beeping. 'I have to go. Someone's ringing.' Glaring at the screen, he saw *No Caller ID* displayed along the top. 'Hello?'

A noise came through the speaker, struggling as though short of breath – a distorted, nasal rasp that sounded almost inhuman, like the snorting of an animal.

'What have you done with her? Answer me!' In the

distance, Connor could hear the faint sound of whimpering. 'If you lay a finger on her, I'll fucking kill you. Do you understand?'

Again, the breathing seemed as though the person or thing on the line was deformed.

'Connor...' The voice was distant and echoed as though coming from a basement or well.

Certain it was Liv, he jumped up, feeling the charging lead tug from the socket. 'Oh my God. Liv. Where are you?'

'You have to help me,' she sobbed.

'Listen to me. I've called Liam. We're going to come and get you. Tell me where you are? Hello? Can you hear me?' He heard chains rattle, and a clanging noise reverberated as though someone was dragging a stick on iron bars. It became louder as though Liv was not alone – muffled voices crying for help, desperate to escape. A door slammed in the distance, and Liv's gasps became faint. Again, he pleaded, 'Liv, tell me where you are?' His face felt hot, his skin itchy, and beads of sweat dropped into his eyes. 'Can you hear me, Liv?'

Silence. And then, almost like grunting through the phone, resembling a demented animal, the thing that had taken Liv ended the phone call.

4

Saturday Morning

Connor stood in the kitchen, his eyes almost piercing a hole in the phone screen and the battery indicating it was at five percent. Although he knew what the outcome would be, he tried desperately to scrutinise the call. Tapping the info showed only the date and duration: one minute and three seconds. There was no option to call, message, or email the person who'd rung him. Placing the phone on the side, with the charger still plugged in, he rushed into the bathroom, hoping something had been left behind – anything to denote who'd taken Liv and where.

The shower curtain was pulled back, and the bath was empty. The warm, sweet aroma of vanilla from the reed diffuser filled the small space and would be comforting at any other time. Backing out of the bathroom, Connor crossed the hall into the bedroom and, on hands and knees, flung the quilt back, checking under the bed. Boxes of photos, a pair of high heels, and his boots had been pushed to the side. Whatever had been in the flat had been hiding under the bed.

His skin went icy cold as a shiver darted through his body, imagining someone or something lying in wait while his girlfriend was in the kitchen, remembering her hearing the lamp drop during the FaceTime call. Lying in wait, they'd crawled out, ready to pounce.

As Connor stood, his brain became foggy, and the room started spinning. Composing himself, he sat on the bed and reached for Liv's pillow, smelling her fruity perfume. The sense of doom hit him hard. His heart rate quickened, and it felt like a fist was pushing through his stomach.

Only hours ago, they'd watched a boxset on Amazon, sipped wine, and talked about their plans for the future. How, one day, they'd buy a gallery together, displaying Liv's art, and people would come from all over the world to buy her work.

Jumping off the bed, Connor tried desperately to keep optimistic as he rushed from the bedroom and into the kitchen. Grabbing Liv's mobile phone, he tapped in her password and looked at the latest calls. Connor's name appeared numerous times, and a couple of friends in Hastings. There were no withheld numbers or anything that looked suspicious. The last few pictures were of Liv and Connor visiting London – a day out at Madame Tussauds, The London Dungeon, and an Italian restaurant. *Dungeon,* he thought, remembering the phone call and Liv's cries for help fading into the distance.

Placing Liv's phone on the table, the irony was almost too much – the dungeons. The waxworks at Madame Tussauds. A building full of doppelgängers.

His head began racing with images of the figure running at Liv. *It was me. But it couldn't have been. I was on the train. It was like looking in the mirror. Am I fucking losing it? I saw me, behind Liv, running at her. But I'm here. Liv isn't. I'm losing the plot. That's it. I'm going fucking mad.*

Stepping to the drawer, Connor grabbed a packet of Nurofen, placed two into his mouth, and slugged a glass of water he'd left in the room the night before.

An ache worked along the side of his temple, and it felt as though his head would explode.

The phone started ringing, causing Connor to jump.

Looking at the name, he hoped they weren't part of the reason this was happening.

'Ella,' he said, his voice cracking.

'Hi. How are you? Sorry. That's a dumb question. Erm, Liam just called. I'm so sorry.' She sounded concerned, with a tinge of embarrassment as she stuttered her words. 'Have you found her?'

Like Connor and Liam, Ella was born in Rye, and the three had been friends since school. Recently, they'd drifted apart for reasons they struggled to come to terms with or discuss. An accident that had changed their lives forever.

'Nothing. I don't know what's going on, Ella. I feel like I'm cracking up.' After a moment's silence, he continued, 'It's good to hear your voice. It's at times like this I realise how much I miss you and Liam.'

'Christ. I miss you both too. I'm still here. You can call me anytime you need to.'

'You know how difficult it is, Ella, what we all went through. It wasn't just us that suffered.'

'Do you think it's got anything to do with—?'

'Stop! Please, let's not go there. I can't bear to think about that time. It's in the past. We need to leave it there.'

'But what if it's not? I mean, if it hasn't stayed buried. Connor. I need to tell you something.'

'What is it?' he asked, hearing the fear in her voice and bracing himself for the bad news.

'Liam... Liam told me about your FaceTime call. How it was like looking at your twin.'

'Yeah. So fucking weird. It's why I think I'm losing it.'

'Wait. Let me close my bedroom door – one second.' Her voice became faint and difficult to hear. 'You're not losing it.'

'Why do you say that?' he asked, almost clinging to her every word.

'Because I've started seeing things too.'

5

*S*aturday Morning

Frank Dawson
   Retired caretaker, St Michael's High School, Rye

The table jumped as Frank Dawson's fist landed hard on the wood. He gripped the cup, which rattled in his hands, and the coffee began spilling over the rim. The alluring scent of fresh dough and coffee should have been comforting, but nothing worked anymore. His thick grey hair felt damp, and his moustache itched.

'Is everything okay, sir?' A waitress with a bright blue uniform, black leggings and the name Jennifer displayed on a badge wandered around the counter and stood beside him. Her manner was sincere but sceptical.

'Huh? Fine. Yes. Everything is fine,' Frank answered, his deep blue eyes glued to the coffee stains on the table.

'Can I get you anything else?' she asked.

He could see customers were peering over, possibly concerned for his wellbeing. In the far corner of the cafe, a young couple shuffled on their seats and asked for the bill. He could hear parents at the next table ordering their two children to stop staring. 'The coffee is fine,' Frank answered. 'I'm not hungry. Please. I just want to be left alone.' With his finger, he swirled the coffee stain and began patting it, unable to look the waitress in the eyes.

'Okay. Just shout if you need anything.' Looking at the family beside her and back to Frank, she leaned forward and said quietly, 'I don't mean shout. Just ask if you need anything else.' Backing away, she turned, grabbed the card reader from the counter, and walked to the couple in the far corner.

Bang. Again, Frank pounded his fist on the table.

The buzz of the card reader whirled as it printed a receipt.

Two chairs scraped along the wooden floor as the couple stood and shuffled out.

'Leave me alone,' Frank whispered. 'Why are you tormenting me?' He placed his hands over his ears and turned, looking at the family beside him. 'Do you hear it? You must hear it.'

The mother stood, grabbed the kids by the arm, and led them outside. The husband threw a couple of notes on the table and told the waitress to keep the change.

'Thanks, and we hope to see you again soon,' Jennifer said as she approached Frank's table. 'Sir, do you need me to call someone?'

'I said I'm fine!' Staring at the table, Frank began ranting.

'Are you here now? Are you watching me? Maybe you're standing outside and peering in, glaring from the shadows. Leave me alone! Stop tormenting me. Need to go to the supermarket. Washing tablets. What setting? Cotton or silk? Turn dial. Clockwise. Or anti? Never get it right. Press start. Wash clothes. Eat. Maybe cereal. Splash of milk. Not keen on the sour taste. Sleep. I must sleep. Numb nuts. That's what I am. Voices. My head aches. Leave me alone. I don't deserve this. Numb nuts.'

'Sir. I really think I should call someone?' Jennifer pushed.

Frank began gasping for breath. He stood, and for the first time he looked the waitress in the eyes. 'I... I have to go. How much? Two coffees. No food. Your time as a concerned citizen. How much do I owe?'

'Nothing. It's on the house.'

Turning, Frank raced to the door and rushed along the street.

'Excuse me. Hey! Stop! I want to help you.'

Biting on his knuckles, Frank turned, seeing the tall, slim girl from the cafe. The name badge on her blue jumper had turned almost vertical, and as she straightened it, her green eyes softened as though concerned for his welfare.

His breathing slowed, the cold morning air suddenly invigorating. 'Help! No one can help,' Frank said.

Pointing to a bench on the pavement, Jennifer said, 'Would you sit with me for a moment?'

Gazing at the seats, Frank saw carvings etched into the wood. 'Emma loves Matt' and a heart encircling the words. Another name he couldn't make out. 'I need to go. I want to be left alone.'

'Please. I just need a couple of minutes. I... I heard what you said in the cafe.'

They walked over to the bench and sat. Although it was cold, the sun was bright in the cloudless sky. Opposite, a woman placed a key in a lock, opened the door to a boutique shop, and punched in an alarm code. Vehicles crawled past on Rye High Street. A tractor with its raucous engine, the windows vibrating, and the driver bouncing in the seat rolled along the street with bales of hay spilling from its container.

The panic had subsided. His heart rate returned to a more normal pace, and Frank's head began to clear. For the moment, the voices had ceased.

'I want to help you. Is there anyone I can call?' asked Jennifer as she picked at her black leggings.

'I have... have these episodes. Like I... I hear voices. I can't control them. It started with the phone calls. I'd answer. No one was there. Then, the knocks on the front door of my cottage late at night. I'd go and see who it was. But there was never anyone there. I see... I see things. It's like they're haunting me. Sometimes they'll be on the road, and other times they'll be standing at the window, looking inside the cottage. I can't sleep. I can't eat. It's driving me fucking insane. What do they want? I can't bear it any longer. I'm crac... cracking up.'

'Who? Who are they?' she quizzed.

Frank jolted like he had just woken from a bad dream. 'Are you a policewoman?'

'God, no! You saw me. I work in the cafe.'

'Then why all the questions?'

'I want to help,' Jennifer answered.

'No one can help me. I see them everywhere. They're tormenting me.' Frank jumped up. 'I've already said too much. Thanks for your concern. But you can't help.' As Frank stood by the roadside, he saw a white transit van approaching from his right side. 'Hey,' he shouted to the driver, 'can I have a word?' As the van slowly passed, the driver gave a sinister glare without as much as a muscle moving in his face.

Frank stared at the back of the vehicle, reading the stickers: "Honk If You Love Rye"; "This Van May Be Slow, But It's In Front Of You". Glancing behind, he saw Jennifer walking back to the cafe.

Reaching his car, a small red Mini Cooper, Frank opened the door and got into the driver's seat. As he adjusted the rear-view mirror, he saw the van pull a U-turn.

After several deep breaths, Frank was confident the latest episode was under control. He was more relaxed. The heat which had enveloped his body had passed. His airways felt clear. The sweat on his brow had evaporated.

You have this, he told himself. *It's not real. Come on. Get it together.* Starting the car, he glanced at the driver's side wing mirror and pulled slowly onto the road. *I need to get home. Get some sleep and see the doctor. It's happening too frequently now. I have to sort it.*

At the end of the high street, Frank turned onto the A259 towards the outskirts of Rye. Although it was the start of summer season, the road was unusually clear. He jabbed the radio button, listening to a local talk show as they discussed the latest housing crisis in the UK.

With a quick glance to the wing mirrors, he saw the empty road behind him. The speedometer crept to fifty miles an hour. He hated speeding. Easing his foot onto the brake, he brought the car under control and looked to the rear-view mirror, now seeing the Transit van behind him. It gained speed and swerved out, suddenly driving alongside him.

Winding down the window, Frank shouted, 'It's me. Is everything alright with you?'

The driver just stared. Unflinching, with no reaction. Suddenly, he yanked the steering wheel, jerking it left and right, the van's movements erratic, swerving along the road and dropping back.

As Frank reached for his phone, the van rear-ended him, causing him to drop the mobile into the footwell.

'What is wrong with you? Have you lost your mind?'

Jabbing his foot hard on the accelerator, Frank desperately tried to create distance between the two vehicles. The bend came fast, and he swerved onto the other side of the road, narrowly avoiding an oncoming vehicle. The tyres skidded, and the smell of burning rubber pushed through the window, causing him to cough violently. Managing to gain control, he steered the car over to the left-hand lane. His legs were shaking, his face damp with sweat as again the van behind rammed into him. This time, Frank jerked forward, straining his neck. Although the pain was harsh, he had to keep driving. The next bump could knock him off the road and headfirst into a tree.

The narrow lane leading to his cottage approached fast. With pursed lips, his body tense, he hit the brakes and steered into the turning. At the brow of the hill, he undid his seatbelt and glanced behind, searching for the driver. There was no trace of him or the van.

Turning off the engine, he got out of the car and grabbed his phone from the footwell. Dashing along the path towards the cottage, the red brickwork gleaming in the sun and the flowerbeds awash with daisies and petunias, he placed the key in the front door, awkwardly twisting it, his hands trembling, and pushed the door back behind him, locking himself inside.

At the living room window, Frank looked along the path to the main road.

Once he was certain he'd lost the van, he dialled Connor's number and waited for him to answer.

'Hello,' the familiar voice said.

'What the fuck is wrong with you? You nearly killed me. Have you lost your mind?'

'Huh?'

'On the road. Just now. You were driving a white van. Did you not realise it was me?'

'Frank. What are you talking about? I don't own a van.'

'I might be suffering from delusions,' Frank spouted, saliva spraying from his mouth, 'but I'm not completely fucking crazy.'

'I've... I've had the morning from hell. Liv's—' Connor stopped mid-sentence.

The sound of a fist pounding on the front door reverberated through the living room. Ending the call, Frank placed his mobile in his trouser pocket and walked across the living room floor, staring through the spy hole. 'Who's—? Who's there? Hello?' His hand shaking, he reached for the handle, slowly bringing it down and opening the door. The Mini Cooper was still on the drive. The pathway leading to the main road was clear. Leaving the front door open, he turned left and walked around the side of the cottage. The gate leading to the garden was closed, the padlocked chain wrapped securely around the iron bars. He peered over the hedge and into next door's garden, suddenly leaping back as Rufus, the small Jack Russell, raced towards him and began barking.

A deep breath filled his lungs; he blew out hard, strolled to the front door, and closed it, locking it behind him.

As he sat on the sofa, patting the sweat on his forehead with the back of his hand, someone knocked at the door again.

'I'm calling the police.' Frank sat, his breath erratic, his legs bouncing, and his eyes glued to the front door.

Bang. Bang. Bang.

Balling his fists, he leaped off the sofa and rushed to the window, lifting the lock and pushing it back. The sound of distant vehicles hummed in the air. In the trees planted along the drive, birds hopped between branches as two squirrels chased each other on the lawn. There was no sign of anyone at the door. As Frank grabbed the handle and shut the window, he heard the back door open and footsteps race along the living room floor.

6

---

*S*aturday Morning

'It's happening to others too.' Connor was sitting at the kitchen table with his mobile phone held tight to his right ear. His words rushed out with uncontrolled urgency.

'Slow down,' ordered Liam, sounding like he was struggling to swallow a mouthful of food. 'Who?'

'Frank Dawson. I just had the weirdest phone call.'

'The caretaker?' asked Liam.

'Yes. He sounded... like, delusional. Accusing me of trying to run him off the road. Ella told me she sees things too.'

'What do you mean? Have you spoken to Ella?'

'I know you told her,' Connor pointed out, his tone sincere. 'It's fine. We're all friends. But she said... after I told her about Liv being taken and the person looking like me, she said she's started seeing things too.'

There was a short gap in their conversation as Liam digested everything.

'Sees what?'

'Can we meet?' Connor asked. 'I feel like I'm losing my mind.' Panic seemed to swallow him, and he struggled to keep his body from trembling.

'Yeah, no worries,' Liam responded. 'Shall we say The Bell in half an hour?'

Banging his thighs together to stop them shaking, Connor felt momentary relief. 'See you then.'

'Can I get a pint of Peroni, please?' Liam watched as a barmaid he'd never seen before reached into the fridge and grabbed a glass coated in ice. Although the pub had just opened, he could hear pool balls being smashed behind him. Jazz music played softly from the speakers, and the creak of a toilet door resounded, as if someone was already breaking the seal. The start of several trips to empty their bladder.

The barmaid smiled as she tilted the pint glass and began pouring the drink, before pressing the tip of her glasses further back on her nose and placing the drink on the counter. 'Anything else?'

The front door opened, and Connor walked to the bar, giving his friend an awkward hug.

'Do you need a large whiskey?' Liam asked.

'No. It's too early,' Connor stated as he glanced at his watch. 'But I'm tempted. Just a lemonade.'

Once Liam had paid, the two men found a table by the front door. The stale smell of alcohol was overwhelming, and dust mites were visible in the light by the front window.

As they clinked glasses and sipped their drinks, Connor became agitated and began folding the beer mat, tearing small pieces, and dropping them on the table. With his thumb and forefinger pinching the bridge of his nose to ease the stress, he eyed Liam's long, curly blond hair. 'You need a trim. And you've lost weight. Not all it's cracked up to be living on your own, is it? It's good to see you.'

'You, too.' Wiping the beer from his lip, Liam asked, 'Anything from Liv?' His voice was low and solemn.

'Nothing. I feel as though I'm cracking up. I can't call the police. I don't know where to start looking for her. I'm fucking scared, Liam.' Pulling his stool further into the table, Connor looked around the pub. The barmaid was sat tapping on her mobile phone while the young couple playing pool placed money into the slot and stacked the balls into a triangle. The woman chalked her cue while the guy broke off. 'I can't get the warning on the note out of my head.'

Leaning in, Liam checked over his shoulder and whispered, 'What did it say again?'

'It will come for you, too.' As the words left his lips, Connor jolted, spilling some of his drink over the table.

The barmaid shook her head, smirked, and walked over to the table with a cloth, wiping it down. 'Shall I get you a bib?' she asked sarcastically. 'A straw, maybe?'

'Huh? Sorry. I didn't mean to spill the—'

'It's fine. I'm teasing.' As she strolled away and washed the cloth in a sink behind the bar, the waft of her musty, bitter perfume hung in the air.

'What the fuck does that mean?' Liam asked, glimpsing the torn pieces of his friend's beermat on the table.

Shrugging, his shoulders almost level with his earlobes, Connor lifted his drink and took another sip of lemonade. 'I

can't sit here all day. I need to be out there looking for her.'
He stretched his neck, his eyes drawn to the ceiling for a
moment, where thick cobwebs hung in one corner, then he
looked back to his best friend. 'Will you help?'

'Of course I'll help. You don't need to ask. Where do we
start? Liv's missing. Someone broke into your flat. I do think
we need to call the police.'

'No!' Connor responded, his legs bouncing under the
table, indicating his nervous state. 'No police. They've
warned me. They'll... They'll kill her.'

Swigging half his beer in one go, Liam stared at his
friend, his eyes almost boring a hole into him. 'They looked
like you?'

'Yeah.' Connor went on to describe scene by scene what
had happened. 'I know it sounds crazy. I'd struggle if
someone told me the same story.' Dropping his head to his
hands, he whined, his body slumping, resembling a balloon
that had lost its air. Leaning back on the stool, he sighed
heavily. 'The phone call from Frank. It was so weird. He was
adamant I'd followed him. He mentioned a white van and
that I nearly killed him on the road. But I was home. In the
flat. Is it possible Liv's in the van? What is going on, Liam?'

'Drink up. I think the first port of call should be Frank.
He lives on the outskirts of Rye. One of those cottages on the
brow of the hill.'

Behind the counter, the barmaid pointed the remote
control at the TV screen, turning up the volume. A story was
breaking about a murder in Rye.

Connor and Liam spun around, facing the TV, while the
couple at the pool table placed their cues down and walked
closer to the screen.

A woman dressed in a black skirt and jacket with a
microphone pinned to her white blouse began talking.

'Yes, a tragic event is unfolding in the outskirts of Rye as a neighbour reported screams coming from a cottage at around ten thirty this morning. Local police were quick to the scene and found a man lying unresponsive on the living room floor. We'll have more updates throughout the day. We're told police are treating it as a murder investigation.'

Gripping the edge of the table, Liam watched the barmaid staring at the screen, shaking her head. The couple at the pool table appeared frozen, stunned into silence, digesting the breaking story they'd just watched.

'Shit,' the young guy said, aiming the comment to the barmaid. 'This sort of thing doesn't happen in Rye.'

'The world is getting crazier by the minute,' the barmaid fired back.

'It's him,' Connor said in a raised voice, the stool rocking on the worn carpet as he stood.

'Look,' Liam replied, pushing the glass of Peroni away from him, 'we don't know anything yet. It could be—'

'It's Frank! I have to get some air.' Looking at the barmaid, Connor thanked her for the drink and charged out onto Rye High Street.

Liam followed, also thanking her on the way out.

Although it was still early in the day, the streets were bustling with tourists. Families walking along the street, taking photos, gazing at the numerous paintings hung in the many galleries, seeking out antiques, and others going for lunch. The air was full of the smell of vinegar and garlic.

'I have to go. I need to get my head straight,' Connor insisted.

With a hand on his shoulder, Liam said, 'We don't know it's him.'

Rubbing his thick stubble, Connor fired back, 'He rang me and said I was following him. Fuck, he was in such a state. If you heard him, you'd feel terrified as well. Look, I have to wait in... in the hope of another phone call. I'll bell you when I hear something.'

'Okay. Let me know your plan of action. I'm here for you.'

After another awkward hug, Connor turned and walked down Mermaid Street, across the sharp cobbled stones, as more tourists stood on the road taking photos.

As Liam placed his key in the lock, he thought about his mum and dad. They were on holiday with Ella's parents in Marbella and had hired a yacht for a month of sun and relaxation. He didn't want to tell them about Connor and Liv and worry them. *No doubt they'll see the report about the possible murder in Rye,* he thought, closing the front door behind him.

Whiskers, the family's tabby cat, circled his feet, weaving a figure eight around his legs and meowing for food.

'Ah, I can't leave you out. You haven't eaten for a full two hours, huh!' Bending down, Liam stroked her back, hearing the loud purring noises. 'Come on, then. Let's get you fed.' In the kitchen, he opened a tin of cat food, forked half of it out, and placed it by the back door, watching the cat sprint past it through the cat flap and outside. 'Fine. Suit yourself. Don't like my cooking. I can take the insult.'

Light shone through the large double-glazed window as Liam peered into the garden. They had one of the largest on Harbour Street, but the downside was the time it took to mow the lawn. He gazed at the flowers, heathers, pansies, and violas he and his mother had recently planted on the side of the stony path. Although they looked tired now, they still brightened the space and gave a calming feel. Turning, he glimpsed the note of instructions stuck to the American-style fridge.

1. Mow the lawn. (Don't forget)

2. Water the flowers. This is essential if it doesn't rain.

3. Feed Whiskers. This will need to be done daily, or she'll die. You wouldn't like not eating for days.

4. And Liam, please, no parties. Be sensible and lock the door every night, both front and back.

5. Oh, we love you.

6. Lastly, if you get sick of eating toast and pasta, grab one of my cookbooks. You'll learn loads.

Haven't you heard of Google, Mum? Liam thought, shaking his head and laughing. *Note to self. Open cookbooks and leave them on the kitchen counter for when parents return.*

Feeling his phone vibrate, Liam grabbed it from his pocket. 'Hello. Blue Flame. The what? Did you say the sink is blocked? Oh, my dad, he's on holiday. I'm Liam, his son. I can come to you in the next—' Suddenly remembering the urgency with Connor and Liv, he responded, 'I'm sorry. I can't take any jobs at the moment. You'll have to try somebody else.'

Behind him, his laptop pinged – a new email alert. Turning, Liam slid a stool from under the breakfast bar and pulled out the charger from the computer. The lid was still hot as he pulled the laptop open.

The new email looked like spam. It was an address he hadn't seen before.

. . .

From: youneedtoseethis@notspam.co.uk
   To: liamanderson@yahoo.co.uk

In the subject bar, it said, *For attention of Liam. Don't ignore!*

With a deep breath, he slid his finger on the laptop pad and clicked the mouse over the email.

A small box appeared with a play symbol over it.

'What the hell is this?' Debating whether to delete it, he hesitated, blinking his eyes, his fingers drumming on the counter. Composing himself, Liam clicked play.

The video started with a young woman chatting to an older man on a bench. The picture was slightly grainy and, at first, out of focus. As the camera panned in on them, the picture cleared.

A hot flush developed on his chest, and his mouth became dry as he realised the man was Frank Dawson – their old caretaker at school. As the couple spoke, Frank looked unnerved, visibly frightened, and his body twitched. As the young woman placed a hand on his shoulders, he stood and rushed across the road, calling to the driver of a transit van.

As Liam paused the recording and zoomed in, he saw Connor. 'What the fuck?' The cat flap caused him to jump as Whiskers entered the kitchen and began eating her food. The recording became hazy, and a blank screen appeared for a moment. It continued with Frank Dawson closing the window of his cottage, someone holding a camera, filming everything, and another person charging across the wooden floor towards him. Frank spun around, and the person behind him placed a bag over his head.

Liam gasped as he watched Frank struggle, his arms violently thrusting in the air and trying to remove the bag.

He dropped to the floor, his body jerking as the masked person began stabbing and scratching his face with a pen until Frank was unrecognisable.

Then they turned to the camera and said, 'It will come for you, too.'

7

Saturday Morning

'He lived alone. We didn't have many dealings with him.' Margaret Stevens leaned against the brick wall while her Jack Russell continued barking. 'I used to say good morning or wave if I saw him coming up the drive. He rarely responded. A grunt here and there. That's just the way it is now, unfortunately. People keep themselves to themselves.'

'And you heard screams?' Officer Martin Willis asked, seeing the rollers in her hair, the dull blue scarf tied around her head, and the stained apron wrapped around her clothes. 'Is that what first alerted you that something was wrong?'

'That's right. Ooh, eerie it was. I was hanging my clothes on the line. Well, it's a warm day and the price of electricity nowadays doesn't bear thinking about. I told your colleague all this earlier.'

'Thank you. I'm sorry to put you through this again. As you're the only witness, it's vital we get the details correct. What happened then?'

'Well, let me see. I'm not as young as I used to be, so pardon me if I have to get the story straight in my head. After hanging out the clothes – my husband, George, wets the bed, see, and I'm forever running the washing machine. Bless him. It's his age. I'm no spring chicken myself, mind. I have this apron on. I was going to bake cakes, see. Scones. With raisins. It's his favourite. Maybe you'd like one when they're ready.'

'That's very kind,' the officer replied. 'I may take you up on the offer.'

Looking at the yellow tape placed around the gate, which flapped in the light breeze, the police cars lined along the drive, and the people entering the house dressed in white overalls, she asked, 'So was he murdered then?'

'I'm afraid it's still an investigation. We're not at liberty to confirm anything yet.'

'Sod your bloody scone then. You can miss out.' Fixing her rollers, she asked, ''Ere, they won't come for me, will they? Only Rufus, the Jack Russell, is getting old now, and George, my worse half, is almost bedridden. Mind you, seeing him first thing in the morning without his false teeth is enough to scare anyone off.'

'I'm sure they won't come for you. Crimes like this are extremely rare, so please don't worry yourself unnecessarily. Thank you so much for your help. You've been amazing.' As the officer put on overalls, gloves, and a mask over his nose and mouth, he entered Frank's home, glimpsing the plaque on the wall declaring, "Dawson's Cottage."

The body was still on the floor, while forensic experts took photos and measurements. Officer Willis walked over to one of the first responders. 'Whoever did this, done a proper job on him. It's rough. What's the latest?'

The female police officer nodded. 'It seems they marched straight into the cottage through the back door. There's no damage, so it was probably unlocked. Preliminary observations suggest suffocation, but we'll need to wait for the autopsy for confirmation. We found a bag, one of those clear plastic sorts used to hold sandwiches. But the perpetrator wasn't finished there. They hacked his face. The injuries are consistent with blunt force trauma. We haven't found the instrument as of yet.'

Turning, Officer Willis stood over Frank Dawson. Some of the flesh on his face had been hacked away as though ripped by a wild animal, and both of his eyes had been gouged out. His mouth had been stretched open and looked disjointed, hanging at an unnatural angle as though his jaw was broken, and his neck had been ripped so severely that the muscles and tendons showed. The wooden floor he lay on was awash with blood and bone fragments.

'Whoever did this,' Officer Willis suggested, 'wanted to torture him. They weren't satisfied with suffocating him. They wanted to humiliate him. To mutilate his body until he was unrecognisable. We're dealing with one twisted bastard here.'

'I'm knocking off. Care to join me for a drink?' Officer Martin Willis stood outside the cottage, his face still pale from the scene inside.

'Sure,' his colleague replied, pulling off her gloves.

He and Chloe Denham had been friends since joining the force. Although they were keen on each other, dating other officers was often frowned upon and never encouraged.

Removing his protective gear – white overalls, gloves, and mask – Martin carefully placed each item in a biohazard bag provided by the forensic team. Once the bag was securely tied, he handed it to one of the forensic officers for proper disposal. The forensic team would ensure the items were either cleaned or incinerated.

After returning to his patrol car, Martin radioed in to officially sign off his shift. He and Chloe then drove the police car back to the station, ensuring all equipment was accounted for and the vehicle was in proper condition.

'Wow, I needed that,' Martin said, a few minutes later. He took another sip of his Guinness and held the glass up to see its thick, creamy head, while wiping the remnants from his top lip.

Chloe sipped on a straw which rested in a glass containing a large gin and tonic.

Although she'd been an officer for a few years and thought she'd witnessed it all, the earlier scene had clearly been deeply distressing, etching a frown mark between her eyebrows. 'I've never seen anything like that,' she said quietly. 'Christ, his face. What are we dealing with here?'

'A monster,' he responded, shifting on the barstool. 'Can you imagine doing that to someone? The freak needs hanging by his fucking testicles.' Aware they shouldn't be talking about an active case, Martin looked around the bar, making sure no one could hear them. He gazed at Chloe, her black hair tied back, the lipstick fading, and her dull green eyes sunk back inside her head. It looked like she'd aged ten years overnight. 'Are you okay?'

'What choice do I have? It's part of the job. It doesn't make it any easier to deal with, though. My father warned me when I first told him. He said, Chloe, you'll see things that'll make the hair stand up on your head. Things that will haunt you for the rest of your life. Until today, I took it with a pinch of salt. How the fuck do you deal with—?'

'I know,' Martin interrupted. Lifting his glass, he held it in front of him. 'So close,' he said, trying to distract her.

'What?'

'You're supposed to get the drink halfway down the G. It's called splitting the G.'

'Yeah. In one go. How many have you had?' She smiled, staring into Martin's soft blue eyes.

His wavy black hair was damp, and his stubble prickled his hand as he ran it over his face. Grabbing his mobile phone as it vibrated in his pocket, Martin peered at the screen. 'It's George. Hi, mate. Shit! Okay, thanks for keeping me updated. Speak later.' Ending the call, he turned to Chloe. 'The body. Frank Dawson. Forensics at the scene have found a miniature wooden figure shoved deep into his nose.'

'That's disturbing. Why do that?'

'It was a figure of Frank,' he explained. 'Someone carved his exact image as a doll and shoved it inside him.'

'Like a... a doppelgänger?'

'It seems so.'

8

---

*S*aturday Afternoon

Liam leaned against the breakfast bar, trying in desperation to compose himself, as the contents of the email powered through his mind. He staggered to the kitchen sink and grabbed a glass, filling it with cold water and slugging it in one go. His chest felt tight as if it were being crushed in a vice, and his throat seemed blocked as he tried to control his breaths.

For almost half an hour, he'd anxiously tried to find the email again. After he'd watched the video, it had disappeared from his laptop. After refreshing it numerous times and checking his spam and junk folder, he'd slammed the laptop lid and sat, completely numb with shock. His head ached, and panic encompassed his body.

Now, standing at the kitchen sink, his legs weak, he gulped more water and placed the glass in the sink. *Are they watching me now?* he thought, moving to the back door and pressing on the handle to ensure it was locked. *They filmed Frank while he sat talking on a bench. Connor was driving a white van. But it couldn't have been Connor. He was home in his flat. Can they see me?* His mind was warped with images of the recording he'd been sent. Frank Dawson suffocated and lying helpless on the floor. Someone standing over him, mutilating his face with a pen. He rushed to the downstairs bathroom, spilling the contents of this morning's breakfast into the toilet. He wiped his mouth with a tissue and leaned against the wall. A dull ache worked across his forehead and seemed to spread quickly over his face.

After he'd composed himself, he walked back to the laptop, opened it, and checked his emails again. The last one received was yesterday evening at 7.42 pm – a discount voucher from Lidl.

Backing away from the breakfast bar, he placed his hand on his forehead, working his fingers into his warm, clammy skin to ease the pain. At the kitchen cupboard, he opened a drawer and grabbed two Nurofen, washing them down with flat Pepsi that tasted like it had been left on the side for days.

Grabbing his mobile from his jeans pocket, he opened a Facebook group called "Rye News" and looked at the comments. There were numerous pictures of police cars, ambulances, and news teams outside a cottage.

Some were blurry as if people had taken photos on their phones as they drove past.

Liam scrolled through the comments.

Adam Yeats.
Terrible news. RIP. Our thoughts are with you.

.   .   .

Martha Riley.

Does anyone know who it was?

Paul Townsend.

What is going on in this world? Rye is such a quiet, peaceful place. No one is safe anymore.

Julie Hart.

Apparently, the neighbour heard screams. Can you imagine how scary that must have been? Doesn't bear thinking about.

Anonymous.

I live near the person. I'm too frightened to give a statement to the police in case of repercussions, but I saw his body through the window. He was fucking ripped to bits. I also heard the scream. His face was completely disfigured.

Claire Whitehall.

@Anonymous. Bullshit. If you did see him, as you say, you need to speak up. Stop hiding and tell us who you are. It's vital this person is caught.

Sharon Kemp.

It sounds like it was a wild animal if @Anonymous is telling the truth. That's some scary shit.

. . .

As another picture appeared on the thread, Liam zoomed in and saw the small red Mini Cooper on the drive.

'Any news about Liv?' asked Liam optimistically.

'No. Nothing. I'm going out of my mind.'

'It's breaking on social media. It's... It's definitely Frank. Go to Rye News on Facebook.' Liam was sitting at the breakfast bar in the kitchen with his mobile on loudspeaker.

'Wait a second. Let me look. I can see all the comments, but Frank's name isn't mentioned.'

'The picture. Can you see it?' Liam pushed.

'There's a few. Which one am I looking at?' Connor asked.

'The... The clearest one. Near the top. It's Frank's Mini. See it on the drive.'

'Erm... hang on. Yeah, I can see it. Oh shit!' After a brief pause, Connor said, 'I'm never going to find her. I know the same psycho who did this has Liv. What if she's already—?'

'Stop! Don't even go there. We have to remain optimistic. Keep calm. We'll find her. Something else happened.'

'What?' asked Connor. 'What else happened?'

'I wasn't going to tell you. Christ, you have enough on your plate.'

'Tell me what, Liam?'

'I... I received an email. As soon as I watched it, it disappeared from my laptop.'

'What was on it?'

'Someone filmed Frank.'

'Filmed him. In what way?'

'Sat on a bench, chatting to a younger woman.'

Pushing hard, Connor asked, 'Who was the woman?'

'I don't know. But when Frank left and rushed across the road, I saw... I... There was a white Transit van. I paused the recording and zoomed in. Mate, you were in the driving seat.'

'Me? But you know that isn't possible. I came straight home after the call ended. After Liv... I've been here in the flat.' Through gritted teeth, Connor stated, 'Frank was right. The phone call. He asked why I was following him.'

'I know it wasn't you,' Liam remarked, his voice low and controlled. 'It gets worse. The recording finished with Frank being suffocated and stabbed with a pen. It was so sick I vomited. I don't feel safe. I'm here alone and paranoid that someone or something is after us.'

'And the email is definitely gone?'

'Yeah. I checked everywhere.'

Digesting the conversation, Connor went silent for a moment. His choppy breaths resounded through the speaker as though anticipating their next move. 'I need time to think. It feels like my head's about to explode. I'll call you if I hear anything.'

'Okay. I'll wait by the phone. Connor, we'll... we'll find her.' As Liam ended the call, he heard an intense slamming noise by the front door. Rushing along the hallway, he saw a leaflet lying on the mat. 'Didn't you see the sign above the letterbox? No flyers or junk, arse wipe.' Bending down to pick it up, he flipped it over. At the top of the A4-sized paper, written in large red letters, it said:

It will come for you, too.

Beneath was an old high school picture with Connor, Liam, and Ella sitting together in the front row.

Behind them stood their teacher, Greta Franklin, and the caretaker, Frank Dawson.

9

S aturday Afternoon

After pulling over to the side of the road, Connor killed the engine and messaged Liam.

I'm outside.

A few seconds later, Liam opened the front door, holding the flyer which had been pushed through his letter-box. His eyes were wide, and he bit the corner of his lip as he scanned the road. Approaching the car, he turned around, glancing behind as though expecting someone to jump him. He sank into the passenger seat and closed the door. Turning to Connor, he handed him the A4 flyer. 'Thanks for coming so quickly.' Then, watching Connor's face he remarked, 'It's coming back to haunt us.'

As Connor read the words and looked at the high school photo, his mouth widened as though he had lockjaw. His hand began shaking, the paper trembling, and he placed the knuckle of his left thumb against his forehead. 'Shit,' he muttered softly. 'Only a handful of people know what happened. They're all in this picture. It's too coincidental,' Connor declared, his fingers massaging the skin on his brow. When Liam didn't answer, he continued, pointing at the caretaker standing roughly in the middle of the back row. 'There's Frank.'

'Dead!'

'I know that. Christ, Liam.' Resting the flyer on his lap, he began recalling the names. 'Ella. She said she's seeing things too. Then there's you. The email you received. The flyer. Me. I don't have to go into what happened this morning with Liv going missing. There's only one other person who was involved.' Connor pointed to a woman standing next to Frank. 'Mrs Franklin.'

Taking the flyer back and placing it on the dashboard, Liam put on his seatbelt. 'Do you know where she lives?'

'I haven't a clue,' Connor answered, his mind so distracted that he struggled to think.

'The church,' Liam suggested with a wave of intensity.

'What about it?' asked Connor, his eyes glazed over as he stared through the windscreen.

'Mrs Franklin. She works there, right?'

'I... I think so. I haven't been there for so long,' he answered, feeling a tad guilty. After losing his father to cancer a couple of years ago, Connor had struggled with his faith.

'So,' Liam continued, his voice eager and brimming with energy, 'that's as good a place to start as any.

The grounds were immaculate, with a stony path leading to the church doors. The grass was a deep green and looked like it had been recently mowed. On each side of the path were bushes trimmed and shaped to within an inch of their lives. Further back, there were gravestones, their edges chipped and crumbled with old age and the granite etched with words they couldn't read.

Inside, the church smelled of incense and old wood from the benches, and the scent of candle wax was overbearing.

A large crucifix hung over the altar, and robust stone pillars lined each side of the nave.

'Hello,' Connor called out, hearing his voice echo through the church.

A young priest appeared from one side of the altar, dressed in a long black cassock that reached his ankles, a stiff white clerical collar pressing into his throat. His hair was thinning, and the clumps on each side were messy and chaotic.

'Connor Murphy,' he said with a smirk as he strolled down the steps and along the aisle. 'To what do I owe this pleasure?'

'Hi, Father Maloney. We were hoping you could help us.'

'If you're expecting a confession,' he said with a hint of satire, 'there are not enough hours in the day for me to hear your sins, young man.'

'Er, no, not confession,' Connor replied, his voice strained with embarrassment.

'I'm pulling your leg. Although I must admit, it's been a while since you've been here. We don't charge, you know.'

'You do. What about the offertory?' Liam stated as both men's eyes seemed to bore a hole in his skin.

'That's voluntary! And young Liam Anderson. It's been a

minute. I hope you haven't burned the house down while your parents are away. How are they doing? Enjoying the holiday?'

'Yes, they're good. Thank you,' answered Liam.

Connor wondered how it always seemed priests knew everything about everyone. Who needed social media?

'So,' Father Maloney said, interlacing his fingers, 'how can I help?'

'We were hoping to have a word with Greta Franklin,' pushed Connor. 'Is she around?'

The priest turned full circle with his hands out. 'Oh, that lady is a blessing. A gift from above, wouldn't you say? We'd be lost without her. Look around you. Sparkling, right? Look at the glint of polish on the wooden pews. The gleam of the floor. That would suggest she's gone home for the day. Her job is done. The woman is quite simply a marvel.'

'Where is that again?' Liam asked sheepishly. 'I mean, her home?'

'Young Liam Anderson,' the priest said, creases appearing on his brow and his eyes almost bulging in their sockets, 'if you think I'm foolish enough to give out staff addresses, you're very much mistaken. Now, I must get ready for a home visit. A parishioner is sick. Needs must. If that's all, then I'll bid you good day.' With that, Father Maloney turned, climbed the steps to the altar, and disappeared around the back.

As the young men left the church, Liam pointed out a shop at the back, displaying prayer books, rosary beads, and holy water.

On a shelf behind the counter, they found an address book with the staff's details.

❧

'I can't believe you did that! In a church, as well.' Connor followed the sat nav with instructions to Mrs Franklin's address.

'It's not like we're robbing the place. And I did return the address book where I found it.'

'You better say three Our Fathers to seek forgiveness.' Connor pulled into a parking spot on a side road a couple of miles outside Rye. The street was lined with trees and there was a small play area opposite with a couple of swings, a slide, and a rickety old roundabout. A group of adults supervised their children while a dog ran back and forth, fetching a stick.

Greta Franklin lived at forty-nine Dead Man's Lane, a large semi-detached house painted white with a black-coloured door. There was no Ring doorbell or security cameras, and the gate at the front of the house was permanently open, strapped to a wooden pole. The front lawn was small and tidy, with a water feature, the pump buzzing loudly, and two bins by the front window.

They sat in the car, the windows cracked open, watching the house. The only sounds were children playing in the park and the occasional vehicle passing along the top of the road.

With a deep exhale, Liam whispered, '*It will come for you, too.*' As their fearful eyes met, a hand rapped on the passenger window, causing them to jump.

'You can't park here! Look at the signs.' A traffic warden pointed across the road as Connor got out.

'Sorry. I'm paying now. I'll do it on the app.'

'Yeah. Well, make sure you do. You've already had ten minutes free. I see everything.'

The two men walked past the open gate and approached Mrs Franklin's front door. The smell of rotten food and decaying grass in the bins was overbearing, and they had to swat flies that buzzed around their heads.

Reaching for the front door knocker, Connor pulled it back, tapping it twice against the wood. Looking at the bins, covering his mouth with the sleeve of his tee-shirt, he imagined Mrs Franklin, her body cut into small pieces and dumped in one of the bins. He decided to keep the horrific image to himself. As he went to knock again, the front door swung open, and Mrs Franklin stood in the hallway, to the sound of their relieved sighs. Her brown eyes were tired, and her skin was weathered-looking. The shock on her face was evident. Her mouth opened, and she bit hard on the middle part of her lip. It was obvious she wasn't best pleased to see them. Her eyes widened, the heavy wrinkles etching deep into her skin. Her hand covered her mouth, and she stepped back as though unsteady on her feet. With a cautious gaze, her eyebrows knitted together. 'What are you doing here?'

'Erm, hi,' Connor said awkwardly, his chest tightening. 'This is slightly weird.'

'Weird?' Mrs Franklin asked. 'What's weird?'

'So,' Connor said, looking at Liam and shifting on his legs. 'I, we, have some bad news. Erm, Frank's... Frank's dead. We...er, think he was murdered.'

'Murdered?' Her eyes dropped to the doormat, and a high-pitched shriek spilled from her mouth. Looking between the two men, she said, 'That's awful. He was a good man.'

'Can we come in?' Connor spoke in a low, soothing tone to ease her mood.

'I'm rather busy. I have things to do.'

'Please,' Connor pushed. Gazing back at Liam and

seeing him nod, he turned to the elderly woman. 'I fear you may be in danger. Not just you. All of us.'

'Danger?' Mrs Franklin dropped her chin to her chest, waited a few seconds, and stood against the wall. 'Wipe your shoes.'

They followed her along the dark hallway and into the living room.

The side units were filled with ornaments, everything from figurines of animals to religious artefacts. A couple of pictures hung on the wall, possibly her and her husband, who'd died almost a year ago – another of a couple with a small child. The TV was small, balancing on a table, and the cream carpet was spotless. There was a pleasant smell of lime polish and also fresh bread coming from the kitchen.

'I heard a report on the radio this morning,' Mrs Franklin stated. 'A death here in Rye. They said they're treating it as a murder investigation. I thought it might be gang related. You know, drugs. That's often the case. But Frank. Are you sure?'

'We're sure,' Connor confirmed.

'Where are my manners? Please, sit,' she said, beckoning to the comfy-looking sofa against the back wall. 'How did you get my address?'

Liam looked at Connor and back to the woman. 'Er, Father Maloney. At the church.'

'Well, I'll be having words with him when I see him. He shouldn't be giving out people's addresses.'

Shit, Connor thought. *Get out of that one.*

'Mrs Franklin,' Connor said, seeing her face awash with embarrassment. It was as though she struggled to hold eye contact.

'Greta. It's Greta.'

'I'm so sorry that we've turned up here like this.' Gazing

around the room, Connor declared, 'You have a lovely place.'

'Thank you,' she fired back with a curt tone, 'but I doubt you're here to judge my living conditions.'

'I think you're in danger! All of us are.'

'Sorry,' Greta said. 'I don't understand.'

Clearing his throat, Connor began telling her about Frank. How distressed he had been this morning and that he'd called with an array of accusations, stating that he'd seen Connor chasing him along the road driving a Transit van. The paranoia in his voice. He explained the email Liam had received, nodding at his friend to continue the story.

Liam didn't hold back. He went into detail about the recording and its contents, how it showed Frank running across the road and, later, butchered in his cottage.

Closing his eyes momentarily, Connor's body stiffened. 'Mrs Franklin, Liv went missing this morning.'

'Missing.' Coughing to clear her croaky voice, she said, 'Have you called the police?'

'No,' he answered abruptly, explaining the warning and phone call he'd received. 'I can't. They'll kill her. Liam received this through the post earlier today.' As he removed the flyer from his jeans pocket and handed it to Greta, watching her unfold it, Connor urged, 'It's a high school photo. We're all in it. See.'

'I can see.' It looked like the blood had drained from her body. She began shivering, and her lips seemed to change to a deep purple. Looking between the young men, her voice feeble, she asked, 'What does this mean?'

'Well,' Liam took over, 'Frank's been murdered. It was the most sickening act of brutality I've ever seen. Unfortunately, it will live rent-free in my head for the rest of my life.' Nodding at his friend, he continued, 'Connor's girlfriend,

Liv went missing this morning. Ella said weird things are happening to her, too.'

With the palms of her hands tapping on her lap, displaying her uneasy state, she responded, 'It proves nothing.'

'Mrs Franklin, Greta, we were all part of it,' pushed Connor, seeing her look to the wall behind them. 'We all—'

'Stop!' she roared. 'It was so long ago. What choice did we have?'

'Oh,' Connor said, his tone stern, 'we had choices. We came to you, remember? You dismissed us as though we didn't have feelings. As though it didn't affect us. Do you know all the sleepless nights and torment we all suffered? And still do! You threatened us! You dismissed it without one regard for our conscience. You should have let us do the right thing. We were children, and you left us to deal with the horror alone. We were terrified.'

The silence was choking as the three of them digested the conversation. None of them had ever been allowed to express their feelings, and it was like the air had thinned out, slowly suffocating them.

'Someone has already been killed,' said Liam. 'It's only a matter of time.'

Greta looked down at the flyer, reading the words, "*It will come for you, too.*"

Her eyes fixed on the two figures in the back row of the photograph. The tall, handsome man standing proud next to her. Both Frank and Greta had huge smiles. The three children sat in the front row, legs crossed and grinning. 'We didn't mean for any of it to happen,' she said. 'But it did. We can't change the past. Leave it buried, for Christ's sake.'

'Do you have anyone who can stay with you?' Connor

queried. 'A friend or relative, perhaps? Just until this blows over.'

Standing, Mrs Franklin walked to the window, looking at Connor's car parked outside. Across the road, children played tag. A dog was chewing on a stick, and a parent pushed a child on a swing. 'I have no one.' Turning, her voice sharp, she said, 'I think you both need to leave. Thank you for the warning. I'll keep the doors locked.'

Connor stood. 'Would you mind if I used the toilet?'

'Upstairs, first on your left.'

'Thank you.' He opened the door, climbed the stairs and pushed back the bathroom door, locking it behind him. Connor was drained, but it had to be said. Greta had to hear his frustration and how the past had affected all their lives.

When he'd finished, he flushed the toilet and washed his hands, using a towel draped over the bath to dry them. Something stirred towards the end of the hallway. A creak. Possibly a door closing. Connor was certain Mrs Franklin lived alone. While standing at the living room window, she'd remarked, "I have no one." So what did he just hear? The breeze from an open window, perhaps? It was the start of summer. Sliding the lock back, he stood, peering along the hallway. The door at the end was open moments ago. Another loud shuffle resounded along the hall, and Connor was sure the handle was thrust downward. It was as if someone wanted him to go and check. Voices came from below. Mrs Franklin and Liam were making small talk. Suddenly, the door cracked open.

His skin tingled, and he struggled to catch a breath as he crept along the hallway, praying the floorboards kept silent. Again, there was an eerie creak as the door closed.

Deliberating whether to go back down, grab Liam, and

leave, he summoned the courage to reach forward and open the bedroom door.

The windows were closed. A duvet was pulled high to the pillows and folded back at the left corner. To his right, a door leading to an en-suite bathroom was ajar. On the floor by his feet was the same high school photo. Only this one was slightly different.

Frank's head was circled with a red pen.

10

*S*aturday Afternoon

Ella walked through the kitchen and into the bathroom at the back of the house, where she turned on the light and stared at her reflection. Her long blonde hair was tangled, and her blue eyes appeared dull and lifeless. Lack of sleep had played havoc with her skin, with red blotches on her cheeks and spots developing across her chin.

Undressing, she got into the shower, feeling the warm water wash away the stress.

The recent developments with Connor freaked her out. His girlfriend Liv was missing. The person appearing on the FaceTime call had apparently looked exactly like him. As the water poured from the shower spout, she thought she heard a tap on the bathroom door. But it wasn't possible. Her parents were on holiday. She was alone. Reaching the control panel, she flicked it off. 'Is someone there? Hello?

Who's out there?' A cold, sharp jolt pounded through her body as she turned the water back on. Steam filled the bathroom, and goosebumps appeared on her skin despite the hot water. Lately, odd incidents had unsettled her, things she couldn't explain. A couple of days ago, she received a phone call from a mate. Ella had been spotted in Winchelsea, and her friend asked why she'd ignored her. Only Ella hadn't been to Winchelsea for months. And then last week she'd had a call from a withheld number late at night while she got ready for bed. When Ella answered, a voice had whispered, '*Go to the window.*' Freaked out, Ella had turned off the light and looked out, seeing a woman the same height, with long blonde hair and dark glasses, standing on the street, looking up at her. Thinking she was overtired, her mind playing tricks, she'd pushed it to the back of her mind. That was until Connor told her what was happening to him.

Once she'd washed her hair and body, she grabbed a towel, dried herself, and stepped into the same long black dress she'd worn that morning.

In the kitchen, she opened the fridge door, thinking about putting a pizza on. Her mobile phone ringing caused her to jump. Ella picked it up, looking at the local number and not recognising it. About to decline it, she changed her mind, pressed the answer button and lifted the phone to her ear. 'Hello?'

'Ella. It's Martha Strong.'

'Martha Strong,' she repeated, trying to place the name.

'From the boutique shop in town.'

'Oh, God. Sorry. Martha, how are you?' It was a store she and her family often frequented, and Martha sold everything from tat to designer clothes and suits.

'About today.' Martha's tone was direct, cold, and lacked

empathy. 'Drop the money down or return the garments. I'm willing to forgive and forget. Well, forgive, anyway.'

'Sorry? I'm not sure what you mean,' Ella asked, her words jumbled and stuttering.

'Look, you and your family have been regular customers for years. I class you as personal friends. Your mum and I play bridge every Wednesday evening. I've been to your house for parties, and you've all visited mine numerous times. So either drop the garments back or pay for them. Please, Ella. I don't want to fall out with you.'

Her head started spinning, her eyes became blurry, and she placed a hand on the kitchen unit to steady herself. 'Martha, honestly, I've been home all day. I don't know what you're talking—'

'It was you,' Martha said abruptly, her voice loud and brash. 'You came in here an hour ago. I saw you, Ella. You placed four garments in your bag and strolled out of the shop, calm as you like and ignoring the alarm. I rushed out onto the street, stunned that you'd do this to me. You heard me calling. What is going on with you?'

'Martha. Please, you need to believe me. I would never, ever—'

'Drop the garments back. I don't want to call your parents. I adore your mother. This could conclude our friendship. Not to mention the embarrassment it will cause.'

'Are you still at the shop?'

'For another hour, yes.'

'Wait there.' Ending the call, Ella stepped into her sandals and grabbed her coat from the front door, Martha's accusations swirling in her head.

Outside, Ella stood by the front gate, unable to comprehend the phone call, stepping from one leg to the other, her brain foggy and disconcerted.

Bringing her hand to her mouth, eyes squinting, she doubted her own mind, pondering if there could be any truth in what Martha had said. She had been adamant Ella had stolen from her shop, throwing bizarre accusations.

Placing her phone in her coat pocket, she walked along Rye High Street, her heart pumping hard in her chest, panic rising slowly from her stomach.

Seeing the sign on a wall, "Martha's Boutique For The Chic," she braced herself and opened the door.

A bell rang above the shop, and she eyed a handrail with an alarm fitted.

The store was empty except for Martha, who stood behind the counter with a measuring tape. Her cheeks were bright red and etched with broken veins, her short blonde hair immaculately styled as though she'd just walked out of a salon, and her long green dress was elegant. The shop smelled fruity, as though a strawberry-scented air freshener had been sprayed.

'Martha, I assure you—'

Lifting a hand, she commanded Ella to stop. 'I'm not a stupid woman.'

Reaching the counter, Ella replied, 'I know you're not. No one is saying that. But please, you must believe me. I've never stolen anything in my life. I'm as confused as you are.'

Martha leaned over the counter, almost face to face with Ella, her voice controlled and stern. 'Oh, I'm not confused. Where is the stuff?'

Backing away and turning one way and another, Ella said, 'I... I don't have it.'

Reaching for a calculator behind the desk, Martha began tapping digits. 'We'll call it two hundred.'

'Two hundred! Are you mad? It wasn't me. Martha, come on.'

'Right. Then I'm calling your parents and then I shall ring the police. I'm sorry to do this. But I'm not a mug. You can't make a fool of me.'

The panic which had started in the pit of Ella's stomach worked fast through her body, seeming to grip her skin like a vice. *I have to pull a trump card,* she thought. *Innocent until proven guilty, don't they say?* 'Show me the evidence!'

'Very well. Come with me.' Martha steered Ella to a small room at the back of the shop with a monitor perched on the long table. She grabbed a remote control and sifted through the footage.

The time in the top right corner showed 2.56 pm and today's date.

The door opened, and a woman wearing dark glasses strolled over to a railing holding clothes. Martha was behind the counter and greeted her. The woman waved back. The recording clearly showed the woman placing items in her bag. She wore the exact black dress Ella was wearing.

11

S aturday Afternoon

Charging down the stairs, Connor stumbled, gripping the railing for support, and then rushed into the living room. He saw Greta Franklin jolt as she stared out the front window. As she turned, the creases on her face were more evident.

'What on this earth are you doing, young man? You nearly frightened me half to death.'

Connor pointed at her, shaking his head. 'Do you have something to do with all this?'

'Come on, mate. Calm yourself,' Liam instructed. 'What's happened?'

'I'll tell you what's happened. I went to the toilet. I heard a noise in the bedroom and found this.' Holding out the flyer with Frank's head circled, he glared at Greta and hissed, 'You did this.'

'I think you'd better leave. You have no right going into my bedroom. It's one thing to blame me for the past, but to accuse me of having something to do with Frank's death. Oh, no. You've overstepped the line. I've a good mind to call the police. You come round here again, and it's exactly what I'll do. Go on, the pair of you. Out! I said out!'

The front door slammed as the two men walked along the drive, their heads bowed in shame.

'It was her. Circling Frank's head in the photo and pretending not to know about his death. I bet she pushed the flyer through your door as well. She's fucking with us,' Connor speculated as he got into the car.

Liam joined him, slamming the door shut. 'Listen to yourself!'

'What? Listen to what?'

'Do you really think she's behind this? Taking Liv. Killing Frank. For fuck's sake, Connor. Get a grip!'

'Sorry. It's all too much. My head is swimming with shit. I'm paranoid. I can't think straight. I'm tired. Liv's gone.' As he broke down, wiping the tears from his eyes, Liam placed an arm around his shoulders.

'Mate. You need to keep it together. We'll find her.'

Once he'd composed himself, Connor looked to Greta's house. 'She doesn't seem like the type of woman to play sinister pranks.'

'She has nothing to do with it,' Liam stated.

Resting his head back against the driver's seat and closing his eyes, Connor tried to slide the pieces of the puzzle together, but the more he did, the more disoriented it appeared. 'I heard a noise while in the toilet. It was like someone was there, wanting me to hear them. They wanted me to find the flyer on the bedroom floor.' Looking at Liam, he said, 'The flyer. Frank's head was circled. It had to have been done today. Someone's upstairs.'

'Open the door, Mrs Franklin. It's Connor. Open the door.' He peered through the letterbox, looking along the empty hallway. After rapping the knocker several times, they rushed around the side of the house.

Liam pressed his face to the kitchen window and knocked on the glass with his knuckles. 'She's not there.'

'She's ignoring us.' Connor tried the lock to the back door, pulling the handle one way and another. Stepping back, he stood on a knee-height brick wall and gazed at the upstairs bedroom. The curtains were open, and a shadow passed across the room. At the same time, Mrs Franklin appeared at the back door.

'What do you want?' she said through the glass. 'I told you I'll call the police. Now piss off.'

'Liam, someone's in the upstairs bedroom,' announced Connor. 'We have to get her out. Please, Mrs Franklin, you're in danger. Open the door. Hurry!'

'Go away. I'm not listening. You have three seconds, or I'm making the call. One.'

'Open the door. There's someone inside. You need to listen,' Connor bellowed.

'Two.' As she said three, she spun around, seemingly aware of a shadow in the hallway behind her. She grabbed the keys from the rack, hands shaking, and tried to place the key in the lock. 'Help me!' she cried as the keys dropped to the floor.

Break a window,' Liam shouted.

As Connor grabbed a brick, he threw it at the glass, watching it bounce off like a tennis ball. The figure raced through the kitchen as Mrs Franklin screamed, picking up the key and ramming it into the lock this time. She wriggled it for a second before Connor and Liam managed to kick the door back. As it pounded against the wall, the shadowy person turned, charging along the hallway and out through the front door.

Wheezing heavily, Mrs Franklin bent over as the men supported her arms. 'What have you brought to my house?'

'They've gone.' Connor looked across the road at the park. The same few people were there, and the dog was still running with the stick. A couple walked along the pavement, pushing a pram and oblivious to what was happening around them. They suddenly saw Connor and smiled. To his right, the road was empty. On his left side, a group of teenagers walked towards him, possibly going into town for the evening.

'Anything?' Liam asked from the front door.

'No. He's long gone. Did you get a look at him?'

'It was difficult with the sun reflecting on the back door glass,' Liam stated. 'I'd say he was male in terms of size and shape. You?'

'Same. But yeah, it looked like a man.' With another glance along the road, Connor joined his friend, and they both walked through to the kitchen, seeing Greta sitting on a chair by the table, slumped forward, with her hands clasped together.

'Can I make you some tea?' Connor asked, realising the stupidity of his question as he closed the back door and locked it.

'I... I want to be left alone. I'm in... in shock. You know, for all the years I've lived here, I've never once, not once, had anyone try to break in. It's a safe place, Rye. You could leave the doors unlocked and sleep sound, knowing you're secure in your home. We have a neighbourhood watch thingy on our phones. If someone so much as farts, you'll see it on WhatsApp.'

'They obviously don't work on Saturdays,' Liam quipped, seeing the curt expression on the woman's face as she frowned and almost hissed at him.

'I will have a tea,' she stated, directing her order at Connor. 'And then leave me alone!'

Next to the sink, Connor found the kettle, filled it with water, and switched it on. 'Where are your cups?'

'The cupboard above your head. Milk's in the fridge. No sugar.' Reaching a shaky hand out, Greta took the cup from Connor, sipped the tea, and placed the cup on the table, spilling some of the contents into the saucer. Eyeballing the two men and looking between them, she asked again, 'What have you brought into my house?'

Connor sank slowly into the seat. Pulling his mobile phone from his jeans pocket, he held it in front of his face and unlocked it. 'I'm going to call the police. Please don't tell them we were here or about Liv being missing.'

Banging the palm of her hand on the table, she shouted, 'No!'

'He may come back,' Connor urged.

'I said no. No police. That's an order. Just... Just leave it.'

Sipping her tea, she placed the cup back on the saucer and looked Connor in the eyes. 'I know who it was. I saw his face. Darren Franklin. My nephew.'

'Okay,' Connor said, slightly more optimistically than he'd meant. 'Great. So call him. Find out what's going on and why he was here. This is positive, in a way.'

She looked to the wall and then back to Connor. 'I can't call him. He's been dead for ten years.'

12

Saturday Afternoon

They're watching me, Ella thought as she scrutinised the footage for the umpteenth time. Looking down at her garment, she thought, *They're wearing the same black dress. They've been watching.*

Martha had left her alone in the office while attending to the shop, sarcastically telling her not to pinch the monitor when she left the room. The woman who'd entered the shop was roughly the same size and shape as Ella, and she'd waved to Martha as though knowing her. To any layperson, it looked identical to her. But it wasn't Ella.

'Who the heck are you?' Pushing slowly off the chair, Ella stood in silence, her eyes closed, trying to comprehend the situation, mulling it over in her mind. The black dress. Exactly what she wore today. Fear drove through her body, and she felt vomit rise to her throat. The door busting open caused her to jump.

'Well?' Martha asked, standing with her arms folded, her lips twitching as though uncomfortable with the circumstances.

The consequences were too much for Ella. Her strict father. The shame on the family. The relationship between her mother and Martha. The police. 'I'll pay,' she hissed.

At the counter, Martha produced a credit card machine, tapped in the figure of two hundred pounds, and watched as Ella inserted her card and entered her PIN. 'Thanks, love. It's all forgotten about now. Would you like a receipt?'

'Stick it as far up your fucking arse as it will go. Bitch.' Ella turned and walked out the front door.

'Connor, it's me. Any news on Liv?' Ella steered around the droves of people on the pavement. Many of them stood taking photos, others with dogs on leads, and groups of tourists pointed and chatted in colourful languages.

'Nothing. We're at Greta Franklin's place. Something's happened. I'll tell you later.'

'Can you talk for a minute?' asked Ella.

'Of course. What's up?'

After explaining what had happened, the phone call from Martha, the visit to the shop, and her seeing the footage on the monitor, she said, 'It wasn't me. I was home all day. I feel like I'm losing my mind, Connor.'

Hearing the panic in her voice and how she stuttered her words, he said, 'You're not.' Briefly, Connor explained what had happened at Mrs Franklin's house. How he'd found a photo with Frank Dawson's head circled and had a visit from her dead nephew.

A shiver bolted through Ella's body as she listened to her friend. Her legs felt flimsy as she stopped, placing a hand against the front wall of a house. 'Do you think this has something to do with what happened to us?'

'I don't know. Very possibly. Where are you now?'

'The high street. I'm going home. I've had too much drama for one day. I have to get my thoughts together. And I'm two hundred pounds down just to save face,' Ella stated as she looked over her shoulder.

'Okay. I'd say it's safer to stay indoors until we find out what's going on.'

'I'm so scared, Connor.'

'Me too. Look. Get home quickly. I'll call you later.'

'Thanks. I will.' Ending the call, she turned around, peering along the street, wondering if someone was watching her.

A wave of anxiety swept through her body at the thought of being alone. Standing in the hallway by the front door, Ella secured the chain and twisted the double lock.

Slowly, she climbed the stairs, entered her bedroom, and slumped on the bed, her mind addled by today's events. Martha had humiliated her with the threats and she wondered if she'd still meet her mother every Wednesday for bridge. Would she tell her? Maybe they'd have a drink, and it would slip out – an off-the-cuff remark. *Oh, how's the thief doing? She's barred from most of the shops in Rye now, the little peasant. Sticky fingers, that one. She's a bad sort, is Ella. Take the coat off your back, she would – a proper little Swind-*

Ella. Ella. Ella. She nicked a pint of Stella, and the landlord's locked her in the cellar.

The mess of the bedroom was daunting. A black top and leggings hung over the back of a chair. Her makeup strewn over the dressing table. The curtain rail hanging lopsided and coming away from the wall. The wine stains on the white rug. Reality bit hard. She was quickly outgrowing this place, and it suddenly felt as though the walls were closing in as the claustrophobia gripped tight.

Her mobile phone rang. Ella grabbed it off the bed, seeing a withheld number. 'Hello, Ella speaking. Hello?' When no one answered she hung up, dropped the phone on the bed and leaned against the wall, turning her head side to side to ease a crick in her neck.

The phone rang again.

'Ella speaking. Who is this?' she asked with a sharp tone. 'Hello?' The phone pinged with an email. Jabbing the end call button, she looked at the screen.

From: youneedtoseethis@notspam.co.uk

To: EllaMcKenzie@gmail.com

In the subject bar, it said, *For attention of Ella. Don't ignore!*

Biting on her lip, Ella debated opening it. Her fingers twitched, her heart raced, and she pulled her left knee to her chest. Inhaling, she clicked on the link, seeing a photo of a woman standing with a carrier bag. The dark glasses. The black dress and the long, blonde hair. The same person she'd seen in the footage at Martha's shop. Dropping the phone on the bed, she sprang up and rushed to the window, to see her standing on the street, looking up at her.

Quickly, Ella stormed out of the bedroom, charged down the stairs, and flung open the front door. The woman was gone, but the carrier bag she'd held was sitting by the front door. Ella grabbed it, looked inside and saw the four garments Martha had accused her of stealing. As she tipped the contents onto the ground, she saw labels on each piece, held with a safety pin. Each label held writing.

It will come for you, too.

13

*S*aturday Afternoon

Standing in the back garden, Connor stared at the blank phone screen and digested the call with Ella, taking a second to try and clear his head. The stranger the day became, the more he worried about Liv. He wanted to scream at the top of his voice until he went hoarse. The frustration was building, and it felt like he'd spontaneously combust at any moment. Each breath was a struggle. His vision was impaired by tears, and with every second that passed, hope was dissolving. With a gulp of air, he felt his chest expand, as he tried to clear his head and stem the panic that threatened to engulf his body. When his skin had cooled and stopped tingling, he turned, opened the door, and walked into the kitchen.

'You okay, mate?' Liam asked.

'Oh, just great,' he answered with a touch of sarcasm. To

Mrs Franklin, Connor asked, 'Your nephew. Are you certain it was him?'

'Yes, you heard me correct.' Greta was clearly shaken, and it looked as though the blood had drained from her face. Her complexion was deathly white, the bags under her eyes were more apparent, and it seemed as though she'd aged ten years in the last hour.

'Darren was a problem child. Oh, he was always missing school, getting detention, in trouble with the teachers. He... He was my sister's only child. She and her husband tried for so long to conceive. Darren broke her heart. Then she discovered he was on drugs. At her wit's end, she was.'

Placing a hand on Mrs Franklin's, seeing the tears in her eyes and trying to comfort her, Connor asked, 'What was he taking, if it's not a rude question?'

She looked to the ceiling as if thinking. 'The white powder stuff. Sniffing and snorting all the time. Then, he moved on to stronger drugs. Oh, what was it called? My sister told me, but I can't remember. It's the same name as a long-legged bird.'

'Jennifer Lopez?' Liam quipped, and Connor slammed his foot into his shin.

'Heron. That's the name. Injecting it, he was.'

'*Heroin*,' Connor mouthed to his friend, ensuring she couldn't hear him.

'Then he was crossing the road and staggered in front of a car. Gone like that. Killed instantly. Off his bloody face. That's the term you young ones use. Ten years ago, it was. I remember it like it was yesterday.'

'I'm so sorry for your loss,' Liam offered.

'It was him. I know it. I saw his face. I'm not stupid.' Looking at Connor, she again asked, 'What have you brought to my house?' Standing, the chair toppling backward and hitting the tiled floor, she raised her voice. 'Get out! Now. The two of you. Get out this instant!' Pointing at Liam, she said, 'And you, you imbecile. Obnoxious brat! I thought you'd make something of yourself when you left school. How wrong I was.' Her tone became less dramatic. 'There are many more so-called birds, as you put it, with longer legs than that J-Lo.'

'Father Maloney, it's Greta Franklin.' She spoke slow and stern, with intent in her voice, jabbing the loudspeaker button and holding the phone in front of her mouth.

'Greta. Hello there. How can I help?'

'It's a... a tad awkward. I need to speak with you in person.'

'Confessions are usually done at the church,' he said.

'I went yesterday. It's urgent. Can you come over?'

'I'm actually passing your road as we speak. Wait, let me hang a right. Be with you in a few minutes.'

'Thank you, Father.'

There was a knock at the door, and Greta hurried along the hallway, stopping to fix her hair in the mirror. 'Thank you, Father. Come in, won't you?' She led him back along the hallway and into the kitchen, filling the kettle and switching it on.

'Can I use the toilet?' the priest asked.

'Of course. You know where it is, don't you?'

'Yes. Along the hall. Unless it's moved.' He returned a few moments later and sat with a huge sigh, straightening out his cassock. 'Is everything alright, Greta?'

'Two sugars, isn't it?'

'Oh, go on then. It's the weekend.'

Greta placed two cups on the table – one for Father Maloney and one for her. 'I had... I... I had a visit from my nephew today.'

'Okay,' he said, studying her face. 'And did something happen?'

'Father, he's been dead for ten years. I know it sounds crazy. Bonkers, even. But I saw him. He was standing behind me in the kitchen.'

Leaning back on the chair, the priest was clearly pondering what Greta had said, choosing his words carefully. 'How did you feel seeing him?'

'I'm terrified. I don't want him here. He was vile while alive, and he'll be vile as a spirit, too. Could you... bless the house, Father?'

'Greta,' he said, placing the palms of his hands on the table, 'has this happened before?'

'I haven't lost my mind if that's what you're insinuating.'

'I'm not suggesting that for a minute. I know it was a tough time for you last year with losing your husband. You were married for... remind me again?'

'Forty-six years. And yes, it was a horrible time. I still suffer every day. I miss him, but life goes on as they say. What choice do we have?' Her eyes dropped to the table, watching as the priest drummed his fingers. 'Please, Father, bless the house, would you?'

'Of course. I have holy water in the car. Don't move.'

Father Maloney returned a couple of minutes later and said a few prayers as he sprinkled the holy water over the kitchen. Greta joined him, and they finished by making the sign of the cross.

'Right,' the priest confirmed, still holding the holy water, 'I believe the spirit will be laid to rest now and at peace.'

'Thank you, Father,' Greta said as she walked behind him to the front door.

'You're a good woman, Greta. You do lots for the church. It's a pleasure.'

As the priest opened the door, he turned. 'Oh, I almost forgot. I found this on the bathroom floor. It must have fallen.' He handed her a miniature wooden figure.

'That's not mine,' Greta insisted as she examined it. 'I've never seen it before.'

'Well,' Father Maloney said, 'it must be yours. It looks exactly like you.'

14

Saturday Evening

Ella had placed the garments into the carrier bag, stepped back into the house, and closed the front door, twisting the lock and pulling the chain across to secure it.

Now, in the kitchen, she emptied the contents onto the table, holding each piece in front of her. The clothes were shredded as if cut with scissors. Taking them back to the shop was not an option. The message on each label was disturbing, written with a black felt tip pen. Ella read the labels over and over as though in a trance.

It will come for you, too.

. . .

Aggravated, she shoved them into the bag, opened the back door and dumped the whole thing into a large bin. Staring down the garden, along the muddy path which wound to an old rickety shed and a small fence along the back, she thought how easy it would be for someone to climb over, race to the back door, smash a window, and get into the house. It was getting dark, and thick black clouds smothered the sky. Through a gap, she glimpsed the half moon, almost transparent and nestled between the branches of a distant barren tree, casting a faint glow over the tranquil landscape.

Turning, Ella viewed the house. Her fashion course at university had finished. She didn't have a job. Her parents were away for a month. How would she survive all alone in the house?

Realising the urgency of the situation, her mind raced. *I have to forward the email to Connor,* she thought, her heart pounding. She rushed into the house, locked the back door, and charged up the stairs. Grabbing her phone from the bed, she opened it, only to find that the email had vanished.

'No. Where's it gone?' With her right finger, she scrolled down the page, seeing newsletters from authors she followed, updates from the local jazz bar, Rye festival promotions, and an Amazon audiobook offer.

After checking her junk and spam folders, Ella stepped to the window, looking down to the street. Two young guys dressed in jeans and shirts walked along the pavement, deep in conversation and smoking cigarettes.

An older couple linking arms came towards them, stopping and taking selfies. There was no sign of the woman who'd dropped the bag.

'Who are you?' Ella whispered against the glass, seeing her breath form condensation. 'What the fuck do you want?'

In a single day, she thought, *this person has ruined my reputation and is causing me to cower in my own home.*

Her body jerked as her mobile phone rang from the bed. Placing a hand on her chest, hoping to control her heart rate, Ella turned slowly. The name was familiar, and she answered. 'Hi, Connor.'

'Ella. I'm with Liam. Can we come over?'

His words immediately seemed to stem her panic. 'Yes. I'd like that. I hate being alone in this house.'

'Okay. We'll be there shortly.'

Stretching her neck, eyes resting on the ceiling momentarily, Ella began picking at her nails, her thighs bouncing under the table. Then, looking between her friends, she told them what had happened, finishing with the chilling message written on the labels.

The deathly silence which fell over the kitchen was a testament to their angst.

Shifting his chair closer to the table, his fingers in his mouth as he bit his nails, Liam said, 'I had the same thing this morning. The email was a recording. Frank Dawson, ripped to bits. Fucking mutilated, Ella. The person responsible turned to the camera and said, "It will come for you, too." Then, it disappeared from my laptop.'

'"It will come for you, too,"' repeated Ella, her voice sounding as though she was drugged. 'The labels.'

The letterbox pounded. Ella squealed, turned, and peered along the hallway.

'Wait there. I'll go.' Connor got off the chair and walked along the dim hallway, feeling his friends' eyes almost bore a hole in his back. His fingers were twitching, and his cheeks were hot as he reached the front door. Something had been pushed through the letterbox. Quickly, Connor stooped, picked it up, and unfolded it. His fingers were warm and sticky as he fumbled with the A4 size page. It was a copy of an old news report from the local paper, Rye News.

The headline read:

Tragic accident at St Michael's as one pupil dies and another is disfigured.

Beneath was a picture of a small group of parents, standing, huddled together by the school gates.

Across the article, written in black felt-tip pen, were the same words – the same stark warning:

It will come for you, too.

Outside, the air had turned cold, and faint drizzle pushed against their faces.

'Let's go this way?' Connor suggested, pointing along the high street.

He and Liam ran side by side, aware people were watching them, passing the many restaurants, bustling pubs, and art galleries.

They sidestepped the families and couples sauntering on the pavement, groups of friends standing outside restaurants reading menus, and a woman bent over with a bag cleaning up her dog's poop. No one appeared suspicious.

'Shit. Who was it?' gasped Connor, his face almost glowing with the colour in his cheeks.

'Let's backtrack.'

They turned, jogging back along the road, past Ella's house and down the hill, stopping at all the side roads.

'They've gone.' Connor bent over, steadying himself and catching his breath. 'Let's go back to Ella.'

'It's us,' Connor shouted through the letterbox. 'Open the door.' He heard the clunk as Ella removed the chain and pulled the front door back.

'Anything?' she asked, her eyes wet and fearful.

'Nothing. They disappeared into the night,' Connor stated.

They assumed the same positions at the kitchen table as before.

'We're not safe, are we?' Ella mused, almost like she was talking to herself.

Connor grabbed his phone, opened Facebook, and clicked on Rye News.

A picture of Frank Dawson, standing in woodland, wearing a brown jumper and jeans, appeared at the top. Flipping the phone, he showed the picture to his friends. 'They've released a statement.'

It is with a heavy heart that we announce the passing of a wonderful member of our community and the Rye family. Frank Dawson, fifty-three, who has lived in Rye for over twelve years, was found dead at his cottage this morning after a neighbour alerted the police.

We won't go into the gruesome details as that is not what we're about. I'm sure the local police will be releasing statements over the coming days.

Frank's parents are deceased, and he has no siblings, partner, or children.

We would like you all to keep him in your prayers tonight and may he rest in peace.

Funeral arrangements will be posted here in due course.

Again, please keep Frank Dawson in your prayers.

Admin. Rye News.

Scrolling down the page, they read the messages of condolences that began filtering through.

Shaun Kemp

Top man, Frank. So sorry to hear this.

Mary Hemsworth

Go fly with the angels. Best caretaker St Michael's ever had. RIP.

Paul Richards

We love you, Frank. Bless you, mate. Rest easy.

Daisy Riley

Oh, this is too sad. Rye is in mourning tonight. Take it easy, Frank.

After scrolling through the many comments, Connor closed his phone, placed his elbows on the table, and dropped his head in his hands.

'This is all coming back to haunt us, isn't it?' Ella said as she stood, pacing the kitchen floor. 'What happened at school, I mean.'

'Stop it!' Liam snapped, his voice harsh and stern. 'It was a horrible accident. We didn't mean for it to—'

'She's right,' Connor said, cutting his friend short. 'It's coming for us. It's only a matter of when.'

15

T he Past

The words didn't slur in her mind. Odd, that. Only when she tried speaking. It confused Sinead. But then, so much had lately. For the moment, the stomach cramps had eased. She'd been up several times during the night, vomiting. Sometimes, she felt like she was possessed, like the young girl in *The Exorcist*: a demon or some other monster taking her body over, causing all these bizarre symptoms.

Generally, Sinead was healthy. She exercised regularly. Ate well and only had the odd glass of wine at the weekends. Her mother was well into her eighties and still fit, but her father had died from a heart attack, being the only one amongst his siblings to die so young.

Although she'd drunk almost a pint of water through the night, remembering someone somewhere telling her water cures everything, her mouth was parched, her lips chapped, and her tongue felt raw as though it could easily snap off.

The bedroom door opened, and Roy Kipler, her boyfriend of a few months, walked in with two cups of tea. His curly brown hair draped over his forehead, his tee-shirt was too tight, and he stumbled awkwardly as one of his slippers dragged on the wooden floor.

'Careful. I'll be wearing the tea,' she laughed, her voice hoarse and dry sounding. It hurt to talk. It hurt to do anything lately.

Setting the tea on the side, Roy pulled the blanket back, pressing his hand to her forehead. 'I don't think you have a fever. How are you feeling? Geez, you were up half the night.'

'Death. That's the only way to describe it. I feel like a corpse who's missed their calling. Everything aches.'

'I'm so sorry you're going through this. Hopefully, the results of the blood test will come through soon.' Pressing his lips to the cup, Roy heard clanging noises coming from the twins' room. 'Christ's sake. Boys! Boys, simmer down!' To Sinead, he asked, 'Can I get you anything? Tablets? More water?'

With a hand on her stomach, she shook her head. 'I just need to sleep.'

'Okay. I'll drop the boys in and head to work. If you need me, I'll have my phone. I love you.'

'Love you too,' she slurred.

No sooner had the bedroom door closed than a gentle rap resounded on the wood.

'Ah. Nathan. How are you?'

'I'm fine.' Approaching the bed, his eyes sincere and with a concerned look on his face, he held a vase with flowers. Handing it to Sinead, he said, 'I'm thinking of you. Get well soon.'

'Nathan. You are such a sweetheart. Thank you.' Holding him, she could smell vanilla shampoo on his hair, and his skin was sticky and smelled of sugar. 'Have a good day. Love you loads.'

'You too,' Nathan answered as he left the room.

Smiling, she placed the vase on the bedside unit. In her peripheral vision, she saw a shadow at the door. Fred Kipler, Nathan's twin brother, stood with a menacing expression on his face, his eyes screwed tight and a wicked smirk, staring at her.

'Aren't you going to ask me how I am? Fred, I'm talking to you.'

The young boy was frightening. All her life, no one had scared her as much as this fourteen-year-old boy. It was sinister. As though he was pure evil. In the few months she'd dated Roy, the twins' father, he'd done wicked things, and she feared it was only the beginning. Their mother, Angela, had walked out a few years ago, and although it wasn't gospel, Roy had claimed on more than one occasion that Fred was at fault. 'I asked you a question, Fred. Fine! Ignore me, then. Close the bedroom door.'

Pushing it further open, Fred turned and walked down the stairs.

It was just gone 10 am when Sinead's mobile phone rang. Blinking tears from her vision, she pawed at the bedside unit, pushing her body along the mattress and leaning against the headboard.

Withheld number.

She hated those. Usually sales calls or someone trying to con you out of all your money from your bank.

As she blinked, the words cleared further, and she pressed the answer button. 'Hello?'

'Sinead Pearse?'

'Speaking.'

'It's Doctor Adams here. Are you able to talk?'

'Yes,' she responded, the pain in her throat just bearable. 'How can I help?'

'Mrs Pearse. We have the results back from your recent blood test. Can you come into the surgery? It's a matter of urgency?'

'I... Oh, God. I'm sorry. I can't. I'm so unwell at the moment.'

'I suggest you call an ambulance. Sooner rather than later. Is there anyone who can be with you at this time?'

'My... My partner, Roy. But he's at work. What's going on?'

'Your results show the presence of a... a toxic substance – ethylene glycol. It's commonly found in antifreeze, and this explains the symptoms you've been experiencing. I need to ask if you've been exposed to anything unusual, like chemicals or contaminated food or drink?'

'Erm... No. Not at all.' Visions of Fred Kipler standing at her bedroom door pulsed through her mind. *Surely not,* she thought. *Oh, God, no. It can't be true. This cannot be happening.* 'Look, I'll ring my partner. I'll get him to come home. Thank you for calling.'

'Mrs Pearse. I cannot stress this enough – you need to call an ambulance now! Without immediate treatment, your condition will deteriorate rapidly.'

Ending the call, Sinead wept. The nausea returned hard,

and it felt like the contents of her bowels would empty all over the bed as she rushed to the toilet.

While on the loo, she dialled 999.

'I was poisoned,' Sinead stated. 'I told them I didn't know how it happened. But they may investigate it further. The hospital staff have to report these things. The police aren't stupid.'

'So what are you saying?' asked Roy. 'That I did it?'

'No. I'm not saying that. I'm so confused. I know you wouldn't do it.'

'You need rest, Sinead. You've just come out of hospital. We'll get to the bottom of it. But poisoned. They must be wrong, surely.'

'It's driving a wedge between us. Can't you see?' Grabbing her boyfriend's hand, Sinead stopped him from opening the fridge. 'You have to do something about him!'

Slamming his fist on the worktop, Roy Kipler bent forward, acting as though he'd run a hundred-metre race, pushing his fingers into the skin of his temples. 'Don't go there. Don't fucking go—'

'You're too frightened to admit it! You're not stupid. You must see.'

'What, Sinead? See what? You... You think Fred is doing this to you? You're out of your frigging mind.'

'Get him help!' She stood behind him and placed a hand on his shoulder, only for it to be shrugged off.

'I've tried.'

'Really? Tell me what you've tried?'

'The... The school counsellor.'

'Wow. How did that go?' questioned Sinead, not wanting to get into another row.

'She didn't think there was anything serious wrong with him.'

'Roy. They had two sessions. In that time, Fred never said a word to her. Not one word. You told me yourself. How can she assess his mental health without having a conversation?'

'He told me he was shy.'

'Oh, and you believe that? Is he shy when he's hurling abuse at me? The nasty things he does to me behind your back. You know, last night I took a shower. He shut off the feed.'

'Kids do that,' Roy assured. 'It's just a laugh.'

Rolling up the sleeve of her jumper, Sinead pushed out her arm, showing burn marks. 'Only hot water came through the mixer. He fucking knew what he was doing.'

'They're going to be late for school,' Roy stated, opening the fridge and grabbing two sets of sandwiches he made last night.

'Nathan doesn't act like that. He's an absolute sweetheart. Compared to Fred, he's an angel – a pure gentleman. I can talk to him. Have great conversation. We laugh together. He has a wonderful sense of humour.'

'They just have different personalities. I know they're twins, but you can't expect them to function the same.'

'I don't. But I swear, unless you do something about that... that little shit, I'm gone.'

'Whoa. Don't. Please, Sinead. Don't go there.'

'You mean the part where I'll go or Fred being a shit?'

He backed down, softening his eyes. 'I don't want you to go. I'll sort it. I'll get him the help he needs.'

'Is it why your wife left?' Sinead pushed, obviously hitting a nerve.

'We... It was complicated.'

'What did he do to drive her away?'

'I can't do this now.' Strolling to the bottom of the stairs, Roy called the boys. 'Fred. Nathan. We're going to be late for school. Let's go.' As footsteps charged down the stairs, Roy kissed his girlfriend on the cheek. 'I'll sort it.'

'Bye, Nathan,' Sinead said. 'Have a good day.'

'Thank you. See you tonight,' he replied.

Fred trotted into the room behind his brother. Droplets of sweat dripped from his curly brown hair onto his red cheeks.

'Bye, Fred. Have a good day,' she forced, digging her nails into the palm of her hand.

As Fred closed the door, he stuck his middle finger up.

'*Evil bastard*,' she mouthed, returning the gesture.

The burn from the hot water was only the tip of the iceberg; Sinead had held back so much more. One morning, she'd woken to find her favourite blouse slit with a knife. She'd binned a pair of her slippers that felt soggy and stunk of urine. Often when she'd pass the twins' room, Sinead would hear him saying the word 'slut' over and over again. It had reduced her to tears many times.

But she was crazy about Roy. They'd met on a dating app a few months ago. The first thing that attracted her was his aftershave. That woody, lemon scent as he'd approached the bar, hugged her, and bought drinks. As they'd sat, their eyes locked, the conversation flowing, Sinead had felt an attraction like never before. He was her type – a perfect match. Tall, handsome, with amazing eyes and a great dress sense. The only thing spoiling it was Fred. She had to do something about him. Although he was only fourteen, he terrified her.

The quiet tranquillity was a welcome relief from the usual mayhem.

A headache was developing, and she worried it would quickly turn into a migraine. She'd suffered with them more recently.

She pressed a hand to her forehead, feeling relief, climbed the stairs and walked along the hallway to the double room she shared with Roy.

As she passed the boys' room, a pain formed in her stomach, as if it were turning over. Hesitating, she pushed the door back, fearing the young lout would be standing there, ready to do something to cause distress.

Posters hung on the wall with Blu Tack: famous rock bands with scary masks, and motorbikes in the background. A height chart, the left corner peeling away, was marked with a felt-tip pen at five feet four, and the desk was cluttered with toys from movies and exercise books.

The room stunk of dirty socks and a pungent sweat only teenagers could produce.

As she approached the desk, Sinead saw a scrapbook with "Fred Kipler" written on the front. Licking her finger, she gripped the bottom corner and opened it. The gasp that left her mouth was so intense that she felt dizzy.

Drawings of Sinead, naked and being raped by wild beasts, were scribbled across the pages. Others showed a person looking like a half demon, half dog shoving a hot pole into her private parts.

'He's... He's sick.' Crouching, she opened a cupboard with a sticker on the front saying, "Private. Fred's stuff. Keep out." She felt her breath catch in the back of her throat. There were bottles of antifreeze at the back of the cupboard. *It was him,* she thought. *He has done this to me. He's been poisoning me.*

As she turned, her mouth locked open, and her muscles froze, seeing miniature wooden figures aligned along a shelf.

One of them was identical to her.

16

Saturday Night

The TV was muted as Greta Franklin sat on the sofa, flicking through the channels. The soaps she loved to watch, like *Coronation Street* and *Eastenders*, never aired on a weekend. Unless you were willing to watch repeats. Quiz shows frustrated her if the questions were too difficult, and she despised reality talent competitions. Anyway, she couldn't concentrate. Her mind was occupied with her dead nephew, Darren Franklin, visiting and the tiny wooden figurine Father Maloney had found in the bathroom. Greta racked her brains and could say with absolute certainty that she'd never seen it in the house before. There had to be a reasonable explanation.

Examining it and seeing the resemblance to herself, she'd placed it in the bin, fearing it may be cursed.

After finding an old episode of *Columbo*, she turned the

volume up, pushed back on the sofa, and placed her legs on the soft footstool.

'Just one more thing,' she said in a low voice. 'You always bloody solve it. That's the problem. Maybe, just once, have him completely stumped. It's not real life – complete nonsense. And you're always squinting. Just one more thing.'

It was at times like this that Greta missed her husband the most. Truth be told, she missed him all the time. The void Albert had left behind would never be filled. His company, his companionship, and how he always knew the right things to say to ease her worries.

The incident with Fred Kipler had been extremely traumatising, and Greta knew she'd never have gotten through it without Albert by her side. His reassurance had added comfort and relief.

He'd died suddenly just before his sixty-ninth birthday. A massive heart attack. The paramedics battled to save him, but in the end, it was God's plan. Greta still spoke to him, believing Albert was looking down and guiding her every step. The silence was daunting; it was something she would never get to grips with. Staring at the old black-and-white photo perched on a shelf by the TV, Greta's mind flooded with wonderful memories.

She grabbed her mobile from the table next to where she sat. The vision of her nephew plagued her. *I'll call my sister, May,* she thought. *If she says anything about seeing Darren, I'll feel more at ease.* Carefully dialling the number, she waited, hearing the perky voice on the other end of the line.

'Darling sis,' May said. 'Hello. I thought you'd forgotten the number.'

'They're smartphones,' Greta remarked. 'I only had to search your name.'

'I'm pulling your leg. How are you?'

'I'm doing alright,' Greta lied. *Seen anyone lately? Any dead people? Your toerag of a son been to visit recently?* It was how she wanted the conversation to go, but it was too delicate a matter. 'How's Brian?'

'Oh, his usual grumpy self. He's watching *The Wheel.*'

'Washing what?'

'Not washing. Watching. The TV show. With Michael what's his face? Are you going deaf, sis? So how come you're calling so late? You're normally in bed by this time.'

Greta wanted so badly to tell May everything. The visit from her deceased nephew, Darren. Connor and Liam calling over. The priest blessing the house. The figure that he'd found in the bathroom. But May lived in Kent, a good forty-minute drive, and she didn't want to worry her, knowing she'd come over in an instant. 'Oh, I wanted to say hello is all.'

'Are you sure everything's alright? You sound... You sound distracted. Like something's on your mind.'

'Honestly, I'm fine. Let's speak tomorrow.'

'Okay. Night, sis.'

Ending the call, Greta placed the mobile phone back on the side unit and looked at the TV. 'Just one more thing,' she sneered. 'Get a new coat!'

A boisterous groan resounded above her. Gripping the arm of the sofa, Greta again muted the TV, shuffled to the edge of the seat, and stood. The curtains were closed, the side lamp provided soft light, and the only sound was the clock as the second hand swept around the face. Easing back the living room door, she stepped into the hallway, her body suddenly cold, causing her teeth to chatter. She moved silently into the kitchen, and checked the back door was locked. Pushing her face to the glass, she was relieved to see the security light off. With memories of her dead nephew standing behind her only hours ago, she quickly turned, seeing the empty hallway.

The place has been blessed. Get it together, Greta, she thought.

There was a crash from upstairs, as though the loft hatch had slammed against the wall, causing her to flee her thoughts. It felt like her heart was in her mouth.

Hurrying along the hallway, Greta stood at the bottom of the stairs. 'Is... Is someone up there? Hello?' Placing a foot on the bottom step, she stumbled sideways, slamming a hand against the wall for support. 'I said, is someone up there?' Waiting, the silence deafening, she could feel her heartbeat in her ears. Gripping the bannister, Greta began climbing the stairs. Her mind raced. Images of her dead nephew pounded through her brain. A vision of Frank, the caretaker, lying dead on a slab. The miniature wooden toy Father Maloney had handed her. A carbon copy of Greta, carved to look exactly like her. How did it get there? How had her dead nephew visited her earlier? Connor and Liam must have thought she was a crazy old lady losing her mind. But she knew what she saw. Greta didn't care what they thought.

At the top of the stairs, she glimpsed along the hallway to the back bedroom.

'I'll ask again! Is there someone in my house?' Greta grabbed the doorknob to her right, easing the toilet door open. Empty. Ripping off some toilet roll on the holder, she blew her nose, suddenly feeling lightheaded. She dumped it in the toilet, then turned and stood at the top of the stairs, peering at the ground floor.

A gasp spilled from her mouth, and she was certain she saw something rush along the downstairs hallway.

'If there's somebody in my house,' she called out breathlessly, 'you need to leave.' Again Greta waited, still and silent, afraid to make a murmur and trying desperately to detect the slightest sound coming from between the walls.

She went back downstairs, and as she reached the bottom step, she heard a heavy pounding noise charging towards her from the kitchen.

She screeched, her legs giving way, and Greta fell to the ground. As she covered her face, the footsteps suddenly stopped. Worried her mind was playing tricks, she stood and she charged to the front door. She pulled down the handle furiously, but it resisted, stiff under her grip. It was locked from the inside. Searching the floor for her keys, she found the small figurine that she'd earlier placed in the bin as footsteps rushed up behind her.

17

Saturday Night

Standing outside the flat, Connor felt everything was futile. So much rushed through his mind. Had he taken enough care of Liv? Was he doing enough to find her? Why had he been on the train going to meet an artist who probably wouldn't have signed with their gallery anyway?

He bent his thumb under his fingers until he heard it crack, then pushed his fists together, trying to relieve the pain of Liv being missing.

He climbed the steps leading to the front door and eyed the communal buzzer. Flat two. Their happy place. Smiling, he recalled the day they'd moved in and how they'd stood outside, holding hands, excited about creating memories and building their life together.

Swallowing hard, he opened the front door. A pile of letters sat on a shelf, along with flyers displaying local mechanics and pizza restaurants. Thankfully, no threatening messages had been left in the time he'd been away.

Bracing himself, he walked to the far corner of the hallway and entered their flat.

'Liv,' he called, not expecting an answer as he switched on the light. The long, narrow hallway was glum. The atmosphere harrowing. 'Liv, are you home?'

In the kitchen, he sank into a seat by the table and sobbed.

Managing to pull himself together, Connor slugged a glass of water and walked into the bedroom. The duvet was still pulled back on Liv's side. Her slippers rested by the bed.

As Connor removed his clothes, he got an alert on his mobile to join Liam and Ella on FaceTime.

Dropping on the bed, he answered. 'Hey. I'm home. You both alright?' Ella was fixing her hair and brushing it off her shoulders.

'Mum and Dad called from Spain,' she declared. 'I haven't told them about the clothes or the visit we had earlier and I didn't mention Liv or Frank. They never look at social media while away. I think they're pretty sloshed, so they went to bed. Anything?' she asked, meaning news on Liv.

'Nothing. The more time that goes by, the less hope I have.'

'Mate,' Liam urged, 'don't give up!'

'I'm scared. They know where we live,' Ella said.

An alert appeared on the screen. A friend of Connor's had sent a messenger note through Facebook. Exiting the call, Connor tapped into it, still able to hear his friends talking.

Dan Harvey had written, '*Hey Connor, is everything okay? I saw you a few minutes ago. Well, I think it was you, slamming the front glass of the gallery and kicking the door. You looked distressed, mate. Hope you're alright.*'

Rereading the message, Connor said, 'Shit! Guys, I've got to go. I'll call you later.'

'What's wrong?' asked Ella, but he ended the call without answering.

He pulled on his jeans, a tee-shirt, and a jumper, then slipped into his trainers and ran to the car.

It has to be him, thought Connor as he started the engine and pulled onto the main road. It felt like his body was drowning in adrenaline; he hoped he could catch this guy and force him to take him to Liv. His left leg bounced, his right leg pressed the accelerator to the floor. He opened the window to feel the chilly air push against his skin, awakening his senses. Although it had been only a matter of hours, it felt like forever since Liv had been taken. Seeing the figure in his mind, racing towards her, he struggled with his anger, pumping his leg harder, grasping the steering wheel between his hands, and biting down.

He took a side road off Rye High Street, turning into an alleyway, closed the window, and killed the engine.

Fear had been replaced with apprehension and Connor felt he was moving on autopilot. It didn't matter what happened to him. Liv was his priority, and getting her home.

He walked back up the street and stopped a few metres from the gallery.

It was late. The last few people were eating and enjoying a few drinks. Further along the high street, a small queue had formed outside the jazz bar – the only place with a late license. The street lamps glowed along the road, revealing a thin mist in the air. A boiler kicked in, the plumes of smoke harsh as they blew towards him from the flue.

Connor stepped to the corner of the gallery's front window, crouching low and pressing his face against the glass. It seemed empty. The shop was alarmed, and if anyone was inside, the owner, Mr Humphries, would get an alert and call the police.

The glass was intact, as was the front door.

Moving back along the street to the rear of the shop, Connor crept along the alleyway. Something jumped in front of his path. Holding his chest, he swung around, hearing cats screech as they darted over a fence. Above his head, a security light blinked on. The gallery's back entrance had been smashed, and the door was standing open.

Someone was inside.

He stepped back, his chest tightening, his fingers tingling, and he felt his knees buckle. Holding onto the side wall for a moment, he turned his phone torch on and stepped to the door. Shards of glass lay strewn over the floor inside, suggesting the window was broken from the outside. Connor pushed the door wider, unable to see into the shop front. The alarm must have been deactivated, Connor assumed. *They must have gotten the code from Liv.*

Although it was the start of summer, the cold hit him instantly as he went inside. The lights were off, and he lifted the torch, scanning along the corridor, the many paintings in boxes waiting to be collected by delivery companies. The smell of cardboard caught in his nose, and he managed to stem a cough that threatened. Shining the torch into the shop front, Connor heard a shuffling sound. Something scurried along the floor.

'The police are on their way,' he called out. 'They'll be here any minute.'

Approaching the counter, he shone the light on the till and unlocked it, seeing it empty.

Then it dawned on him. The message his friend had sent earlier declaring he'd seen Connor outside the gallery.

The security camera would show this person breaking into the gallery, turning off the alarm, pinching money from the till, paintings, and anything they could get their greasy hands on.

Connor would get the blame, lose his job, and possibly go to prison – the end of his and Liv's future dreams.

They were trying to ruin him. Take everything away that he cared about.

Suddenly, someone was behind him. As Connor turned, he felt a harsh thud land across the side of his face, and he fell to the ground.

When he came around a few minutes later, the pain severe in his head, pounding in rhythm with his heartbeat, Connor pressed his fingers to his skin, feeling a wet, sticky liquid running down his face. He wiped it, got to his feet, and went into the office.

The small monitor was on, perched at the side of the desk, scanning through various angles of the shop floor. Security cameras recorded the front and back entrances.

Connor entered the password, rewinding the footage.

At the back of the store, along the alleyway, a white Transit van pulled up. The van door opened, and a young man got out.

Gasping louder than he'd expected, Connor watched

him, standing at the side of the road, glancing at the gallery. He looked left and right, then made his way to the front of the store. The light from the street illuminated the figure as he stepped to the front window with his hands cupped against the glass.

No wonder Dan messaged, he thought. To any layperson, it was Connor. Down to the dark glasses, the size, build, hairstyle, and stubble. Christ, even the way he walked. His shoulders swinging, arms moving back and forth. At school, other kids mimicked it, taking the piss out of him.

Captured on the CCTV at the rear of the gallery, the Transit van reversed back along the alleyway. It was too dark, and Connor struggled to see the driver.

They're slowly trying to ruin us. He thought about Ella. The story she'd told earlier about her double, pinching garments from the shop. Brazenly walking in, grabbing clothes right in front of the owner. One of her mother's best friends.

A chill drove through his body. *What next? They could do anything. Frank had already been killed. How much worse would it get?*

In the top right corner of the monitor, Connor could see the guy, or whatever it was, standing outside the shop on the high street. He pulled the front door, kicked it, slammed the glass with the palms of his hands, and backed away, watching the gallery from the street. Brazen as you like.

Someone passed on the other side of the road, staring at him – Connor's friend Dan. Connor's doppelgänger shifted, looking conspicuous, swinging his head left and right, then rushed to the back of the shop. Their demeanour suggested stress. An urgency. It was like they were aware people were watching, but it didn't matter. They wanted to be seen.

Moments later, the doppelgänger smashed the glass at

the back of the shop, reached an arm inside, and opened the door.

On the monitor, Connor could see the light from a torch as it danced on the floor and the figure moving through the shop.

Then Connor himself entered through the back door.

Someone rushed him and dropped him to the floor.

With no answers on the footage and knowing he'd get the blame, he deleted everything.

Outside in the back alley, tyres spun, and a vehicle pulled away.

Connor rushed out, seeing a white Transit van pull onto the high street.

He had to follow it.

'Liam, sorry about ending the call. Something's happened.' Connor reached the high street and saw the Transit van heading out of town. Turning left, he floored the accelerator, fumbling with his seatbelt and locking it into its holder.

Sounding as though he'd been woken, coughing phlegm from his throat and clearing it, Liam asked, 'What's happened? Have you found Liv?'

Explaining the recent developments, listening as his friend turned on the bedroom lights, Connor rushed his words, stumbling over them, sounding breathless.

'I'll come and meet you,' Liam said. 'I can take Dad's car.'

'No!' insisted Connor. 'There's no time. I think... I think it's a ruse.'

'In what way?'

'I was forced here. They were too conspicuous. I know so many people in town. They made sure they were seen.

During our FaceTime call, Dan Harvey messaged, asking if I was okay. He'd shouted over, and being ignored, alarm bells rang. Then just now the van pulled away, making sure I'd hear. It may be a trap. But I have no choice.'

'Shit! Connor, be—'

'I have to go. I can't lose the van.' Finishing the call, Connor reached the end of the high street and pulled onto the A259. The van was travelling at a steady pace, making sure not to exceed the speed limit.

Pulling back, sure the driver was aware of his presence, he allowed space between the two vehicles.

Grabbing the phone from the passenger seat, he debated calling the police. But this person had all the cards. He'd threatened him. As soon as sirens were heard, he'd kill Liv. There was no way Connor could chance it. This person was a lunatic. Frank Dawson's death was a testament to their capability.

Ahead, the van swung left, turning into a country lane.

Easing on the brake, Connor saw the empty road ahead and a sign warning to slow down glaring in the headlights. Approaching the turning cautiously, he steered into the narrow lane, seeing the lights ahead disappearing around another bend. Bushes on either side whipped against the wing mirrors. The car bounced over potholes in the road, and although the windows were closed, the smell of manure from the fields was stifling.

The van's lights dipped over a hill and out of sight.

Shit! I'm going to lose them. Connor put on his full lights, illuminating the narrow road ahead. The car seemed to swallow the tarmac as he pressed harder onto the accelerator and switched gears. There was only blackness around him. As he peered at the fields, just a dark void for miles on either side, he suddenly felt completely alone.

Touching the brake, he slowly rounded a bend, almost losing control as a rabbit raced onto the road, skidded, and rushed back into the ditch. Reaching the brow of a hill, he hoped he'd see lights in the distance.

There was nothing.

Connor slapped the dashboard as he steered down the other side, glaring at a road to his left. *Had they gone down there?* Certain it was a dead end, he continued straight, watching the speedometer hit almost fifty. Branches whacked the glass of the windshield and passenger door, and the potholes were so bad he thought the tyres would burst.

As he rounded another bend, at last he saw the van, stopped in the middle of the road with its hazard lights on.

What now? he thought as he sat, half expecting another vehicle to show in the rear-view mirror and trap him. He felt vulnerable. *This person always seems a step ahead. Why stop in the middle of the road and wait? He can see me. Why is he not driving away? Unless... he wants me to catch up with the van. Maybe he'll spring out from the ditch, kill me, and bury me where I'll never be found.*

Although it was only minutes, it felt like hours. Connor sat not fifty yards from this maniac. Something had to give. It seemed like a game of chess. He was tired, frustrated, and needed to get out of there.

Suddenly, he stamped on the accelerator, too tired to think straight. Connor was going to ram it from behind. Do something they wouldn't expect.

As he approached the van, it began to pull away.

In his headlights, he saw the rear doors open, and the person who'd taken Liv was standing, stumbling slightly from side to side. Over their shoulder, they held what appeared to be a body wrapped in a blood-soaked sheet.

Connor was going too fast to stop.

As he closed the distance to a few yards, the person in the back hurled the figure onto the road and closed the doors.

He tried to stop, but there wasn't enough time, and Connor ran straight over it.

18

T he Past

'Leave me alone. You're so irritating.' Ella tried to steer around Fred Kipler, seeing his chubby red cheeks glistening with sweat. His breath was rancid, like sprouts cooking in a pan of water, that foul, putrid odour filling the kitchen, and he wheezed as he laughed. 'Fred. I'm going to tell Mrs Franklin,' she threatened.

'Ooh. I'm so scared. I'm going to tell Mrs Franklin,' he repeated, putting on a baby voice, his eyes almost slit-like, his mouth full of crooked yellow teeth.

'Let me pass,' Ella yelled.

Fred Kipler watched as she went one way and the other, even kicking a chair into her path and watching her attempt to step over it. As she lifted her right leg, he kicked the other one, causing her to lose balance and fall hard on the floor.

'Leave her alone!'

Connor held out an arm and helped her up, as Fred glared at him. 'Or what?'

'Nothing. Just leave her.'

'I asked you a question. What are you going to do about it?' Fred urged, pushing his face into Connor's. 'Go on. I dare you.'

'Are you okay, Ella? Your knee. It's bleeding.'

'I'm fine. Just leave it.'

As Connor walked to his chair, Fred gave him a harsh shove on his back, knocking him over the desk. Gasps filled the room as shocked pupils watched Fred stamping on Connor's hand.

'Er, how dare you! Fred Kipler. Stop this instant.' The room went silent as Mrs Franklin charged towards him, ripping him away by his grey jumper. 'How many times, Fred? How many times must you pick on the other pupils? Always looking for trouble? You're never happy unless you're hurting someone. Well? Answer me, Goddammit?' As she stared into the horizontal slits, resembling a pig, she felt utter disgust. She'd never hated another human being more than Fred Kipler. She despised him, although she could never admit it. Fred Kipler was ruining her life. The numerous detentions after hours and weekends, the disruption he'd brought to her classroom, and the way he stared at her. She was frightened of him. He sometimes kept her awake at night with frustration. And she was certain the boy was possessed. Could any normal child be this evil? A huge puff of air left her mouth as she ordered him back to his chair.

'Fucking old slut,' he murmured.

For peace, she ignored it. What could she do? Give him a hundred lines. Five hundred. A thousand. A weekend detention. Plead with the headteacher to suspend him. *Oh yeah,* she thought. Mr Conway was a personal friend of Roy, Fred's father, and they often played golf together. The countless times she'd gone to the office to complain about the boy had always fallen on deaf ears. Mrs Franklin had to accept it. She was stuck with this prick until the year was up.

Turning to the board, she could feel the eyes boring into the back of her skull, knowing the pupils wanted her to retaliate, to do something about Fred. 'Open your books. Page fifteen.'

The door swung open, crashing against the back wall.

'Liam Anderson, it's nice of you to join us. You can be the first person to read from the Bible during today's lesson,' Mrs Franklin demanded, 'seeing as you stroll in here like you own the place.' Thumping her desk with the side of her hand, she shouted, 'Tuck your shirt in!'

'Sorry, I'm late,' came the muffled excuse. 'The traffic—'

'Traffic,' she said, with a hand in the air to stop him talking. 'Lost your keys. Locked out. Locked in. Dog pissed on your homework. Broken washing machine. I've heard them all. Sit and read. Now!'

As Liam wandered to his desk at the back of the classroom, Fred Kipler stuck out his foot, tripping him up.

'I heard what happened. Fred attacked you again. Are you alright?' asked Liam, unable to hide the annoyance in his voice, aware of a telltale blush on his cheeks as he stared at Ella.

'I'm... I hate him so much. Why doesn't Mrs Franklin do something? You know,' Ella continued, 'I've heard the rumours and what the other kids say about him, but I didn't think he'd be this much of a dick. Christ, he's intolerable. It doesn't let up. The constant jibes and always looking for a reaction. The names he calls me and the shitty stuff he mumbles about my family. I hate him!'

'Can I help you carry your books?' asked Liam.

Pressing them into his chest, she smiled. 'You're a gent. Thank you.'

Connor joined them, and the three walked out to the playing fields.

'I have a plan,' Liam announced as he looked at the kids kicking a football around. A small group sat under a tree, puffing on vapes, trying their best to keep them hidden from the teachers with their hands, while others texted on their mobiles.

'A plan? Go on, I'm intrigued,' Ella asked.

'Nathan. Fred's twin brother,' Liam said.

'What about him?'

'Right,' Liam said, his hands pressed together, trying not to make his enthusiasm too evident. 'Fred Kipler has gotten away with this shit for too long. Agreed?' Watching both his friends nod, his mind buzzing with vengeance, he suggested, 'Let's lock Nathan in the store room. Leave him there for a few hours.'

'What?' asked Ella. 'Nathan is so sweet. He wouldn't harm a fly.'

'Yeah. Leave Nathan out of it,' added Connor.

'No. Come on, guys. Listen. Fred loves Nathan. He adores him. He's the only person on this planet he respects. You know the connection twins have. It's like doing something to one is doing it to both. It's just a laugh. Fred will be fuming when he finds out.'

'Mate,' Connor interjected, 'locking him in the store room. No. It's not fair!'

Lighten up, you two!' urged Liam. 'It's not as if we're going to hurt him.'

'Can you give me a hand? Mrs Franklin asked me to get some books from the store room.' Liam pulled open the door, glancing into the darkness beyond.

'Er... I have to get to class. I don't like being late,' Nathan responded. 'I get embarrassed.'

'It's fine,' Liam fibbed. 'I told her I'd ask you to help. It won't take long.'

'Oh, okay then. I can help.'

Backing against the wall, Liam turned, pointing down the stairs. 'The lights don't work. I'll use my phone torch. It shouldn't take us long.'

'What about Connor? Can't... Can't he help?'

'He's hurt his back. He's at medical. It won't take long. You're not scared of the dark, are you?'

'Me? No, I'm not scared,' Nathan answered, his voice rising a half an octave.

'Good. Then you can go first.' Nathan hesitated at the top of the stairs for a moment, then began to descend. As Liam watched him, he could hear Fred screaming in the classroom.

'Mrs Franklin's gone walkabout again. Has anyone seen Nathan?' Fred spouted.

A door slammed, and feet pounded along the corridor. A few moments later, Connor and Ella appeared, their faces twisted with concern.

'Nathan,' Connor yelled into the stairwell.

'Shush, will you!' Liam hissed. 'It's just a laugh,' he

insisted as he followed Nathan, closing the door to the store room and turning on his phone torch.

The smell of cardboard hit hard. Shelves were lined with old books, newspapers, empty boxes, and felt pens.

Liam kept his right arm extended, shining the torch to the corners of the store room.

'Keep going. I think the boxes are at the back. Thanks for this, Nathan. I appreciate your help.'

'I heard Connor call to me. He was with Ella. What are they doing?'

'No. I told you, he's at medical. Again, thanks for your help.'

'It's okay. I like to help. I'm just worried I'll get in trouble.'

'You're fine. Just a little further.'

As the two lads reached the far wall, Liam pushed Nathan onto a rickety chair.

'What are you doing? I thought you needed help.'

Without saying a word, Liam removed his tie and quickly wrapped it around Nathan's wrists and between a robust shelf, securing it with double knots.

'Please!' shouted Nathan. 'Don't leave me here.'

Moving close to his ear, Liam whispered, 'Your brother is a prick. He has to learn we can get to him in other ways.'

Locking the store room, Liam placed the key on the rack by the door.

When Liam got back up the stairs, he grabbed a triangular hazard sign with the words "Caution. Slippery Floor" from the cleaners' cupboard and placed it outside the store room door.

'I hate this, Ella said. 'Half hour tops. That's it. Then we let him out.'

'I'm with you, Ella,' urged Connor. 'Nathan's done nothing to—'

'Hey! You three. What are you doing in the lab unsupervised?' Frank Dawson walked towards them, shaking his head. 'No one is allowed in there without a teacher.'

A door opened, and Mrs Franklin joined them in the corridor. 'What's the racket?'

With his arms folded, Frank said, 'I found these three in the science lab unattended.'

'What were you doing in there? Connor. Ella. Liam. Answer me!' Mrs Franklin waited, and they stared back at her with blank expressions. 'Right, well, detention then. Starting now. Go and wait in Mr Conway's office.'

As the three trudged along the corridor, listening to Frank and Mrs Franklin talking, Liam turned to his friends. 'Let's bunk off.'

'No. I got in so much trouble the last time,' Ella said, 'I was grounded forever.'

'I've got alcohol. Mum and Dad are away for the weekend. We can get smashed.' Liam watched the concerned expressions on his friends' faces as they hesitated for a moment, swaying Mr Conway's office and walked into the playing fields and onto the road.

'I can't leave him in there.' Turning, Connor looked at the school. 'I'm going back.'

'I'll come, too,' Ella announced. They ignored Liam's

plea to leave it a while longer and made their way back to the store room.

'I'll deal with them. They're good kids. I'm sure it was something innocent. What's wrong?' Mrs Franklin asked, seeing the concerned expression on Frank's face as he sniffed hard.

'Can you smell that?' asked Frank.

Inhaling heavily, Mrs Franklin walked further along the corridor towards the science lab. 'Oh shit! A fire. Oh my God. There's a fire. Quick.'

With his mobile phone, Frank smashed the glass on an alarm. The piercing noise that ensued was almost deafening. Kids charged from classrooms as a small explosion came from the science lab.

As Fred stood outside the open window, pleased the fire was spreading so quickly, a muffled cry for help came from the store room.

19

*S*aturday Night

Almost hysterical, Connor felt his body shake with such force he thought he'd end up breaking a bone. Through the windscreen, the lights of the Transit van disappeared over the horizon.

In a daze, as if comatose, he sat in the driver's seat, his mind blank and unable to develop thoughts.

The skin under his eyes stung, his cheeks were hot and flushed, and his hair damp with sweat. He could feel heat rising through his body, saturating his bones.

Lights appeared in the rear-view mirror, approaching fast and stopping behind him.

Suddenly, a hand grabbed the door handle and pulled it open, and a torch shone in his face.

'I told you not to follow it! What did I say? Shit, Connor.' Liam helped him out of the car, hugging him for support.

'It's... It's her. I know it is. I've run over her. I couldn't stop. There wasn't enough time.'

'It's okay.' Glancing back and shining the torch at the blood-stained sheet, Liam clearly feared the worst, although he didn't say it out loud.

'You'll have to take a look,' instructed Connor. 'How did you find me?'

'Snapchat. It wasn't difficult.'

'Can you please take a look?' pushed Connor.

'Me? I don't think I have the stomach for it.'

'Just... Just pull the sheet back. Tell me who it is.' The two men were silent, suddenly interrupted by a fox screeching in the distance.

'What was that?' asked Connor, dread creeping through him.

Liam shone the torch into a field. 'Don't start. I feel like Jack and David on the moors. All we need is to find the Slaughtered Lamb. We can shelter there.' He felt guilty for making a joke in such a dire situation. But it was either that or crack up. 'Okay,' Liam said. 'But you'll have to hold the torch.'

'Fine. Let's do it.' So much flashed before Connor's eyes as they stepped along the narrow road. The first interview after which he'd recommended Liv for the job. Their first day at work. Their hopes for building a business together. He missed her desperately. The fruity smell of her skin, how she held his hand, often gripping it too tight during scary movies, and how she hogged three-quarters of the bed and kept him awake talking in her sleep. He couldn't imagine a life without her.

Above, the moon glowed bright, peering down on them, partly illuminating the fields, the trees casting ominous shadows over the path ahead.

Liam had almost reached the body.

Turning, Connor glanced behind himself, half expecting to see the lights of the Transit van coming back their way. He watched as his friend crouched, composing himself, quickly looking around him, and then reaching a hand towards the middle of the sheet.

'It's... Er, it's crushed badly. It seems the middle has gone flat.'

'Holy shit. Do you think they're alive?'

'I doubt it.' Standing, Liam looked at him. 'I can't do it. Sorry, mate. I can't.'

'You have to, Liam!'

'This is way beyond my friendship realm. Do you know what you're asking of me?'

'Yes, but if it's her, I... I can't see her like that. Just pull the sheet back.'

'I said I can't!' insisted Liam.

'Yes, you can. I'm here. Just pull it back.'

'You're here,' Liam said sarcastically. 'Oh, like that makes all the difference.'

'Pull it back!'

Again, Liam crouched, reaching an arm out and touching the sheet.

'Go on.'

'Stop! Will you stop? I'm trying to psych myself up.' With the tips of his fingers, he gently undid the rope tied around the body and pulled it away. The sheet was covered with bloodstains, but there wasn't the smell he'd expected.

Connor watched from a few feet away, biting his nails and trying to hold the torch still.

Removing more of the sheet, Liam tried to balance by placing his hand on the ground. 'Throw me the torch, will you.' Catching the phone, he placed it between his lips. 'It's—'

'Who? Who is it?'

'It's Liv,' Liam said, pulling the sheet further back.

'Oh, no. Don't tell me that! Please, Liam. Don't!'

The top part had come away. The middle was just mush from being squashed under the tyres. Liam lifted the head with a picture of Liv stuck to the front. 'No. You don't understand. It's a mannequin.'

I was lured out here. I played right into their hands. 'It's him. It's Fred Kipler. It has to be. The high school photos. The mannequin. The doppelgängers.' Connor pulled the rest of the sheet back, smelling what he now realised was red dye rather than blood. He scrunched it up, and placed it into the boot of his car.

'He's dead. Dead Fred. He died,' Liam quipped.

'Did he?' It felt like the blood had returned to his body. The trembling had stopped, the bloody patch on his head had dried, and the tension had eased. But for how long?

'Yes. No one has seen him since the fire. He disappeared.'

'It doesn't mean he's dead,' Connor fired back.

'Everyone said it at school. Don't you remember?'

Digesting the conversation, Connor looked around, searching for the lights of the Transit van.

'What if Fred is still alive? No, hear me out for a minute,' Connor stated. 'Maybe he's lost in the system. With his mum washing her hands of Fred and no siblings left, it would have been possible to disappear. And now he's come back.'

It was as if Liam turned in slow motion, finally facing Connor.

'Are you serious?'

Connor knew deep down it made sense. Liam may doubt Fred was still alive, but he had to admit the recent events must have something to do with their past.

'How else would you explain all the shit going down?' pushed Connor. 'He's come back to avenge what happened to Nathan.'

'Mate,' urged Liam, 'he died. Fred Kipler hasn't been heard of since that tragic day at school.'

'So how do you explain everything happening to us? Go on?'

'I don't have an answer. But Fred isn't back. Maybe someone is trying to freak us out.'

'Freak us out! Liv's gone! You saw Frank and how he'd been mutilated. That's way beyond someone trying to freak us out.'

'If you think Fred's still alive, and he's doing all this, let's check his old place out – their family home.'

'It's abandoned, isn't it?' asked Connor.

'As far as I'm aware. With everyone missing or dead, the farmhouse has been forgotten about.'

'Right,' Connor said, 'then let's check it out. There may be something to give us answers.'

Nodding, Liam turned to his car, which was parked behind Connor's. 'Let's go.'

20

E arly Hours of Sunday Morning

Almost three miles outside Rye on the A259, Connor indicated and pulled into a side road. Behind him, Liam followed, keeping close to his rear bumper.

Their conversation ran on a loop in Connor's mind, his friend adamant that Fred Kipler was dead.

But if he was, then who was doing this to them?

A friend revenging the terrible tragedy? No, he thought. *It isn't possible. The only people who knew what happened were Frank Dawson, Mrs Franklin, and Liam and Ella.*

Now, one of them was dead.

Could Fred still be out there? he pondered. *Did he know Liam locked Nathan in the store room?* Gazing into the barren fields, he saw specks of light on the horizon, almost like eyes staring at him and scrutinising his every move.

His mind reverted back to that fateful day and how

they'd learned about the tragic events. Liam had locked Nathan in the school store room, and he'd been burned alive. A horrific accident that had changed their lives forever. Frank Dawson and Mrs Franklin had kept silent about who was responsible for locking him in. The chemicals and other flammable substances in the room had added fuel to the flames. All evidence had been wiped away.

What if Fred had seen them outside the store room as they left? Although Connor had pleaded with Liam to leave it and not involve Nathan, it's possible Fred had seen the three friends together and blamed all of them.

If Liam was right, and all this was coincidental, then finding the culprit was like looking for a grain of sand on a beach.

As he approached the abandoned farmhouse, a shudder pulsed through his body, making him jerk.

After pulling over by a ditch, Connor got out of the car and watched Liam park behind him. There was no sign of the Transit van, but he didn't know if it was a good thing. It could easily be hidden in the darkness.

The first detail he noted was the remoteness. There were no other houses for miles each way. No lights and no sound. It was eerie, and he wondered how anyone could have lived so far from civilisation.

Liam joined him, and the two walked together side by side towards the building.

Shining the torch, Liam said, 'What is it they used to sing?'

Without hesitation, Connor replied, '"Nathan Kipler trapped in the fire, burning to a crisp, and about to expire. Freaky Fred tried to save his double, but the fire got him, and now he's in trouble."'

'That's it. All the kids were singing it at school. It spread like wildfire. Excuse the pun. I had nightmares for months afterwards. I struggled to sleep. I woke so many times through the night with cold sweats. I often saw him standing at the end of the bed. I think about it all the time. It haunts me.'

'Me too,' responded Connor. 'The fact Fred was an evil bastard doesn't take away from what happened. His brother didn't deserve to die.'

'We were kids though,' Liam fired back. 'How many times do friends lock each other in store rooms, or toilets, or... or play pranks? We didn't think Fred would burn the school down and disappear.'

Connor so badly wanted to respond. To scream in Liam's face, shake him until he understood. Connor and Ella had told their friend to leave it. That there were other ways to get to Fred. They'd pleaded with him not to involve Nathan. Sweet, sweet, Nathan. Their appeals had been ignored.

But now wasn't the time or the place. 'She put the frighteners on us,' Connor remembered. 'Mrs Franklin. She hated Fred. Remember when she got us all together? "If you admit to this, you'll be taken away and locked up. You'll never see your parents again. Is that what you want? Keep silent." They were her words. We didn't know what to do. The longer it went on, the more trouble we'd be in with admitting what had happened. We were terrified kids with no one to turn to! The trauma we went through trying to deal with the agony internally. It was hell!'

Nearing the farmhouse, Connor took the torch and shone it over the ground-floor windows. Thick boarding was in place and nailed to the frames. The barn-style double doors were locked with padlocks to prevent people from entering. Ivy clung to the outside of the building, almost vice-like, weaving its way around as if trying to smother the farmhouse. The smell of damp and burnt wood was in the air, as though something knew of their presence, and was trying to remind them of the terrible accident.

Leaning against the wall, Connor felt light-headed, as though his head was spinning out of control. He didn't want to be here. It was as though the farmhouse was dragging up all the terrible memories, and at any minute Fred Kipler would burst through a bush in the fields, engulfed in flames and swearing to get revenge.

Nathan Kipler trapped in the fire, burning to a crisp, and about to expire. Freaky Fred tried to save his double, but the fire got him, and now he's in trouble.

The song played over and over in Connor's head. Then Mrs Franklin's voice: *If you admit to this, you'll be taken away and locked up.* Crouching on one knee, he shouted, 'Stop! Just stop it.'

'Mate. Are you alright?' Liam walked towards him, placing a hand out and helping him stand. 'Deep breaths. Come on. You can do it.'

'We... We didn't mean for it to happen. We told you not to do it!'

'Stop! Mate, you need to get it together. We were kids. It was a tragic prank that went wrong. We can't let it ruin the rest of our lives.'

'But it has. I wanted to own up. I wanted to tell someone what had happened. Fred's coming for us. We're fucked.'

A shuffling noise startled them, followed by a loud thump.

'What was that?' asked Liam.

'I... I don't know. I think it came from inside. Rats, maybe?' Inching along the ground, Connor continued to walk around the farmhouse. Every so often, he turned, pointing the light into the fields to see the long grass almost still and lifeless. It was the perfect place for someone to hide. No one would know they were there.

He turned right at the end of the ground floor and continued walking around the side of the farmhouse. There were more windows, once a gateway to the majestic views over the hills, now closed up, boarded, shutting out the world and everything with it.

'It's pointless,' Liam said. 'We're never going to get inside. It's like a prison.'

Suddenly, they saw a small window above the back door. Someone had used a crowbar or other tool to rip the board away. The glass had been smashed, and the shards had been pushed away.

'We can get in here,' Connor suggested. Trying the door handle first and conceding it was locked, he placed his foot against the door, gripping the frame, and pulled himself through the window above, the broken glass tearing his clothes. He landed head first with his arms out to protect him. Once on his feet, he helped Liam through.

'What a mess,' Liam said, looking around.

The kitchen table leaned slightly to the side, one of its legs missing. The wood was grubby and worn, part of it eaten away, presumably by bugs. The ceiling had large, black patches of damp and gaping holes. Cobwebs clung to the corners and onto a light bulb held with a flimsy wire. The floor was sodden from grease, and as they stepped over it, their trainers stuck to the lino.

An old-fashioned brown oak unit leaned against the back wall. Photo frames were tipped on their sides and smashed, the pictures within unrecognisable due to the stains and condensation.

The smell was rancid and could only be described as decaying meat, like a slab of pork infested with maggots.

They covered their mouths, but the foul air filling their lungs was increasingly uncomfortable.

'Someone's been here,' Liam said through the sleeve of his top, his voice muffled. 'That smell.'

'It's probably a dead rat.' Looking around himself at the dire state of it, Connor said, 'No one in their right mind is living here. They've left this place long ago. It's useless. Come on, it's late. We need to go.'

'Hey, look at that.' Strolling over to the side unit, Liam picked up a cardboard box. 'An old cereal carton. I haven't seen one of these for years.'

'Put it back. It's probably contaminated,' said Connor. 'Let's get out of here.'

As the men left, driving back along the dirt road, a figure crept to a window, watching them through a crack in the board from inside the farmhouse.

21

T *he Past*

'There's someone down there.' Over the din, Frank Dawson could hear shouting coming from the corridor. 'I have to try and help.'

The pupils were out at the far end of the playing fields. Most of them stood in disbelief.

'Are you sure?' Mrs Franklin asked. The heat from the flames was so intense it felt like it could melt flesh. 'We need to get out of here.'

In desperation, Frank rushed to the store room, trying to reach the fire extinguishers. 'Who's down there?' he called at the top of his voice.

'Nathan... Nathan Kipler. They've tied me up. I've worked the gag off my mouth, but my hands are tied. Help!'

Another explosion caused Frank to stumble backwards, the heat intense.

'Please help me!' Nathan roared.

Grabbing Frank by the arm, Mrs Franklin ordered, 'Leave him. It's not worth risking your life.'

Frank rushed out into the schoolyard.

Fred Kipler was crouching by the window. A look of horror had replaced his smirk as he'd learned his brother was trapped. He'd seen Mrs Franklin and the caretaker talking, deciding to leave him there. Anger coursed through his body as he clenched his fists and climbed into the science lab through the broken window. The heat was intense, like being trapped inside a sauna. It felt as if his body was being crushed, burning from the inside out. The flames had engulfed half the science lab already, and the thick black smoke made him cough. His lungs felt like they were boiling, and the hot air was unbearable.

Closing his eyes to ease the stinging, tears streaming down his face, he felt for the door to the store room. It was locked, and the handle was hot. He grasped around on the rack next to it for the key. Finally he got the door open, and pushed further into the store room. 'Nathan. Are you down there?'

'Help me! Please, Fred. You have to get me out of here.'

A piece of timber fell from above, and Fred steered around it. 'Who did this? Who tied you up?'

'It doesn't matter. Get me out of here.'

Pushing for an answer, Fred asked again.

'Liam Anderson. Please. Help me, Fred.'

Liam Anderson, thought Fred, automatically putting Connor and Ella in the frame as well.

As the sirens blasted behind him, so did a waft of fire.

Fred Kipler pulled closed the store room door against the flames, and descended down the stairs.

Roy Kipler sat at the kitchen window, looking over the vast land around the farmhouse. The sun was shining, the sky was a deep blue, and the clouds were minimal. His laptop was open, and today, the boss had let him work from home. In all aspects, he should be in an incredible mood.

The letter lay folded on the table, and Roy reached for it, reading it for the umpteenth time.

Dear Roy. I don't know where to begin.

These last few months have been incredible.

The best times of my life.

So, it's with the greatest regret that I'm doing this.

I have no choice. Believe me. If there were another way, I'd surely find it. But there obviously isn't.

The pain has been unbearable as you know.

I've been for tests, and they've proved I'm being poisoned.

Poisoned by your son. Fred Kipler.

The bottle of antifreeze is a testament to what he's capable of.

I packed a bag last night, collected my belongings, and hid it from you. It was too painful to say goodbye this morning. I hope you understand that siding with your son against me is unacceptable. He could have killed me. Maybe that was the intention. I know Fred drove your wife Angela away as well. It's possible you'll find a partner that will tolerate his narcissism, but that's not going to be me.

Bye, Roy.

Yours, Sinead.

. . .

Scrunching up the note, Roy walked to the bin, stepped on the pedal, and dumped it with the rubbish.

He'd thought she was the one. The person he wanted to spend the rest of his life with.

He and his wife, Angela, had argued about Fred for months. In the end, she couldn't tolerate his behaviour a second longer and walked out of their lives, minus a note. He'd tackled it. Asked himself what kind of mother walked out on their family. How she could do this to her children. Her flesh and blood. How depressed had she been to run away and never look back.

The more Roy thought, the angrier he became. The parties they'd held at the farmhouse had become thinner. The circle of friends diluted. Parents turned away at the school gates and refused to give the twins a lift home. All the excuses in the book: *I've got a full load already. We're not going your way. Oh, I'd love to, but we have a meal booked.*

Bent over, Roy pressed his fists into the table, feeling his body tremble with anger. He didn't know what to do with Fred. At his wit's end, he pictured Sinead. Kind-hearted Sinead. The letter had broken him.

As he wiped his streaming eyes, sniffing hard, the phone rang. It startled him as he turned, facing the mobile on the side unit.

'Hello. Roy speaking.' As he gazed at the words across the screen – St Michael's, Rye – it felt like his heart dropped to his feet.

'It's Mr Conway.'

'Yes, I know. What's he done now?'

'I... Erm, I don't know how to tell you this. There's been an accident. A fire.'

He felt like a sponge, soaking up bad news time and again. It was like he'd become immune to it. 'Go on, Fred started it. Am I right?'

'Er... that, we don't know. I'm ringing because we're personal friends. I... I wanted you to hear it from me. Your son, Nathan, is trapped in the store room. Our caretaker, Frank Dawson, tried to get to him, but the flames were too severe. The fire brigade is here as we speak and tackling the blaze. You need to come over here and prepare for bad news.'

Hanging up, Roy walked out to the car, numb, dishevelled, and dead inside. His head should have been going crazy with thoughts, plagued by them as they swirled around, causing mass confusion. But it wasn't. This time, a calmness seemed to drift over him like a scented cloud.

Starting the car, he shook his head, wondering what he'd be met with at the school. Pressing on the accelerator, he steered into the garage, and closed the door behind him. Then he grabbed a hose and stuck it in the exhaust pipe.

As flames ripped through the science lab, the sound of broken glass was eerie, and an almost constant groan emanated from inside, like a sinking ship, its timber stretching as it descended into the deep water.

A poisonous black fog swirled over the playing fields like a plagued spirit as children stood bunched together, some holding hands while others were in tears, covering their mouths with the sleeves of their jumpers.

Firefighters battled on, shouting for people to stand back as they tackled the blaze with hoses.

Moments later, Fred Kipler came running out through

the doors, his arms and legs ablaze and deathly screams ringing in the air.

His classmates leaped back, some running away, too frightened to act or do anything.

One of the emergency crew grabbed a fire extinguisher and put out the flames, wrapping a blanket around Fred's body.

A paramedic placed him on a stretcher in an ambulance, closed the doors, and raced with blaring sirens to the nearest hospital.

It was the last anyone saw of Fred Kipler.

Among the onlookers were Connor, Ella, and Liam, who stood, mortified at what had happened. The prank had backfired in the cruellest of ways.

It would haunt them for the rest of their lives.

22

T *he Past*

'I can't sleep. I can't eat. I'm going completely nuts. We have to tell them what really happened,' Connor said, fiddling with his school tie and pulling the knot tighter. He was standing outside class and waiting to speak with Mrs Franklin. Ella and Liam were with him. Part of the school, including the science lab, was cordoned off and the smell of burning wood still drifted in the air, lingering over their heads, a stark reminder of the tragedy.

'I'm the same,' Liam answered. 'I keep hearing Fred's cries for help in my head. Sorry, it wasn't supposed to sound corny. Mum and Dad keep asking me what's wrong. I woke up early this morning, roaring in the bed. The hot sweats were crazy. I can't concentrate. I think it's best. We need to come clean.' He saw Ella nod, and the three of them each placed an arm out, hands on top of each other in a silent pact.

They opened the classroom door, the three of them shuffling in. Mrs Franklin was marking papers. The school was empty as most of the pupils had gone home.

'Er, is it okay to have a word?' asked Connor, seeing the teacher biting on the end of a pen.

She pushed the chair back, straightening her dress. 'Of course. What is it?' Her voice was stern and resolute.

'Erm... Well... Mrs Franklin,' Connor began with tearful eyes, 'Nathan Kipler was tied up in the store room.'

Looking between the three of them, seeing the glum faces, the look of shame, she said, 'I don't know what you're talking about.'

'I did it,' Liam said urgently. 'It was my fault. My friends tried to stop me but I didn't listen. Nathan died because of me. Don't you see?'

'What I see,' she answered, standing from the chair and walking to the window to look out over the playing fields, 'are three children, bright pupils who have their whole lives ahead of them.' Spinning around, she slowly drew her eyes over each of them. 'Are you telling me you want to throw it all away? Because that's what will happen. If you, Connor Murphy, and you, Ella McKenzie, knew about this and didn't come forward, you'll be taken away from your families, a police record for manslaughter will hang over your heads, and your lives will be completely ruined. You may never see your family again. And Liam Anderson, you can kiss goodbye to the rest of your life! Think long and hard about that! Oh, it's a tragedy. Make no mistake about it. But you're kids with a bright future. You want to chuck away everything you've worked hard for. I won't let you do that.'

What Mrs Franklin wanted to say was that Fred

deserved it. She was glad it had happened. Fred Kipler was a demon, and she despised him with every fibre in her body. He'd almost caused her to have a mental breakdown, and this was his comeuppance. It was like he haunted her. She still took medication to try and shake the evil bastard from the shadows and help her cope.

Clearing his throat, Connor said, 'What happened to Nathan was so wrong. That poor kid. We need to tell the police!'

'Can I ask the three of you a question?'

They all nodded.

'Do you like me as a teacher? Connor, you first.'

Feeling a flush cover his face, he answered, 'Yes. You're the best teacher we've had.'

'Liam. Do you respect me? Ella, I'm asking you, too?'

In unison, they both answered, 'Of course.'

'Good. Then here's something I'll pose to you all. I will tell the police I knew Nathan was down there and I ran. It's called leaving the scene of the crime. It's kind of like a hit-and-run. I'll get the brunt of the blame, too. How's that? No answer? Right, that's the last on the matter. Now if that's all, keep your gobs shut and live your lives.'

As the three pupils left her classroom with confused expressions, Mrs Franklin pushed the door, feeling a hand grab it from the other side before it closed.

'Greta, got a minute?' Frank Dawson, the caretaker, entered the classroom.

Glancing at her watch and knowing the pressure she was under to finish her marking, she lifted the papers, waving them in the air and replacing the stack on her desk. 'It will need to be quick.'

'The police were sniffing around. They're no closer to finding out how the fire started. But they're asking questions. They think it may have been arson.'

'They may be right. I think we both know the culprit. It's just a shame his twin had to die in such tragic circumstances.' Mrs Franklin went on to explain how Connor, Liam, and Ella had spoken to her and how she had had to divert their guilt with scare tactics. She picked up a stress ball, squashing it in her hand. 'I can't lose this job. I've already been reprimanded,' she insisted.

'Have you heard anything else in regards to your punishment?' Frank asked.

'Nothing. But I can't risk those pupils stoking the fire and bringing attention to me. I can't have the spotlight shining on my face. So far, the police aren't able to pin it on anyone. They haven't a clue who tied Nathan in the store room. That's how I want it. They'll give up soon enough.' She stood and walked over to Frank, pulling him close and kissing him heavily on the lips.

'Steady,' he said as she pressed her leg against his groin. 'We might be seen!'

'I thought you loved a risk,' she replied.

'Can you keep a secret?' Frank asked, kissing her hard on the face and undoing her blouse.

'I won't tell if you don't!' she answered, knowing this was the reason she needed her pupils to keep silent. While she was supposed to be looking after the class during break time, she and Frank had been in the toilets sharing a kiss.

23

unday Morning

S

It was just gone 8 am when an alert came through on Connor's phone. Although he wiped sleep from his eyes, blinking to focus, he had been awake most of the night. No closer to finding out who had taken Liv, he'd slumped into bed at around 1 am, staring at the ceiling.

The mobile pinged again.

Turning on his side, he grabbed it and tapped the screen. The WhatsApp message was from a number he didn't recognise. Hesitating, he sighed. His mouth was dry, and his skin felt tight due to dehydration. Pushing his body against the headboard, he eyed the other side of the bed, seeing the empty space. Liv's perfume was still present, possibly coming from her pillow or blanket.

He brought the phone screen closer to his face, tapping to open the message. His fingers twitched, shoulders arching together as he saw a picture of Liv, a knife at her throat, and the words, '*We're watching. Tell the police anything, and the next picture you receive will be me holding her head.*'

Pushing away from the headboard, Connor sat on the edge of the bed. Anger festered in his stomach, like a flame pulsing through his body. A panic attack threatened, causing him to shake.

Breathe, he told himself. *In for five and out. Slow, controlled. You have this. Ride the storm.* As he closed his eyes, a vein at the side of his head began throbbing, and Connor imagined a dark cloud drifting past, melting into the atmosphere.

Once he'd regained his composure, he pinched the screen with his thumb and forefinger, zooming into Liv's face. The look of complete terror was obvious. Grubby marks like oil or dirt clung to the skin under her eyes. Her lips were pressed to a thin line, veins protruded from her neck, and it looked like she was trying to pull her head back. The knife was held to her throat, but Connor couldn't make out if it was piercing her skin.

'Bastard,' Connor whispered. 'You won't get away with this.' Slamming one hand on his thigh, he dialled the number, waiting for the person to answer.

He wasn't sure what to say, but he needed to know Liv was alive.

On the fourth tone, someone picked up. He didn't wait to be greeted.

'Where is she? Hello? Where the fuck are you holding her?'

Then, Liv's voice. 'Connor. Get me out of here. I'm begging you. I'm going to—'

The call ended.

Connor dialled back several times, each call ringing out.

Sat on the edge of the bed, Connor stared at the picture. The feeling of hopelessness was overwhelming. Liv's cries for help haunted him. They seemed to fill their bedroom, seeping from the walls and ceiling, gripping at his throat.

Standing, he walked into the bathroom and took a shower, hoping the hot water would allow the frustration to melt away.

After drying himself, he put on a clean pair of boxer shorts, tee-shirt, and jeans and walked down the stairs. In the kitchen, he filled the kettle, placed two slices of bread in the toaster, knowing he needed to eat to keep up his mental strength, and waited, staring into the communal garden. It was overcast, and the dull sun tried fruitlessly to push through the grey clouds smothering the sky.

The toast popped at the same time as his phone rang. Reaching into his jeans pocket, feeling the dread which was now a typical occurrence, he was relieved to see Ella's number.

'Hey. How are you doing?' he asked.

'Any word on Liv?'

'No. The same. She's still missing.' Knowing he could trust Ella, he continued, 'I was sent a—'

'Have you seen Rye News on Facebook?' she cut in.

'Er, no, not this morning.'

'It looks like... there's another.'

'What do you mean? Another what?'

'It's sketchy. Nothing's been reported yet. But people have posted pictures of emergency responders. Police, ambulances. It's chaos.'

'Where?' asked Connor.

'Rye News on Facebook.'

'No. Where did this happen?'

'Oh. Dead Man's Lane.'

It was as if Connor felt a knife slicing his skin. He jolted, pushing his shoulders back and hearing the bones crack; his body seemed riddled with knots. 'Mrs Franklin lives there.'

'How do you know?'

'We... Liam and I called over to her yesterday. Remember?'

'Oh, shit. Please don't tell me she's dead. I don't feel safe. I have to call the police.'

'No!' he insisted, his voice more harsh than he'd intended. Connor told her about the picture. A knife at Liv's throat and the sinister threat. 'They'll do it. They'll send Liv back to me in pieces. Please, I'm pleading with you, no police.'

'I need to get out of here,' Ella insisted. 'I'm bloody suffocating.'

'Have you spoken to your parents?'

'They phoned early this morning. I think they're worried about me being alone in the house. They haven't mentioned anything so hopefully they haven't seen the news reports.'

'Did you say anything to them?'

'No. Nothing. What would I say exactly? Oh, there's a person that looks like me, trying to destroy my life. And, by the way, remember that accident at school? Well, it wasn't an accident. And now, it's coming back to bite us on the fucking arse. Two people are dead. I'm on that guest list.'

'Get a grip, Ella!' fired Connor.

'Get a grip? Are you for real?'

'Look, make sure the house is secure. I'll call you soon.' After hearing Ella hang up, Connor buttered the toast, reboiled the kettle to make tea, and sat at the breakfast bar, typing 'Fred Kipler' into Google.

There were no pictures of him or his twin brother, Nathan. The first headline at the top of the page read:

Tragic Fire at St Michael's: Student Dies in Horrific Prank Gone Wrong.

A devastating fire at St Michael's High School in Rye has claimed the life of 14-year-old Nathan Kipler.

It's thought that classmates lured Nathan into a store room, where he was then bound and gagged.

His charred remains were later discovered in the basement.

His brother, Fred, suffered serious burns as a result of trying to save Nathan and was rushed to a local hospital.

Overwhelmed with grief, Roy Kipler, the twins' father, reportedly took his own life shortly after the incident.

Investigators are continuing to probe the circumstances leading to the fire, as the community mourns this devastating loss.

In a tragic twist to the story, it's thought Fred Kipler is in a coma after being moved to a private facility.

'Private facility,' Connor whispered. 'What private facility?'

It was time for him to hunt the hunter.

24

S *unday Morning*

'I need to try and find someone. It's urgent.' Connor watched through the glass of the hospital reception as the young man pushed his legs against the floor, bringing the swivel chair closer to the desk, and squinted at the computer screen. His white uniform was pristine, with not a crease in sight. Above him, a sign displayed Rye Hospital Accident And Emergency.

'What's the name, please?'

'Er, Connor. Connor Murphy.'

'And when was Connor brought in?'

'Oh, that's me. Sorry. I thought you wanted my— Never mind. I'm looking for Fred Kipler.'

The young man tapped a few keys and puffed out hard as though stressed, his breath forming condensation on the glass. 'I don't have a Fred Kipler at this hospital.'

Groans came from over Connor's shoulder as a man hobbled to reception, shouting to be seen.

'Sir,' the guy behind the counter said, 'please take a seat! You'll be seen as soon as someone is available.'

'I've been here for hours. Bloody useless. I need someone to see me now.'

'As I said, you have to wait.' To Connor, he asked, 'When did you say he was admitted?'

'Oh, I didn't. It was a few years ago.'

'A few—' Knotting his eyebrows, a corner of his lip curled. 'I'm sorry, sir, our records don't go back that far.'

'I think he may have been moved to a... a private facility. Would you mind checking?'

'Are you a relative?'

The thought made Connor cringe. 'Er, I'm... Look, it's urgent.'

Tapping more keys, the man looked up. 'Unless you're a relative, I can't help. But I can assure you, he's not here.'

'Where's the nearest private facility?' asked Connor, his voice urgent. 'Surely you can tell me that?'

'The closest is Mill House. You can try there. Next person to the front, please. How may I help?'

Stepping away from the glass, Connor knew it was a long shot. But it was a start.

Having first tried Mill House, which drew a blank, Connor drove five miles to Fairbank. Again, the receptionist was unhelpful, assuring Connor he couldn't give out details without identification. The next closest facility was Abbeymore, nine miles outside the town of Rye.

Abbeymore Hospital wasn't at all what Connor had

imagined. He'd pictured a rundown, grubby building with patients hanging around outside, just like the previous facilities he'd visited, wearing tatty dressing gowns and dragging on cigarettes.

A single lane that looked recently tarmacked wound up to a bright blue two-story building, and a carpark with ample spaces.

A sign warned customers of CCTV being in operation and a hundred pound fine for anyone disobeying the rules and parking without a valid ticket.

Connor parked, paid on the app, and walked to the intercom by the front door. He pressed the button for the main reception and waited. It sounded as though someone was trying to tune a radio, and a voice lost in the noise tried to speak.

A moment later, the crunching stopped.

'Sorry about that? How may I help?' The female voice was friendly and sincere.

'Hi, I'm looking to see someone who may be staying here,' answered Connor.

'What's the person's name?'

Footsteps sounded behind him, and he span around, seeing one of the nurses sit on a bench and light up a cigarette. *So it's the staff that smoke,* he thought. *Not the patients.*

The nurse had a pleasant smile with white teeth and a crisp uniform. Her hair was held in place by netting.

'Er, the name, please, of the patient you're wanting to see?' repeated the voice through the intercom.

Turning back round, Connor apologised. 'Fred Kipler.' As the name passed his lips, he could hear the nurse behind him stir on their seat.

'There's no patient here with that name?'

'Are you sure? Connor asked, pushing his face closer to the intercom. 'Fred Kipler.' Then he slowly spelt it letter by letter.

'I'm looking through the names of our patients. There is no Fred Kipler here. And if you want to see a current patient, you would need to show some ID with proof of your connection and make an appointment.'

'Right. Well, can you tell me if he ever stayed here? It's urgent.'

'Like I said, I can't give that information unless you show ID.'

'He was badly burned in a fire. Maybe you don't recognise him now.' Feeling a tad guilty for the sarcasm, he continued. 'Look, I just need to know if Fred ever stayed here or if you know what happened to him.'

'And again, I'll stress, I am not able to give you any details.'

Backing away, Connor knew it was a dead end. The receptionist had clocked him, and a camera perched on the wall pointed to the door where he stood.

'Fine. Suit yourself.' As he trudged away and opened the car door, he heard a voice.

'Excuse me.'

Connor turned, seeing the nurse who was sitting on the bench. Her cigarette had finished, and as she walked towards him, she lit another one. 'Hi.'

'Can I have a word?' she asked.

'Of course,' he answered, eyeing her skeptically.

She acted suspiciously, giddily, fidgeting with her fingers and darting looks towards reception.

'I heard you mention the name Fred Kipler.'

'Yes. I need to know what happened to him. I asked at Rye Hospital, but they weren't very helpful.'

'Are you related to Fred?'

Connor watched her eyes, seeing apprehension. Her pupils widened and she shifted her gaze to the side.

'No. I just need to find him.' Plagued by the picture sent to his phone, the knife pressing into the skin of Liv's throat, he pushed harder, not wanting to give anything away. 'Look, I just need to know where he is. The reports online are shady. No one knows what happened to him. I feel like a dog chasing its tail.'

The nurse diverted her eyes to the main entrance and back to Connor.

He needed to be more persuasive, even if it meant telling someone the turmoil he was going through.

On the spur of the moment, desperate, he grabbed his phone, clicking into the photo he'd been sent on WhatsApp this morning. 'This is Liv. My girlfriend. She's missing.'

The nurse's eyes flicked to Connor's face, studying it briefly, and then to the phone. As she zoomed in, she gasped as if air had caught in her throat. 'Missing? Oh, Christ. They... They have a knife to her throat.'

Taking the phone back, he placed it in his pocket. 'It's going to sound ludicrous, but I believe Fred Kipler is orchestrating this. I have to know what happened to him. Most believe he's dead, but not me.' Connor stopped, not wanting to delve too deep into his reasonings.

The nurse turned as though contemplating her next line of conversation. Pressing her hands together like in prayer, her forefingers touching her two front teeth, she spun back around to Connor. 'Fred Kipler was here.'

It was like a bullet hitting his chest. He felt suddenly numb, and as he tried to speak, it seemed like his brain couldn't process the words.

The nurse continued. 'He suffered severe hypoxia,

swelling of the brain, and was in a prolonged coma. He recovered at the facility.'

Processing her words, he looked at the building. *I wonder if they knew they were housing a monster,* he thought. To the nurse, he pushed, 'Are you sure? Are you absolutely sure it was Fred Kipler?'

'Yes. A hundred percent. It was him!'

Connor took a minute to process the information, feeling a buzz as adrenaline coursed through his veins. It was a lot to process, but this was proof. He felt like progress was finally being made. 'Do you know his background?'

'I'm aware there was a fire. He had burns to his arms and legs. But it was the smoke he inhaled which caused hypoxia. He's a lucky guy to be alive.'

'So what happened to him?'

'He was in a coma for a long time. When Fred was transferred here, we thought it would be his final resting place.' She looked at Connor, her eyes squinting, biting on her lip. 'But he recovered.'

'Recovered?' said Connor. 'How so?'

'Although he had permanent scars on his arms and legs, he came out of the coma and made a full recovery.'

'Came out,' Connor pushed, aware he was sounding like a parrot.

'Yes. His brain was still sharp. He could talk, hold conversations, and after months of care and nursing, he was back on his feet.'

'So what happened then?' he pushed, not wanting to sound too desperate. The nurse had given answers he'd thought he might never find.

'I read up on Fred. His story, you know. I heard about his brother being locked in a store room. A freak accident. And I know the police were unable to pin the fire on anyone. In my eyes, Fred was extremely courageous, trying to save his twin brother. The head nurse here did everything for Fred. She went above and beyond. As time passed, people forgot about him being here. It's like Fred Kipler was lost in the system. His father had taken his own life, his brother had died, and no one came to visit. When the head nurse had done all she could, she left. Then, one morning, I brought Fred breakfast and boom. He'd gone. Left of his own accord in the middle of the night.'

'And the head nurse? Whatever happened to her?'

'That's the strange part. Her name was Angela Bennett. After she left, Fred walked out shortly afterwards. But while searching for keys in her office, I found an old family photograph at the back of one of her drawers. She was Fred and Nathan Kipler's mother.'

25

T wo Months Ago

It was perfect. Like sitting at a poker table and being dealt two aces.

The Universe was looking down on him, or so he hoped. As the rain lashed against the window, Fred gently eased the blankets back, pawed for the light, and got dressed. It was early morning. The alarm clock next to his bed showed 3.01 am, and the red neon lights seemed to blink.

It was too risky leaving the facility during the day. The staff were in and out of the rooms like bees, padding his pillow, straightening the blankets, and constantly checking on him unnecessarily. It was arduous.

Fred grabbed his bag and filled it with clothes. Nothing flashy. No designer labels. A few plain tee-shirts, jeans and jumpers.

His mother had nursed him to health and then left.

Now, it was Fred's turn. As he climbed out the window, jumping onto the soft ground, he thought he should feel sentimental, maybe even sad. But he hated this place. And besides, it delayed him from doing what he needed.

It was time.

As the rain whipped against his skin, Fred Kipler pushed his arm through the bag, placing the strap over his shoulder, and made off through the fields.

It was an amazing feeling. Freedom. Selfishly gulping the fresh air, Fred thought about his twin brother and how he missed him. He welled up, feeling choked as he glanced up at the full moon, guided by its wondrous light. They were connected. He and Nathan had finished each other's sentences; they'd shared everything and often had the same thoughts. Well, not entirely true. He'd wanted to be more like his twin brother, but Fred had been aware from an early age of his intrusive thoughts, the dark side of his mind, and the evilness that lurked deep within him. Nathan had been different. A gentleman. Always wanting to please people, even when they did him wrong. Always willing to forgive and forget. Not Fred: his mind was tormented with images of retribution. So, was he insane? Fred remembered reading somewhere that if people were crazy they didn't know. But he did know himself, and he was going to act on his longing for revenge. The feeling stirred from deep within, festering in his gut, working its way like the roots of a tree through his veins. It excited him more than anything. He just had to work out how to torture the people responsible.

But he would. Very soon, they'd all pay.

∾

By the time Fred stood outside the farmhouse, the rain had stopped, and light broke through the thick clouds. He felt nostalgic, reflecting on his childhood. He could almost see his father opening the front door and he and Nathan rushing behind him with their lunch boxes, untucked shirts, and red faces. Their father hated being late. It was one of his many bugbears. But Fred didn't. He cared for nothing.

Looking past the farmhouse, at the road disappearing and merging into fields for as far as the eye could see, at the solitude, the tranquillity, he recalled the time the twins had made a treehouse. Their father had helped them by cutting wood and fixing nails into place with a hammer. They were teenagers, and their mother had already left home. Fred didn't feel bitter. He didn't feel anything. But credit where it was due. If it hadn't been for her nursing him back to health, he may have rotted in the facility.

As he glanced at the tree, the small house that had long since fallen and the wood lying scattered on the grass and rotting from the elements, Fred could see his father standing back, arms folded and proud of what they'd achieved.

He'd learned of his father's suicide while in the facility. While his mother explained what happened, Fred had felt his body tense, but his pulse had remained the same. Then he'd turned on his side and slept.

Had he thought about his father since? Did he feel any emotion about his death? Fred couldn't say. His mind was busy with what he was going to do. Maybe that was how he dealt with the tragedies bestowed on him.

Barging his body against the front door to open it, Fred quickly looked behind him and stepped inside. *We'd have to get locks,* he thought, *to stop intruders from wandering in off the road. Board it up as well to make it look unoccupied.*

Perfect was the first word that came to mind as Fred stood, smelling the mould that seemed to fester in his lungs. *This is perfect.*

The floorboards bowed with his weight as he walked across the living room and into the kitchen. The clutter was daunting, but Fred had to leave it exactly how it was. A shit pit. He could see anyone approach for a good half mile along the road, and the bushes hanging over the front windows would partly shield the farmhouse from the fields.

Dust particles floated in the air, catching in the light, and cobwebs clung to each corner of the kitchen. The cold air was stale, and damp patches feasted on the plaster. Fred touched part of the wall, feeling the paint crumble under his fingertips.

There was no electricity, gas, or central heating. No one knew he was here. After the fire, Fred had been rushed to hospital in a comatose state. After recovering at the facility, every day becoming stronger, every passing moment further lost in the system, Fred knew they weren't coming for him. He'd be remembered, but the police had never visited once. They had no proof that he'd started the fire. It was like he was a ghost, a phantom haunting this farmhouse. That's how he wanted it. A faded memory that people mentioned in passing. The spotlight long dimmed, and the candle's flickering light replaced with overflowing wax.

The front door was forced open, and a silhouette appeared in the gap.

'Hello, son. Welcome home,' Fred's mother said as she walked to him, pulling him into a tight hug. 'Are you ready?'

~

'We're going to be a great team, sugar pie. You hear?' Angela rubbed her son's face, seeing him wince and pull back. *Is it embarrassment?* she pondered. *Does he not appreciate all I've done for him?* 'Come, let me show you something.' Grabbing Fred by the hand, she steered him to the far corner of the kitchen. 'It's just us now, and I have the perfect place where we can put our plans into action. Exciting, isn't it? Oh, it's going to be amazing. I've been looking forward to this forever. You have, too. I know it.' On her knees, she pulled the lino back and swung her head up, grinning so wide it felt like her lips would split. 'You're going to love this, Frederick.'

'Don't call me that! I hate that!' His face darkened.

'Oh, don't be a baby. I can put you back in the facility. One call is all it will take. I'll say you lost it and started smashing the house up. Is that what you want?'

'No,' answered Fred sheepishly.

Angela felt herself twitch. The tic had gotten worse lately. It was embarrassing. Her head would jolt to the side, followed by the weirdest grin.

'Good. Then take a look down here!' With the lino peeled back, Angela crawled to a hatch in the floor and slowly lifted it, the groan of the hinges filling the kitchen. As she dropped it back against the floor, dust particles caused her to sneeze. Although plagued with holes, discoloured and rotting, the wooden steps beyond the hatch, which lead to the basement, were stable and robust. Plenty strong enough to take their weight. 'You coming?' She took the stairs one at a time, almost in slow motion, and clicked a light switch on the wall. The bulb blew, which caused her to flinch. 'Bloody thing!' Grabbing her phone, she turned on the torch, aiming it at a heavy metal door. The key was still in the same place, hanging on a hook attached to the wall.

Angela fished for the key, holding it in front of her, running a finger along its rough, cold edges, and then placed it in the lock, twisting hard. After a loud clunk, she leaned against it, shoving it open. 'This used to be a prison, you know. You've never been down here, Fred.' Behind her, she could hear her son gasp.

'You've known about this place and never said anything?' he said, following his mother and watching as she shone the torch across the basement floor. The anticipation thrilled through her body as her head jerked sideways.

Small cells, enclosed by rusted iron bars, resembled grim torture chambers from a bygone era – the kind where prisoners were left to rot in the dark. Each cell had straps attached to the wall and ripped mattresses with the insides spilling out. They looked cold and uncomfortable.

'Your father and I discovered it after moving in. It wasn't on any map, and the estate agent had failed to mention it. It's perfect,' Angela insisted, bouncing on her feet.

Taking the phone and shining the torch into a cell, Fred illuminated scratch marks on the crumbling wall, like someone was desperate to escape. It was like a coffin, with marks in the wood, as if someone had been buried alive. A pipe dripped in the corner of the basement, and the floor had puddles of water. The air was stale, and an odour not too dissimilar from decaying meat invaded their nostrils.

'They're going to pay, Fred – each one of them.' Angela thought about her darling son, Nathan. Christ, she missed him so much. It had cut her more than anything had before. It had torn her apart, limb from limb, and left her dead inside. Her husband killing himself in the barn had been just another reason to drive her on. 'By the time we've finished with them, they'll know what hell feels like.'

26

S *unday Morning*

The street was lined with emergency crew. Flashing blue lights bounced off windows on either side.

Two uniformed officers stood outside forty-nine Dead Man's Lane, guarding the property. Their high-visibility jackets glowed under the harsh artificial light.

The air was thick with the tang of diesel fumes, and a group of onlookers gathered beyond the cordon, whispering among themselves.

Inside the house, Mrs Franklin lay lifeless in the hallway, much like Frank Dawson had; her mouth was locked open as though her jaw had been snapped. Once the windows to her soul, now her eye sockets were nothing but gaping holes. Her face had been ripped apart as though attacked with a blender, and both ears had been torn from her head.

The smell of detergent wafted in the stale air, and cameras flashed as officers took photos and measurements.

'It's barbaric,' one of the female officers said. 'Rye has a serial killer. She's been mutilated in much the same way. What time was the body found?' she asked a colleague.

'The call came in at around 9 am. A neighbour knocked on the door, and when there was no reply' – he pointed at the letterbox – 'he peeked through there.'

'What a shock to get. Is someone with him?'

'Yeah, an officer is looking after him as we speak. I don't know what we'll get here. The place has been wiped to within an inch of its life. This person is meticulous. They scrubbed the place after torturing her.'

'That's good of them,' the female officer responded with a hint of sarcasm.

A young woman from the crime scene unit called to her colleague, 'There's another one.' With a pair of tweezers, she pulled a miniature figure from Mrs Franklin's nose.

A perfect replica of the victim.

'I usually call over on a Sunday morning. We're a tight-knit community,' Mrs Franklin's opposite neighbour, Cecil, confirmed. After stirring the tea, the spoon clanking against the cups, he placed the drinks on the table, and sat, staring at the floor. 'I can't believe it. Her face, I'll never forget it.'

'It must have come as quite a shock. I hope you don't mind, but I need to ask a few questions,' the officer explained.

'Fire away,' Cecil replied, his voice feeble.

'You said you call over every Sunday. Just you?'

'Yes. I lost my wife a couple of years ago. Greta and I

have become close. Oh, it's nothing like that. I don't fancy her or anything. It was just, we loved to talk. And boy, could she. I can't believe she's gone.'

'Did she say anything to you? I mean to suggest she was in trouble.'

Pondering the question, Cecil pressed his fingers together, hearing them crack. 'Nothing. I don't think she had any enemies. Greta was a good person. She cleaned the church. I don't think she ever charged the priest.'

'Sounds like a decent sort,' the officer said, taking notes. 'So, did you see anything suspicious yesterday? Even the slightest thing could make the difference.'

'It was early afternoon. I was watering the plants outside. I live alone, but I take pride in what I do. I can't give up. I like to clean the place myself. Look after things, you know. An Englishman's place is his castle and all that. I don't believe in getting people in when you can do it yourself.'

'Quite,' the officer responded.

'But there was an alert on the street group on Whats-App. A couple of us heard glass smashing. Most of Greta's neighbours within earshot are elderly. You have Mrs Darcy. She's in her eighties. Always has the radio blaring. Then Mr Tibbs. Rarely leaves his bed. His son pops in most days to check up on him. I didn't hear it, but while watering the plants, I looked over and saw she had a visitor. I don't like to pry, but this person was important.'

'Okay. Do you know who it was?'

'Yes, Father Maloney. The local priest.'

'Thank you. You've been very helpful.'

After relaying the information to the investigative team, Officer Martin Willis and Chloe Denham were sent to the local church.

Blessing themselves on the way in as a way of respect, they were met by Father Maloney, who was dashing about around the altar and looking hassled.

'Father,' Chloe said, 'would you mind if we had a quick word?'

The alarm on his face was evident as he stepped off the altar and approached the officers. 'Certainly. I'm sorry if I appear stressed. Our help, Greta Franklin, hasn't turned up, which is most peculiar, and I'm trying to get everything sorted.'

'Father, I'm Officer Martin Willis, and this is Officer Chloe Denham. We're here to speak with you regarding a matter of importance. I'm afraid we have some bad news,' he confirmed, ready to gauge the priest's reaction. 'Greta Franklin was found dead in her house early this morning.'

The church fell into complete silence. Father Maloney bit on his knuckles, tears forming in his eyes as they slowly lowered to the floor. 'No! It can't be. I saw her yesterday.'

'I know it's come as a shock, but it's the reason why we've come to speak with you,' Officer Denham confirmed. 'Please, take as long as you like.'

'Greta was such a good woman. She did so much for us. For the church. And often slogging away without charging. I'm... I'm stunned. How? How did it happen?'

'Well,' Martin stated, 'this is what we need to confirm. A witness said they saw you at the house yesterday.'

'It was most peculiar. Greta called me. She sounded dishevelled. I was practically passing the street after visiting a parishioner and said I'd pop in. On arrival, I could see she was shaken. You know, distracted and... and fearful. That's how I'd describe her.'

In the middle of making notes, Chloe looked up from her pad. 'Did Greta mention anything specific about why she was upset?'

'Yes. Again, most peculiar. Greta said she... she saw her dead nephew. And then asked me to bless the house.'

'I'm sorry,' Martin urged, 'did you say dead nephew?'

'Yes. And earlier, two lads came here looking to speak with her. They wanted Greta's address.'

'Do you know the names of the two individuals?' Chloe asked.

'Connor Murphy and Liam Anderson.'

27

S unday Morning

It felt as though the walls were closing in, the air thin, and she was suffocating. Ella paced the hallway, the wooden floors creaking under her trainers.

Every few minutes, she refreshed the Facebook page, "Rye News," on her mobile, searching for something further regarding the events unfolding at Dead Man's Lane.

The latest post from an anonymous user published a picture taken from the top of Dead Man's Lane. The road had been cordoned off, and police officers stood guarding the scene.

The messages read:

Anonymous:
Scene just now at the top of Dead Man's Lane. Looks

serious. Loads of emergency responders. Police won't let me through. Praying for anyone involved.

ClareDempsey96:

What is happening in our beautiful town? Does anyone know who is involved?

SeanEnnis:

Let's not speculate at this time and fire names about. They'll release a statement soon enough. Praying it's not serious. But by the looks of it, something bad is going down.

Ella closed Facebook, climbed the stairs, entered her bedroom, and stepped to the window. Edging the curtain back, she looked down over Rye High Street. From up here, she was less conspicuous. It minimised her chances of being seen. Peering through the window, she expected to see the woman who'd dropped the bags at her door, standing across the street, staring back. The sinister image was so clear in her head it was almost a reality. But as she blinked, a young couple came into view wheeling a pushchair, their hands clasped tight together. A middle-aged woman strolled past, a teenage girl approaching her, and the two of them hugged and linked arms before disappearing out of view.

Exhaling hard, Ella felt the anxiety seep from her body and decided she needed some fresh air.

She was going to visit the cafe and speak with the woman Liam had described in the footage emailed over to him.

One of the last people to speak with Frank Dawson.

The front door was stiffer than it looked. A bell sounded as it opened, and Ella saw a lady behind the counter, her eyes sweeping towards her and back to the customer paying their bill. The smell of bacon, fresh dough, and coffee was pleasant, although overbearing, and in the kitchen, oil spat from pans resting on grills.

'Take a seat,' the lady said, placing the card machine on its holder, 'we'll be with you shortly.'

Smiling, Ella thanked her. She sat at a table near the front window, picking up a menu and looking over it, but the stress diminished her appetite.

A young woman approached her. Ella saw the name tag: Jennifer. Not wanting to bombard her with questions, she asked for a coffee. Black with no milk or sugar.

'Would you like anything else? I can recommend the apple pie.'

'Oh, goodness, no. It's too early. Just the coffee, thanks?'

Jennifer scribbled something on her notepad and returned a few minutes later with the coffee cup balancing on a saucer.

'Thank you,' Ella said. 'I haven't seen you here before.'

'Oh, I'm new. My family and I moved here recently.'

'How are you finding the place?' Ella asked, trying to ease into her line of questioning.

'I love it. It's so friendly. The people are amazing, and the beach is practically around the corner. What's not to like?'

'Well, most of the people are amazing,' Ella pushed, watching the awkward look on Jennifer's face as she fumbled with her name badge. 'What I mean is, the recent incident.'

Jennifer went to speak but hesitated, her eyes darting

around the cafe and down to her trainers. She looked hassled, almost embarrassed, and began pulling the material of her leggings like a child being told off.

'I'm talking about the murder in Rye,' Ella explained. 'That poor guy.'

The blood seemed to drain from Jennifer's face. Her body tightened, and she tripped as she walked away without answering. The awkwardness hit hard as Ella sat, sipping her hot coffee and feeling judged. She watched as Jennifer approached the older woman behind the counter.

'Can I take my break?' she asked.

Looking at her watch, the older woman nodded, and Jennifer left, disappearing along the street.

Ella kicked her chair back, paid for the coffee she'd only taken a sip from, and followed her.

Outside, tourists had gathered, shuffling along the streets, taking pictures, huddled tight for selfies, while others mulled outside the many shops.

Jennifer stood alone, puffing on a vape.

Stretching her neck and moving her head from side to side, Ella walked over to her. 'I'm sorry if I startled you. I didn't mean to.'

The young woman tensed, squeezing her eyes tight for a moment, and turned. 'It's difficult. Shit! He was in such a state. I tried to help him. But I couldn't get through to him. Later, I found out he was murdered. Do you know what a head fuck that is?'

'I can only imagine. Look, would you mind telling me what he said?'

'I've already given a statement to the police,' Jennifer fired back. 'I hate talking about it.'

'I'm not the police. I knew Frank. He was a friend.'

Although they hadn't crossed paths since high school, Ella did like the caretaker. And he was part of the cover-up.

'Christ! I was scared for him. He was… delusional. I'd never seen anyone like that. I've only been in Rye a short while. My parents moved from London. It's not the start I'd hoped for.'

Needing to push for answers, Ella asked, 'Delusional how?'

'We sat there' – Jennifer pointed to the wooden seat beside them – 'on the bench. I was only trying to offer help. I felt sorry for the guy. Frank said there were episodes, you know, hearing voices and seeing things. Like they were haunting him. Sometimes on the road or standing at the window of his cottage. Phone calls. That was another. The most frightening thing was the knocks on the front door of his cottage late at night.' Jennifer looked hard into Ella's eyes. 'Frank said when he'd answer, no one was there.'

Listening to Jennifer, it felt like Ella's stomach was turning over. A sharp pain rushed across her navel, and she swallowed the phlegm that rose to her throat. 'Did you believe him?'

'I try to put it out of my mind. It's too terrifying to think about. I'm sorry. My break is over. I have to go. Take care.'

Ella watched as the young waitress shoved the front door and disappeared back inside the cafe.

Standing in the busy street, groups of people passing her, oblivious to her situation, listening to their conversations about what to do and where to go, she'd never felt so vulnerable.

Frank had been plagued with visions. They'd driven him

crazy. Phone calls, visits to his cottage. Mrs Franklin, seeing her dead nephew. Now, she's—

She tried desperately to distract herself; it felt like she was in a horror movie. *Watch the videotape,* she thought, *and then it gets you.* But this was reality. Someone was fucking with them, pulling the strings. Avenging what had happened when they were children. The ultimate act of retribution.

Fred Kipler was capable of this with what happened to his twin brother. Now he was committing the perfect crime. But he was dead. Wasn't he?

Her mobile vibrated in her jeans pocket. Retrieving it, she was pleased to see her friend's name across the screen. 'Connor. Hi. Any news on Liv?'

'Still nothing. But I've learned something that may explain all the weird shit and her going missing. I spoke to a nurse. Ella, Fred Kipler is still alive.'

It felt as though she'd been hit in the face with a bat. She fumbled, dropping the mobile on the ground.

'Ella, are you still there?'

'Yes. Oh, Christ!' she replied, checking the screen for cracks. 'Are you certain?'

'I'm certain. A nurse at Abbeymore confirmed that Fred slowly recovered and came out of a coma. He walked out of the hospital a couple of months ago.' Connor went on to tell her about a photo being found in the drawer and the head nurse being the twins' mother.

'So,' Ella insisted through gritted teeth, 'we have to find him!'

'If only it were that easy!' responded Connor. 'Liam and I visited the farmhouse where he used to live.'

'And?'

'Nothing. He wasn't there. It's abandoned. A proper shit pit. Look, I'm heading home. Let's catch up later?'

Placing the phone back in her pocket, Ella reran Connor's words in her mind. *The bastard is alive,* she thought. *He's left the hospital. Now the bogeyman is back.*

Along the street, Ella's eyes focused on a lady sitting outside a pub. She wore a long, cream-coloured coat with the collar up, her stringy grey hair was chaotic, and a walking stick rested against her knees. Although she sat facing the street, her head was turned awkwardly, and she appeared to be looking at Ella.

Abruptly, she grabbed a bag from under the seat, removed a garment, and flicked the label with her finger as if taunting her.

'What do you want?' whispered Ella. 'Leave me alone!' It felt as though ants were crawling over her skin. Scratching her forearms, she stepped away and turned, rushing onto the street. Brakes screeched and a vehicle honked, causing her to stumble onto the ground.

'Are you alright?' the driver shouted.

'Sorry. Yes. I'm fine. I didn't see you.' Ella stepped back onto the pavement, seeing the woman in cream stand and remove her grey wig, placing it in the carrier bag. Kicking the stick away, she began walking towards Ella.

Stumbling backwards, Ella darted along the street, thinking about the CCTV footage from the boutique shop and certain the same woman was following her now. She wanted to face her, to turn, shake her, and ask why the hell she was doing this. *But it's too dangerous,* she thought. *Look at Frank. Look at Mrs Franklin.*

Although she'd only been running a matter of seconds, the lactic acid was building in her calf muscles. She stopped, bending over to catch her breath, and looked back. The woman was still walking in her direction.

Grabbing her phone, she dialled Connor's number, hearing it ring as she continued to run along the road. When it went to his voicemail, she left a message. 'Connor. It's me. Someone is following me. I need help! Call me.' Behind her, the woman was getting closer.

Ella's face was hot, sticky from sweat. She panted loudly, her body panic-stricken. She looked around, wanting to stop and ask for help, but halting would allow the woman to gain on her. They didn't seem to care who watched.

Her house was a hundred yards ahead. The woman was almost upon her. At the last second, Ella dashed into a bookstore, leaning against the door and gasping. It felt like hands were around her throat, constricting her airways.

'Can I help you?' a softly spoken, middle-aged man asked from behind the counter. He placed his glasses on, which hung on a string tied around his neck. 'My, my, you do look like you've rushed here.'

Ella pushed her body away from the door and glanced at the latest books on offer scattered across a table. 'I... I think I'm being followed,' she blurted.

'I haven't heard of that book. Who wrote it? Sorry, a silly joke. I'm pulling your leg. What did you say?'

Hurrying to the counter, Ella stopped abruptly, seeing the gentleman step back. 'Someone is out there. They're following me. You have to help!'

The door opened. Ella span around, seeing a delivery lady with two heavy-looking boxes.

'There is fine,' the shopkeeper confirmed. 'Thank you so much.'

The woman placed the boxes to the side of the door and walked back out.

To Ella, the shopkeeper asked, 'Followed. By whom?' Lifting a hatch in the counter and walking through, he strolled to the shop front and towards the door.

'Don't go out there,' Ella said, thinking how paranoid she sounded.

Ignoring her plea, he opened the door and stood out on the street. 'There's no one looking suspicious. What did they look like?' he called.

'Er... A coat. Cream coloured. And a bag. She had grey hair, but it's a wig.'

The man looked to either side of the shop and across the road. Clearly satisfied, he walked back in. 'There's no one of that description out there now. Would you like me to call the police?'

'No!' she roared, realising she couldn't ask for help. 'Thank you though. I appreciate your concern.' Ella dashed out of the shop.

Did I imagine it? Is my paranoia taking over and making me see things that aren't there? Making her way back to her house, it was as though she could feel a presence. As if a sixth sense had kicked in, and she could feel warm breaths on her neck. She stopped, turning slowly, and saw a figure further along the street, standing in an alleyway leading behind the shops. Ella stepped onto the road to see better, noticing a hand braced on the wall of the alley, a body pressed against it and hiding. Then the woman stepped out and raced towards her.

Ella panicked, dropping her keys. 'No. No, no. Shit!' As she grabbed them, the woman was almost upon her. Ella turned, running to her house. Fumbling the keys in the lock, she dropped them again. This time, it was as though her fingers were paralysed, unable to clutch them. Willing her body to obey her brain's command, at last she grabbed them, opened the door, and pushed it closed behind her. At the same time, she felt a strong arm forcing against it.

'Leave me alone,' she screamed. The door flung open, and Liam stood on the street.

'What's going on?' he asked, as Ella gripped him tight.

28

*S*unday Morning

'Is she out there?' Ella sat in the kitchen, slowly rocking on a chair.

Liam, standing over her, placed a hand on her shoulder. 'Are you certain someone followed you?'

She nodded. 'Go and check!'

After she'd given Liam a description of the woman, he walked into the living room and looked out the window. Nothing appeared suspicious, and the lady she'd described was nowhere to be seen. Across the street, a couple of young lads stood outside a pub, smoking and lost in conversation. Their arms swung wildly, over-emphasising their gestures. A queue had formed outside a sweetshop, excited children pointing in the window at the sweets they wanted.

Backing away from the window, Liam rejoined Ella in the kitchen. 'She's gone. I can't see her.'

The doorbell rang.

Tensing, Ella grabbed at Liam's jeans, scrunching the material in her right hand. 'Don't answer it!'

It rang again.

Placing a finger to his lips, Liam beckoned for her to keep silent. He crept along the hallway, pushing an ear to the front door.

'Is anyone in?' a voice asked. 'I wanted to make sure she's alright.'

'Who is it?' Liam responded, eyeing the back bedroom and getting ready to grab Ella and make a run for it through the window.

'I own the bookshop down the road. The lady was most disturbed. Said someone was following her.'

Flicking a look at Ella, standing in the hallway, Liam saw her give a thumbs up and drop her head.

'Yes. She's fine,' Liam answered. 'Thank you for asking. I'm with her now.'

'And you are?' the voice fired back.

'I'm a friend. She's safe now!'

'Right, you are. Sorry for bothering you both.'

'It's fine. We appreciate it.'

Back in the kitchen, Ella continued to refresh Facebook. There were more posts with pictures of the scene on Dead Man's Lane. 'It's Mrs Franklin. I know it is.'

'It's why I came over. I heard it on the news. We were only with her yesterday.' Liam explained how he and Connor had warned her about Frank and the strange things happening before his death, finishing with her convinced she'd had a visit from her dead nephew.

'I had a call from Connor. He said Fred Kipler is still alive.' Ella relayed the conversation she'd had, followed by the visit to the cafe.

'You spoke with her? To the waitress? Are you mad?'
Liam stated. 'Do you know how dangerous that is? What if
she goes to the police?'

'I have to do something,' Ella pushed, her solemn eyes
meeting his. 'It's like waiting for it to happen. Two people
are dead. Liv's missing. Which one of us is next?'

'What did she say exactly? The girl at the cafe?'

'She said Frank was distressed. Basically in bits. Before
he died, he was plagued with visions. They'd driven him
crazy. Phone calls, visits to his cottage.'

Leaning against the wall, almost trance-like, Liam said,
'That's exactly what happened to Mrs Franklin. Seeing her
dead nephew.'

'What else?' asked Ella. 'Did she see anything else?'

'I didn't ask. She kicked us out.'

Mr Simmonds bent at the knees, his back straight, and
picked up the boxes at the door. New releases, including the
latest thriller novels, had arrived, and he was excited to have
them on display. Often, he hosted local authors who'd talk
about their lives as writers and how they got into literature,
and it would finish with them signing their latest book.
There'd be tea and coffee laid on, refreshments and nibbles.
That's what he lived for. Books were his life. The bookstore
had been passed down through generations, his grandfather
having opened it and passed it to his son, then Mr
Simmonds stepping into the role.

One box at a time, he placed them on the counter,
grabbed a knife, sliced the tape, and pulled the flaps back. It
always got him. He'd never grow tired of the smell of a new

book. The fresh, inviting aroma of crisp new pages, a woody fragrance, and a hint of glue binding everything together.

'Right, let's get you all on display, shall we?' Grabbing a handful of books, he turned, seeing a figure standing at the door. 'Oh, you've changed clothes. That was quick. How are you feeling?'

The young woman didn't flinch. It was like there was a glitch in the matrix, and she was frozen in time. Her long blonde hair glistened in the sun. Her jumper was loose and baggy, and her black leggings appeared to cling to her skin. Her glasses were dark, disguising her eyes.

Mr Simmonds moved towards her, placing the books on the table and arranging them. He grabbed the sign with "Just in, brand new releases at great prices" written in black felt-tip pen and turned it, facing it to the front.

The silence was uncomfortable. He'd helped this woman, knocked at the house to check she was alright, and now she was standing at the door, her expression blank and her presence menacing.

'Look!' he said, his patience wearing thin, 'can I call someone? You've obviously had a traumatic day.'

No answer.

Debating whether to ask her to leave but not wanting to get into a confrontation with this woman – and realising she was possibly unwell – he tried another approach. 'Would you like a book? I can give you one. Free of charge. It's a good way to unwind.'

At this, the young woman pulled a knife from the back of her leggings.

Mr Simmonds cried out, 'What are you doing? No, put that away.'

As she charged at him, he slipped, crashing against a

shelf, books falling onto the floor. Pushing his hands in front of his face, he pleaded, 'Don't do it! I'm trying to help you.'

The woman held the knife in the air, eyed the security camera, and darted out of the shop.

'Weird shit is happening to me. Does it mean I'm next?' asked Ella.

'I'm not going to let anything happen to you,' Liam promised, sounding as sincere as possible, his voice calm and controlled, but inside, he felt as though he was riding a runaway horse, the reins slipping through his hands. And soon, he'd crash to the ground. How long did they have left? How long before it caught up with them?

Looking at Ella, he could feel her vulnerability. He wanted to hold her tight and comfort her in his arms. Ever since school, he'd been crazy about her. Fred Kipler had bullied most of the class, Liam included. But his main target had been Ella, possibly because he fancied her too. Liam had tried his best to stick up for her against the constant goading, the nasty comments, the sly things Fred had done, like tripping her up, pushing her into nettles, standing on her laces. The torment drove Ella mad. One time, Fred had grabbed her and held her on the school playing fields. As she turned, desperate to escape, he'd shoved her face in a pile of dog shit. When Liam and Connor tried to intervene, he spouted lewd profanities about their parents.

Humiliated, Ella had taken time off. Her parents had visited the school, demanding action against Fred. But after numerous meetings and the threat of suspension, nothing had happened. It had fizzled out and been brushed under the carpet, with Fred only forced to apologise.

'Don't leave me tonight,' she asked, her face flushing.

'I... I have to look after the cat,' he blurted, aware it sounded pathetic. He wanted to take the words back and swallow them deep into his stomach.

For so long, he'd thought about being with Ella. But after what had happened at school, they'd all drifted apart. Now, it seemed like a chance he should grab with both hands.

'Fine! That's just fine! Go then.'

'Come on, Ella, I didn't—'

The doorbell rang again.

Their eyes locked briefly before Liam crossed the hallway. Again, he placed his ear to the front door. 'Who is it?' he asked impatiently.

'What's wrong with that woman in there?' the voice asked.

Liam recognised it. The same guy who'd called moments ago from the bookstore. 'I told you she's fine. Please, don't concern yourself.'

The bell rang again. 'Open this door!'

Pushing one hand through his hair, Liam bit on the tip of his other thumb, debating what to do. This guy was obviously poking his nose in where it wasn't wanted. 'I said she's fine. I'm looking after her.'

'Right, I'm calling the police.'

Flinging the door open, Liam saw the guy with his fists balled tight, eyes wild, leaning in to look along Ella's hallway.

'Where is she?' he spat. 'I... I was attacked. She held a bloody knife over me. I'm calling the police.'

The words jumbled in Liam's head as though he couldn't process their meaning. Stepping onto the pavement, he pulled the door closed behind him. 'Please. Can you keep your voice down?' he ordered.

'I most certainly won't keep my voice down, young man. I was viciously assaulted. It's not safe for her to be loose in public.'

'It wasn't her!' snapped Liam, knowing his words would be lost. 'I've been with her. She hasn't left the flat since I arrived.'

'Really? You expect me to believe that? Come with me. Come on.' Mr Simmonds led Liam along the street and into the bookstore. 'There,' he stated, pointing to the CCTV camera on the wall. 'I have the proof.'

'Well, show me,' Liam ordered, feeling like a bear with honey on his claws. He had to act fast. The last thing he needed was his friend being arrested.

The store room at the back of the bookstore was claustrophobic. An old, worn sofa rested against the back wall. A calendar marked with a pencil displayed a couple of book signing events. Clear plastic boxes housed price tags and stationery. It smelled of cleaning chemicals, which caught in Liam's throat, causing a coughing fit. His eyes stung, and he wiped them with his hand.

'Here you are! Check this. You can go back as far as you like. You'll see everything.' Mr. Simmonds showed Liam how to operate the footage and got distracted as another delivery arrived. 'I need to leave you for a moment. It's all there.'

Tapping the mouse, Liam rewound the recording. Ella rushed into the bookshop, breathless, leaning against the door. He could see her and Mr Simmonds liaising. He was standing behind the counter, lifting a hatch before approaching her. Then he checked outside, returned, and Ella darted out of the shop. Liam pressed fast forward, seeing Mr Simmonds behind the counter, making a phone call, getting himself a drink, and unboxing some books.

Then he saw it. The woman in question. *Shit!* Liam thought. *It's... It's Ella.*

This... This imposter is roughly the same height and weight and has long blonde hair. The dark glasses are hiding her eyes. But to a layperson, it's her. With his mouth ajar, eyes locked on the screen, he watched as the woman stood at the front door, still, motionless, and utterly morbid looking. A quiver drove through his body as his heart quickened. Backing away from the screen, he turned, peering into the bookstore, hearing Mr Simmonds thank another delivery person and bring more boxes to the counter, panting like a dog on a hot day. His mobile rang.

'Hello, dear. I'm closing the shop early. I... I was attacked. I'll tell you about it when I get home. Okay. Love you.'

An alert came through on the screen. *Tinder. You have a new match.*

Oh, Liam thought, facing the screen, *interesting.* On the spur of the moment, he highlighted the section of security footage and the few minutes that followed and deleted it.

'Well?' Mr Simmonds asked. 'What do you think?'

'I can't see anything. It's gone.'

Frustrated, the shop owner scanned through the recording, back and forth, and saw that the section was now missing. 'You idiot! You've done something. I'm calling the police.'

'You have no proof,' Liam said as he left the room. 'It's your word against hers. Was that your wife on the phone?'

'Yes, we run the shop together. What about it?'

'I'm sure she'd love to see your Tinder profile.' Feeling guilty, he left the shop, knowing that, the next time, the woman pretending to be Ella could do so much worse.

Liam returned to Ella's and explained everything that had happened. As he finished, his mobile phone rang. 'Connor. Hi, anything?'

His voice sounded concerned and rushed. 'You need to come over. It's urgent! They're coming to the flat.'

29

S*unday Afternoon*

After pressing the buzzer to unlock the door, Connor led Liam into the communal hallway. Liam followed him, and they hugged.

'What's up?' asked Liam. 'It sounded urgent.'

'The police are on their way. They know about our visit to Mrs Franklin.'

'How?'

'I don't know. Maybe someone saw us.'

'Wait,' Liam said. 'The priest. Father Maloney. We asked him for Mrs Franklin's address. He must have told them. What are we going to do? Will they try and pin this on us?'

'Come inside. We can't talk here. It's getting worse by the minute.' Connor entered his flat, his friend following him into the kitchen. 'Do you want a tea or coffee?'

'Just water,' Liam answered as he sat at the table. 'So it is her. It's Mrs Franklin?'

'I... I think so. Why else would they want to talk to us?' Connor grabbed a glass from the cupboard, filled it with water and placed it on the table, joining his friend.

'Ella's not good,' Liam said as he sipped the water, grimacing at how cold it was. 'I feel bad for leaving her.' He told Connor about the woman who'd followed her. And how she'd rushed into the bookstore and, finally, how Liam had gone back and deleted the footage. Connor listened, his eyes fixed on his friend's face, stunned into silence and feeling the panic in his body. He felt light-headed, his fingers pulling at his stubble, and his thighs bouncing together.

'What am I going to tell the police?' asked Connor. 'If I tell the truth, I'm risking Liv's life. Look at this.' Grabbing his phone, he navigated to the last message on WhatsApp, showing a knife at Liv's throat.

'Oh, Christ. I'm so sorry. She looks... petrified.'

'Wouldn't you? I've tried to call the number back so many times.' Standing, Connor walked to the window, looking over the communal garden. The surrounding fence was high, with a wooden gate on a latch for the rear entry. *Anyone could open it,* he thought. *Just march in and come to the window.* The garden table was rickety and leaning to the side with an ashtray filled with water and cigarette butts floating at the top. Three chairs, the wood rotten and discoloured, looked uninviting. 'How do we know they're not watching now?' Connor mused. 'Ready to pounce at any moment.' He flinched as the flat's buzzer rang. It felt like a claw slowly working through his body, tugging at his insides. On wobbly legs, he walked to the intercom. 'Hello.'

'Hi,' a female voice said. 'I'm Officer Chloe Denham, and I'm with Officer Martin Willis. Could we have a word?'

A word, thought Connor. *Yes, there's a word. Of course, officer. There's three more. Now, leave me alone.* It wasn't the time for sarcasm. As he buzzed them in, the picture of Liv with a knife to her throat was at the forefront of his mind.

Greeting them, Connor shook their hands and beckoned them into the kitchen. Both officers chose to stand and refused a drink.

'Connor Murphy, is that correct?' Officer Willis asked, flipping open his notebook.

It felt like he was on a gameshow, ready for a quick-fire round of questions. If only that were the case. 'That's correct,' he said, his voice sounding more like a squeal.

Looking over at Liam, Officer Willis asked, 'And you are?'

'Liam. Liam Anderson. I'm Connor's best friend,' he stuttered, his face turning scarlet.

'Okay,' Officer Denham pushed, 'we're investigating an incident that occurred last night on Dead Man's Lane. You're not under arrest, but we do need your cooperation. Yesterday both of you were asking questions about a Greta Franklin. Can you tell us why?'

Bang. It felt as though all fingers were pointing at them, judging them, scrutinising them, the spotlight glowing on their faces, like the next words that left their lips would carve out the rest of their lives.

'A good friend of mine,' Connor said, glancing swiftly at Liam, 'sorry, ours, was found dead yesterday morning. He was a caretaker at school. A very popular character.' The screams of Fred Kipler as he realised Nathan was trapped pierced Connor's ears. Mrs Franklin's words ordering them to keep silent. The knife at Liv's throat. 'We were looking for Mrs Franklin to comfort her. She and Frank were close.'

'Close how?' Officer Willis asked, pen poised.

'Friends,' answered Connor. 'Very good friends. They worked together for years. We often saw them together, I don't know, hanging out, getting lifts from each other. We wanted to check in on her. To make sure she was alright.'

'How did she seem?' Officer Denham asked. 'Was she relaxed? Did she appear to have something on her mind? Was she worried about anything?'

'Er... I don't think so,' answered Connor, aware he was fidgeting.

'You don't think so,' Officer Denham repeated. 'Did anything seem unusual or suspicious in her behaviour?'

In his mind, the picture of Liv's throat enlarged, floating towards him, widening until it was right in front of him, almost slapping Connor in the face. 'We cared for her. She was so well respected at school. You know, one of the teachers you never forget. That was Mrs Franklin. We simply called over to comfort her. To be there for her. Are we suspects in something here?'

'We have to do our job and follow leads. It's protocol. Can I ask you both where you were last night?' Officer Denham pushed.

'Our friend's house. Ella. She can vouch for us. We were there until late,' Liam added.

'What's her full name?' Officer Willis asked.

Liam hesitated before answering. 'Ella McKenzie. She lives on Rye High Street.'

Scribbling in her notepad, Officer Denham said, 'We'll be following up with her. If your story checks out, that should clear things up for now. We'll be in touch if we have more questions.' Officer Denham gave a curt nod. 'One more thing – if you remember anything else about what you saw or heard at Mrs Franklin's, let us know immediately. Understand?'

Both of them nodded as Connor let the officers out.

At the door, Officer Willis turned, clearing his throat. 'Don't go anywhere!'

The door closed, leaving a palpable silence in its wake.

'I feel so guilty,' Connor announced as he joined Liam in the kitchen. 'How can we tell the police it's Fred? Do I risk Liv being sent back to me in a body bag? Because that's what will happen! I don't know what to do.'

'Guilty? See straight, will you? Mrs Franklin is dead. The police have all but confirmed it. Judging by the events of the last couple of days, they'll be coming for us next. We have to keep quiet for Liv's sake. How bad would you feel if the next picture is Liv's headless torso? It's *us* that's at risk here. So stop with the guilt already!'

Connor went to say something, but Liam needed no answer. His friend was right. Fred Kipler was out there watching them. He probably knew their every move. Had he set up listening devices when Liv was taken? Could he hear them now? How much time did they have, and if Connor was murdered, who would save his girlfriend? The questions swarmed in his mind, while all the time he was no further in finding the bastard who'd taken her. 'I have to check if he's bugged the flat.' Connor rushed around, peering at the walls and ceilings and searching for brick and plasterboard dust. Anything to denote a device had been fitted. He charged into the bedrooms, searching behind units, pictures, and under the bed. There was nothing obvious.

Back in the kitchen, he sat beside Liam, staring at Liv's picture on his phone. 'I miss her so fucking much,' Connor confessed. 'She was my life.'

'I know, mate. But don't talk in past tense. You're sounding defeated already. That's not you. Remember at school, the pep talks you gave Ella and me before exams? You told me I'd get great grades. That I could do it.'

Connor's eyebrows raised, his feet tapping against the floor. 'And did you?' he asked.

'Well. No,' Liam answered, a corner of his lip shifting upwards. 'But that's beside the point. You saw the positives. You got me through when it counted. I remember how proud Mrs Franklin was.'

'She definitely took a shine to the three of us,' Connor said. 'An amazing lady. I wonder why she was so adamant that we didn't own up. Remember when all three of us walked into her classroom? The threats she made to stop us.'

Nodding, Liam bit his bottom lip. 'I think something was going on with her and Frank!'

'No!' Connor said, a confused look on his face as he digested the accusation. 'Why do you say that? They were both married, weren't they?'

'Mrs Franklin was. I think they were having an affair. They were always together.'

'It doesn't mean they were seeing each other,' stated Connor.

'Maybe,' Liam said, 'it's something to do with why she was so adamant we didn't confess. Why she made all the threats. I think she was hiding something. I recall her being on a disciplinary. She'd taken time off for a suspension. They were the rumours.'

'Well,' Connor said, leaning into the table and shrugging, 'she wasn't too pleased to see us yesterday. The scared look on her face. The distraction in her persona and how cold she was. It wasn't the teacher I remember.'

'Maybe,' Liam suggested, 'it's because she saw her dead nephew!'

Mulling over his words and trying to process them, Connor asked, 'Do you believe it was him?'

'Mate, with the shit that's been happening recently, I'd believe she saw Father Christmas in her hallway if she'd said she did.'

It was late evening and getting dark outside. Liam had gone to the spare room in Connor's flat to sleep off a headache.

Connor had spent part of the afternoon Facetiming Ella and looking at social media. The police still hadn't revealed Mrs Franklin's name to the public. But it wouldn't be long until people discovered her death.

Rye had a serial killer. The press would be all over it. It lowered Connor's chances of getting Liv back; he knew the killer's notoriety could make them panic. Though he imagined Fred getting off on being a shadow in the spotlight.

Standing over the bed, Connor placed his hand on Liam's leg and shook him.

As his eyes opened, he drew back, confused as to where he was. 'Bloody hell, mate. You scared the shit out of me!'

'Sorry,' Connor said, turning on the light. 'I need a favour!'

With the back of his hands Liam rubbed his eyes, then pushed up from the bed and pulled the blankets back.

'Naked! Are you for real? Now I have to wash the sheets.'

'Sod off. I showered this morning. What favour do you want?' asked Liam as he stepped out of bed. He pulled on jeans and a tee-shirt, then crouched, tying his trainer laces.

'I'm going back to the facility. If I can find anything about Fred's mother, it may lead us to where he is.'

'Mate, I don't think it's a good idea. These places have security cameras and people at desks watching the doors. They run a tight ship. You can't just walk in there.'

'I can if I find the nurse who helped earlier. If she's still on shift, we'll find a way inside.'

Driving up the narrow road leading to the car park, Connor pulled into the same space he'd found earlier. It was quiet. Security lights shone against the front of the building, and the red brick glowed in the distance.

'What's the plan?' asked Liam as he got out of the car.

I don't have one!' replied Connor, locking the car.

'Are you for real? So what? Waltz in there, evading the rules, and don't expect to be noticed?'

'No. I can't dance. I'm just going to walk in there.'

Following Connor as he set off towards the hospital, Liam muttered, 'You're deluded! This is a stupid idea. It's not even an idea.'

'Just trust me.' When he reached the front door, Connor saw a male nurse sitting at the desk with a mobile phone held to his ear, laughing with whoever he was talking to. Connor thought about shutting off the power, if he could find the consumer unit, but there were possibly patients on life-support machines or watching their favourite soaps. The last thing he wanted was to upset the residents. As he waited, feeling Liam's breath on his neck, the nurse from earlier entered a room at the end of the corridor. She was wheeling a trolley with plates of food on it. 'That's her. Quick. When I message you, press the intercom.'

'Press the intercom,' Liam recited, his voice trance-like and almost flat. 'And say what?'

'You're looking for directions.'

'To where?' Liam spouted.

'I don't know. Think of somewhere!'

'As if he's going to fall for that.'

'Just distract him.' Connor rushed around the building, standing outside a window to the room the nurse had entered. Through a gap in the curtain, he saw her placing food on a table. A patient was lying in the bed, turned on their side and sleeping. He tapped the glass, seeing the nurse turn around at the noise. When he tapped again, she walked over to the window and pulled the curtain back.

Connor sent a message to Liam. '*Press it.*' From around the corner, he could hear the buzz echoing outside the building.

Press it, Liam thought. *And say what? Uh, yeah. Hi, mate. How do I get out of here? Follow the signs, knobhead.* He watched the guy behind the desk becoming rattled, trying to balance the mobile phone against a mug. His voice boomed over the intercom. 'Abbeymore. How can I help?'

'Hi. I think I've taken a wrong turn,' Liam announced. 'Am I on the right road to the motorway?'

'Where are you headed?'

'Erm, Birmingham.'

'You're nowhere near Birmingham! It's about two hundred miles from here. I'm sorry. I can't help!'

The nurse opened the window and leaned out. 'Is someone there?'

Along the path, Connor crouched, keeping still and trying not to make a noise. His phone beeped with a message, and he clenched his teeth. Turning it to silent, he read the message. '*Not budging. Said he can't help. Still talking on phone.*'

Tapping again, he fired back, '*Do it again!*'

'*Prick,*' wrote Liam.

The nurse was still leaning out the window as the buzzer sounded again. 'Who's out here?'

'Hello, Abbeymore,' the male voice over the intercom declared.

'It's me again,' Liam stated. 'Did you say left or right on the main road?'

Behind the desk, he watched the man place his phone down, irritated as he spilled his coffee. 'Shelly,' he called, loudly enough for Liam to hear through the door, appealing to an unseen colleague. 'I'm saying goodnight to the kids. Can you see what that idiot wants at the front door? Sorry about that. I'm here. Yeah, some clown wanting to know how to get to Birmingham.'

As the female nurse walked to the main doors, Liam hid behind bushes on the front lawn.

Connor climbed in the window and hid behind the door. *Please don't wake*, he thought, watching the patient stir and turn in the bed. A soft light glowed from a lamp on the bedside unit. The food was untouched.

From the main entrance, he heard the nurse announce that no one was outside.

'Make sure he's gone,' a male voice answered. 'He was asking for directions. Please check again!'

After a noticeable huff, Connor heard her walk to the main door and return a few seconds later. 'He's gone.'

The footsteps approached the room where he hid. The patient was still sleeping on their side. The handle tipped downwards, and the door opened. Connor took a deep breath, and as the nurse entered and the door closed, he came behind her, covering her mouth.

Abruptly, she swung her right leg back, catching him in the shin. Her words were muffled as she spoke, trying to work Connor's hand away from her mouth.

'Please. You have to help me,' he begged. 'It's me. I was here earlier. You told me about Fred Kipler's mother.'

He felt her body loosen, and she became still.

'I'm going to take my hand away,' he declared. 'Don't shout.' As he did, she span to face him, and Connor was unsure if she'd scream for help or hit him. She did neither.

'What do you want?' she whispered, closing the window. 'I could report you for breaking and entering!'

'Nothing's broken. Look, you're the only person who can help.'

'This better be good!' she snapped.

Choking back the lump in his throat, he peered at the patient in the bed who'd started snoring. Then he gazed into the nurse's eyes, seeing them soften. 'As you know, my girl-friend was kidnapped yesterday.' As Shelly dropped her chin to her chest, he continued with everything that had happened, finishing with Ella being followed and Liam deleting the footage in the bookstore. 'If I can find Fred's mother, I may find my girlfriend.'

Her eyes seemed almost locked into place on his, and her brows were raised high on her forehead as she registered everything that had happened.

'Please,' Connor pushed. 'I don't have anyone else. Do you have staff details? Maybe footage of when Fred was here? Anything that might lead me to Liv?'

'There'll be stuff on the computer. But it's confidential. I could lose my job.'

'I'm desperate.'

Standing back, she eyed him up and down.

Connor feared it could go either way.

She hesitated, shook her head, and then said, 'Fine! I'll help. But you have fifteen minutes. I'll tell Cody to take his break. The password is Abbeymore123. Under any circumstances, it does not come back to me. You got that?'

Connor nodded as the nurse walked to the main desk, instructing Cody to grab a bite to eat.

30

S *unday Night*

'Once you enter the password, you'll find the necessary files. Do not make copies. Get what you need and then go.' Shelly leaned over the desk, watching the staff room where Cody had gone moments ago. 'Christ. If he comes out, I'm screwed. Hurry up!'

'What about the security cameras?' asked Connor as he pointed above the door to the main entrance.

'They're rarely checked. I can delete them once you've finished.'

A door opened.

They both flinched, looking across the main entrance hall.

'Alison. Back in the room,' Shelly ordered.

'I'm hungry!'

'I'll bring you something in a minute. Please, go back inside.'

As Alison's door closed, Connor entered the password, seeing Shelly saunter away out of the corner of his eye.

A list of files appeared along the left side of the screen. Moving the mouse down the page, he saw the name Fred Kipler.

There were records of his stay at the facility.

Please give me something, Connor thought, imagining Liv hanging off the edge of a cliff, their hands clasped tight together, dark veins protruding and his grip becoming looser until finally, his hands let go and— Forcing the thought out of his head, he clicked into one of the most recent files.

At the top of the page was a bio of Fred Kipler, with a report on his condition.

Fred Kipler

Age: twenty-one

Gender: male

Height: 5 foot 10 inches

Condition: Fred suffers from PTSD due to trauma. He also shows signs of psychosis and takes medication to help with these conditions.

Angela Bennett, the facility's manager, has asked for these sessions to be recorded for the benefit of training and research.

Connor hovered the mouse over a recent audio recording and pressed play.

'*Hello, Fred. My name is Doctor Ambrose. How are you feeling today?*' A scraping noise rang out as though the doctor had opened the curtains.

A grunt as though the patient hadn't fully woken up yet.

'*In our last session, we spoke about your brother, Nathan. I want to delve deeper and understand how you're coping with the loss.'*

Then Fred's voice. *'I miss him!'*

As Connor listened, he found it uncomfortable hearing Fred speak. He felt so close suddenly, yet so far away. This was his last hope of finding Liv.

'Of course you do. How was your relationship with Nathan? Tell me your earliest memory. I want a picture of your relationship.'

'Fun. That's the word I think of when I remember Nathan.' There was a bout of coughing and a shuffling noise.

'Fred, during our last session, I asked you to make notes to help you deal with your brother's death. A sort of way to help process your feelings. Did you manage to write anything down for me?'

'I'm sorry. I didn't. I... I forgot.'

'Okay. Could we do it now?'

'I'll do it next time.'

Listening to the conversation, it was obvious Fred was a man of few words. There was no richness in how he spoke. It was just a dull tone, as though he couldn't be bothered.

'I would like you to make a start on it. You know, Fred, writing our thoughts down helps in many ways. It lets us tackle obtrusive thoughts and understand them more. I think you struggle with this. Can you tell me anything that's come into your head recently that is particularly unsettling and tough to deal with?'

'I can't think.'

'Try, Fred. The more we dig into this, the quicker you'll get better. Any recent thoughts? You can tell me anything. Fred! Erm, Fred! For the benefit of the tape, Fred has closed his eyes.'

Staring across the hall, Connor looked at a certificate of excellence in a black wooden frame hanging on the wall.

Other pictures showed the facility when it had first opened, someone important cutting a ribbon with a crowd standing behind them.

He thought about Fred, recalling their school days and how he'd tormented the class for so long. Everyone had disliked him. Even then, he'd barely said anything; it was his actions and how he'd behaved that had made him wicked.

Now, listening to the tapes and understanding what Fred went through, left Connor in no doubt as to who was behind Liv's disappearance and the atrocious murders of Frank Dawson and Greta Franklin.

As he exited the recording, clicking into another recent one, a branch slapped against the window next to him. He grabbed the edge of the table, feeling his heart skip a beat. His body tensed as a door opened at the end of the corridor. Shelly was pushing the trolley, one of the wheels wonky and causing an irritating squeaking noise as she vanished into another room.

I need to be quick, he thought, peering at the room where Cody had gone. Glancing at his watch, he decided he had around ten minutes before Cody came back to his desk.

It was Doctor Ambrose's voice again. *'Fred. How are you doing?'*

No answer.

'This is going to be our final meeting for a while. How do you feel about that?'

No answer.

'During our last session, I asked if you'd make a few notes if you remember. Just a coping mechanism for your obtrusive thoughts. How did that go, Fred?'

A loud burp could be heard, presumably from Fred's mouth.

Rude bastard, Connor thought. *How have you got the patience to talk to him?*

'*Fred. Can you sit up, please?*'

A shuffling noise was heard as it seemed the patient obeyed.

'*That's better. Now, did you make the notes we discussed? Okay. You're shaking your head. Would you like to do it now?*'

Then Fred spoke: '*What happened to my father? He hasn't visited.*'

'*Erm, the records show your father passed away. I'm truly sorry for your loss.*'

The tape went silent. Connor expected howling or at least something denoting Fred's grief. It was eerie. As though the guy had no feelings.

'*Fred. It's a shock. I can only imagine how you're feeling. Do you want to talk about your father?*'

'*I'm hungry!*'

'*I'll make sure they get you something shortly. In the meantime, I'd like to talk to you about your relationship with your father. How was it growing up? Were you and Nathan close to him? Was he strict? Tell me about him. Are they good memories?*'

A knock resounded, and a female voice said, '*Oh, I'm sorry. I didn't realise you were still in here.*'

'*It's fine. We're just finishing up.*' There was the sound of a door closing. '*I'm going to finish here, Fred. I'll pencil in some sessions in the near future. You really would benefit from opening up. Get some rest, and I'll come by again soon.*'

The door opened and closed, and it seemed that Fred was alone. The tape was still running.

Fred spoke, but it was so difficult to understand what he said. It was low, almost distorted.

Pressing the mouse, Connor rewound to the last part,

where Fred had mumbled a sentence. He turned the volume up, listening hard. *Come on, what the hell did you say?*

Again, he rewound the tape, turning the volume up another notch. It sounded like white noise, unpleasant, harsh on the ears. Connor grabbed a pen, dissecting each word he heard and scribbling it on a piece of paper. Over and over, he listened, then it all made sense. The words came together.

'*They killed Nathan. The five of them. Retribution is coming!*'

31

S *unday Night*

Ella's mobile phone pinged. She opened the message and read it.

Sorry I had to dash. Police called to Connor's flat. They wanted to speak with us. We're at a private facility where Fred stayed. I'll bell you later. Liam.

She thought about calling them, but it was late, and all Ella wanted to do was grab a glass of water and sink into bed with a good thriller novel. It was the only way she'd get some sleep.

Placing her phone on the kitchen worktop, she went to the cupboard, grabbed a glass, and filled it with water. Gulping it in one go, she looked at her shadow on the glass of the back door.

The security light is off. All the doors are locked, she reassured herself. Reaching for the handle, she tried to yank it down, feeling it resist.

Ella leaned her forehead against the cold glass, feeling instant relief from the pressure that had swarmed her body. She suddenly felt relaxed, her shoulders dropped, and she felt confident. *You have this,* she told herself. *Nothing is going to happen.*

She grabbed her mobile phone, climbed the stairs to her bedroom and undressed, leaving the main light on. After brushing her teeth in the en-suite bathroom, she picked up a book she was excited to read, resting it on the mattress and hoping the recent events wouldn't impact her concentration. Pulling the covers over her body, she leaned back against the headboard and stretched her legs, pointing her toes.

Heaven, she thought. As her body sank further into the bed, unwinding, it felt like all her thoughts and paranoia seeped like a thick grey cloud into the atmosphere.

Ella opened the book, feeling excited, and the smell of the pages enticing as she started the prologue.

Click.

Her body stiffened. Her eyes were glued to the bedroom door. *What was that?* she asked herself. *It seemed to come from the downstairs hallway. Ignore it. Don't let your imagination run wild. You're safe.*

For a moment she lay still, the book resting on her chest, but Ella had to go and check. She'd heard something, and her mind wouldn't rest until she found out what it was. Lifting the covers back, she got out of bed, tiptoeing to the bedroom door. She leaned over the wooden railing, peering downstairs.

The hallway light was off.

When alone, she disliked a dark house; Ella made a point of leaving the downstairs light on. Sod the electricity bills. Her peace of mind was more important. Still she questioned herself as she crept to the top of the stairs, rerunning her last movements before climbing the stairs to the first floor.

I turned the kitchen light off. I know that. Did I switch off the downstairs hall lights? I can't be certain. This is insane. I'll put them on now. Then I'll be sure. Hurrying down the stairs, Ella found the light switch by the front door, quickly pressed it on, and charged back up the stairs, fearing someone was behind her.

Leaving the bedroom door open, she climbed back into bed and picked up the book again. Her hands struggled to hold the edges still. The paper fluttered between her fingers.

You're fine. You're safe, she told herself.

As she continued reading, a calmness washed over her, but she still struggled to digest the words, having to read certain lines a second time. The frustration was overpowering, and she thought about putting the book down and trying to sleep. But it wouldn't happen. Not now Ella was wound up.

Her phone rang, making her wince. Reaching out to the bedside table, she saw the words on the screen.

Withheld Number.

'Hello?' Her voice sounded timid as she pressed herself further into the headboard. 'Who's there? Hello?' Tutting, she ended the call and dialled Liam's number, hearing it go straight to his voice message.

'Hey,' she said. 'How are you and Connor getting on? Did you just try and ring? Bloody hell! This is all madness. I'm in bed, but call me when you get this message.' Placing the phone back on the side, Ella stared at the ceiling, determined not to be frightened.

The phone rang again. *Yes,* she thought, picking it up.

Liam. Her disappointment was raw when she saw the same words.

Withheld Number.

'Hello? Who is this?' Ella went silent, her ears ringing. She pulled up her knees to her chest, remembering what Jennifer had said at the cafe and how she'd described Frank's state. *There were episodes,* she'd said, *you know, hearing voices and seeing things. Like they were haunting him. Sometimes on the road or standing at the window of his cottage. Phone calls. That was another. The most frightening thing was the knocks on the front door of his cottage late at night.* When no one spoke, Ella ended the call, turned her phone off and slammed it on the bedside table.

Picking up the book again, she tried desperately to digest the words and occupy her mind. But it was like they were in a different language – a blur on the page, the letters in the wrong order and muddled together.

A knocking noise came from deep within the house. As though someone was trapped in the walls.

She leaped out of bed, and leaned over the railing. The hallway light was still on downstairs. *A good thing,* she thought. Again, she heard a light tapping noise, as though someone didn't want to disturb her. As Ella rushed down the stairs, she realised it was coming from the front door. Dropping to her knees, she placed her ear against the wood and listened hard. A raucous thump caused her to jump back. The flap of the letterbox began to slowly flip upwards. Charging forward, she slammed it shut, double-checked the door lock, and darted back upstairs.

In bed, she placed her hands on the sides of her head, softly weeping. 'Leave me alone.' Ella gently rocked, rolling her neck, dropping her head from one shoulder to the other, and waited until her heart rate slowed.

Slipping further into the bed, she closed her eyes and tried to entice sleep. But her ears were on alert, listening for the slightest sound; every one of her senses was heightened. Although it was warm, an icy chill drove through her body. Tossing and turning, she finally gave in, assuming the same upright position against the headboard, book in hand, and trying to decipher the words on the page.

Finally finishing the prologue, she turned the page, seeing chapter one. Continuing to read was the only solution to find sleep.

Swiftly, Ella reached page fourteen, and she was turning the pages faster. The words had started to make sense and fall into place. Temporarily, she was in a different world. Someone else's, with their own problems.

Click.

It was like her heart burst through her mouth, her insides twisting over themselves. The sharp pain in her stomach spread, and it felt as though her airways were blocked.

Closing her eyes, she counted to ten, her throat making a weird gurgling noise. She threw the covers back and stepped to the upstairs hallway.

As Ella leaned over the railing, she saw the hallway light was turned off.

Someone's in the house, she thought. She span around, wanting to grab her phone, but as she faced the bedroom door she saw something. *Is that a shadow? Is someone in there?* Quickly, she grabbed the handle, slammed the door shut, and crept down the stairs. Too frightened to open the front door, with images of the woman who'd followed her waiting outside running through her mind, she turned the hallway light back on and rushed through the house and into the kitchen. Flicking on the light switch, she got on her hands and knees, and crawled under the table.

I'm trapped! I could make it to the garden and call for help. But by the time someone came, whoever was in the house could grab me. The garden fence is too high. I'd never make it. She envisioned her body leaning over the top of the fence and a hand grabbing her ankle.

Light steps seemed to come from the downstairs hallway as if someone was creeping towards the kitchen door. Was her mind playing tricks?

Click.

Oh, Christ. The hallway light's gone off again. Someone's out there, she thought.

It felt like her lungs were under pressure, expanding as if they were about to explode. The sharp stinging in her ears was aggravating. The din only caused more commotion in her head.

And then— *Clunk.*

The house was drenched in complete darkness.

Placing her hand over her mouth, Ella tried to quell the whimpering. Again, there were light footsteps, this time entering the kitchen. Listening hard, she thought she heard breathing. Backing further under the table, Ella blinked so hard her sockets burned, desperate to see through the blackness.

Something dropped beside her. Ella gasped as it rolled towards her thighs.

The footsteps exited the kitchen and disappeared through the downstairs hallway.

Another click. The lights had returned. Beeping noises came from the fridge. The display on the oven flashed, the time showing 0.00.

Slowly, she dropped her eyes to the floor, looking for the

object that had rolled across the floor. A tiny wooden figurine. Ella picked it up, seeing a replica of herself.

Throwing it against the wall, she lunged up and raced into the hallway.

Behind her, the back bedroom door opened; footsteps pounded along the hallway.

There was a knock at the front door, and Connor shouted, 'Ella. Are you awake?'

As she opened the front door, the intruder climbed out of the back bedroom window.

32

S*unday Night*

'I can't stay here. I'm done.' Ella watched from the downstairs hallway as Connor and Liam closed the window in the back bedroom.

'We tried to call,' Connor said. 'Your phone was off.'

Stepping into the kitchen, Ella pulled at her long blonde hair, feeling the tangles, and dug her fingers into the scalp. 'It kept... ringing. No one was there. I heard knocks at the front door and... and the electric went off. They're going to come back.' Looking at Liam, she said, 'I'm staying with you! We have to keep together until this... this animal is locked away.' Bending down, Ella picked up the miniature wooden figure. 'And what's this? A fucking... carving of me. Look. It's me.'

'He was here,' Liam said, his voice stern and deliberate. 'Tell her, Connor! Tell her what you found at the facility.'

Walking across the kitchen, Connor sat at the table. His friends joined him.

'A nurse helped me. She let me look at private records. I told her about Liv being kidnapped. There were therapy sessions.'

'With Fred?' asked Ella.

'Yes. And a doctor or psychologist. I don't know his qualifications. But he was trying to help Fred.'

Wiping a tear from the end of her nose and scratching it, Ella sniffed hard, her voice quiet as though she was beaten. 'How did he sound?'

'He didn't say much. It was mostly the doctor. Thinking about it, Fred didn't say much at school either.' Swallowing, visibly shaken, Connor looked between his friends. 'But when he did speak, it was... how do I describe it? Like hearing the devil speak. It was sinister. As though you could hear evil in his tone. Shit, guys, it gave me goosebumps hearing it again.'

'As if the bastard couldn't be scary enough,' Ella threw in. 'It was horrible. I've never been more frightened.' Glancing around the kitchen, she added, 'I can't stay. You have to let me sleep at yours, Liam.'

'I'm no closer to finding Fred's mother,' Connor said. 'I'd hoped breaking into the facility would lead us to him, but there are no records with her current address. I have to tell you, at the end of the session recording, Fred muttered words I couldn't make out at first. The audio tape ran for a couple of minutes, and Fred was alone.'

'What did he say?' Ella asked.

'After listening to it repeatedly, I made out a chilling threat. "They killed Nathan. The five of them. Retribution is coming!"'

Ella let the words digest, thinking about the intruder

fleeing out the back bedroom window which she obviously hadn't locked and how close she'd come to being murdered. The skin on her arms tingled, and goosebumps developed. 'I'm locking up here. They've been in the house once before, and they'll try again.'

Standing, Connor pushed the chair under the table. 'I have to stay at the flat in case Liv returns.' Ella and Liam slowly nodded, but Connor didn't look optimistic. The minutes were ticking, and they'd got no closer to finding Liv.

After Ella locked up, they got into Connor's car. From the passenger seat, she watched the house as they drove away, wondering if it would ever be safe to return.

'We need petrol,' Connor said, eyeing the gauge, the needle in the red. He pulled onto the A259, watching bright lights in the rear-view mirror.

Ella was silent in the passenger seat, her legs pulled to her chest.

Behind them, Liam rested his head against the window, his eyes blank, watching the bleak horizon.

It was gone midnight, and the road ahead was clear. Connor turned the heater to mid-position to tackle the slight chill. He switched on the radio, finding a local jazz station, hoping the music would lighten their mood.

In the right wing mirror, the vehicle lights behind were blinding.

Bloody arsehole, Connor thought. *Dim the lights – selfish prick.* Tilting the rear-view mirror dulled the glare, making it more bearable. 'How are you doing?' he asked Ella.

'Oh, great. Just great.' She placed her hand on his, feeling his cold, clammy skin. 'You?'

'Terrified,' he whispered, feeling Ella's hand return to her lap.

Ahead, the bright lights of the petrol station glowed so hard it stung his eyes. The neon sign read, "Open 24 Hours". As Connor slowed, flicking the indicator, he noticed the vehicle behind slow down too, as if the driver was following them.

He pulled onto the forecourt and got out.

Ella and Liam joined him.

Without saying anything to the others, Connor watched as the following vehicle stopped, the hazard lights blinking in the darkness.

'You want anything?' asked Liam as he set off to the main entrance.

"Er, no, I'm good,' Connor answered. He opened the fuel cap, pulled the nozzle, and began filling the car.

'I love that smell,' Ella said as she leaned against the vehicle. 'It's weird, isn't it? Almost hypnotising. Always reminds me of day trips with my parents as a kid.'

'Yeah. So why have they never brought it out as a fragrance if everyone loves it?'

'Bit dangerous, I'd say,' Ella laughed. 'It's flammable, duh!'

The conversation made Connor think about Fred, the fire, and the tragic accident. It would always haunt him. The hose vibrated in his hands, the numbers on the pump swirling like a broken clock. Ahead, the vehicle that had followed them was still parked in a lay-by.

Once the car was full, Connor replaced the nozzle and fuel cap and walked with Ella to the main entrance. The doors separated, gliding open.

Liam had a few packets of crisps, a chocolate bar, and a can of coke, balancing them in his hands as he walked to the till. 'You sure I can't get you anything?' he asked. Both of his friends refused.

'I need the loo quickly.' Looking out through the window, Connor noticed a couple walking along the dark country road, holding hands. *That's odd,* he thought. *Where are they going?* The town was behind them, and the nearest house was a few miles away. *Maybe they've broken down.*

He went to the toilet and returned a minute later, shaking his hands as the dryer wasn't working. 'Just the petrol, please. Pump number two,' he said at the counter, tapping his card on the machine and grabbing the receipt.

Liam and Ella were standing outside chatting by the main doors.

The couple had crossed the road now, and were turned away towards the fields.

'Ready?' Connor asked as he walked to the car.

Suddenly, the couple shifted and turned to face them.

Both wore dark glasses.

'Stop!' ordered Connor.

'What's up?' asked Liam.

The neon light illuminated their faces as they stood, peering across the road.

'Over there. Those two. I saw them walking past the petrol station seconds ago. They crossed over. They're watching us.'

'Let's just get in the car,' Ella whispered, her anxiety level peaking again.

'Do you think it's them?' Connor was positive it was the man who'd taken Liv.

'I... I think so. Oh, shit.' Glancing behind him, looking vulnerable, Liam seemed to weigh up the options. 'I say we get in the car and drive over there.'

'I think that's a plan,' said Connor. 'But it could be a trap.

Liam, will you tackle them with me? If it is them, we'll force them to bring us to Liv.'

'Yes, mate,' assured Liam, but his frail, broken voice told a different story.

Across the road, the couple were still facing them. It seemed as though they were statues frozen in time.

'Guys. I just want to get out of here!' said Ella. 'This isn't good.'

'Let's get in the car.' Walking to the driver's door, Connor pulled it open and sank into the seat. Ella and Liam joined him, and he began reversing.

With his knees on the seat, looking out of the back window, Liam announced, 'They're still standing there.'

'What are they doing?' Connor asked, edging closer to the bush at the edge of the forecourt.

'Nothing. They're just bloody... staring at us.'

'It's definitely them. I'll pull the car around, and we'll jump out. Ella, will you help?'

'I have no bloody choice. Let's do this!'

As he pushed the gear stick into first, a Transit van shot from the car wash.

Connor didn't have time to pull away, and it rammed into the side of his vehicle, crushing the metal against their bodies.

The driver pulled away, picked up the couple across the road, and fled into the darkness.

33

E*arly Monday Morning*

'You can't keep me here, you sick bastards. People will be looking for me. I... I need to pee again.' Liv sat on the cold ground, one of her arms wrapped in a heavy chain which was bolted to the wall. It was pitch black, exactly like having her eyes screwed tightly shut. The first few hours had been the worst, held in a makeshift cell as she'd drifted in and out of consciousness, the result of being whacked over the head and having a cloth doused with liquid held over her mouth. Its vile odour had knocked her out. She'd screamed so hard it felt like her throat had ripped, broken, and she feared she'd never talk again. Her pleas for help were pointless. The cell was insulated, her cries lost in the night, and eventually, it sounded as though she was under water.

There were others, too. Close by, held against their will. Liv could hear the muffled, gagged voices, desperate to escape. Every so often, chains clanked with the hope of escape. With her free hand, she'd worked at the knot behind her neck and pulled the cloth away from her mouth. Her lips were still raw, chapped, and bloody. She could taste it with her tongue. *Had the others pleaded to be released?* she thought. *Had they tried to escape? Or were they just too weak or addled to even consider crying for help? Maybe,* she surmised, *they've been down here so long they've surrendered, waiting for the moment their lives will end. Maybe they're embarrassed for me. Maybe they're laughing as they're held in the cells. But I can't give up.*

Blinking, Liv tried in desperation to focus on something. Earlier, she'd seen a light across the ground as the heavy door unbolted and slowly creaked open, but her head had ached so profoundly that the only relief had been to close her eyes.

As she yanked her arm down, the chain echoed through the dingy basement, cutting into her wrist. Unable to hold it any longer, Liv began to pee herself. The warm sensation was uncomfortable as she scratched between her jeans legs with her free hand.

Crying to herself, she recalled waking in the back of a van, arriving at a farmhouse, the fresh air a relief from the vile cloth. And then suddenly it had been placed over her mouth again.

She struggled to work out how long she'd been held down here. Hours? A day? Maybe two? She couldn't remember. The last vivid memory she had was of talking to Connor on FaceTime. And then her world had gone dark.

The smell of urine was strong in her lungs. In the distance, something squealed. *Rats.* Liv hated them more than anything. A fear of getting bitten and being poisoned with rabies overwhelmed her. Pushing her feet against the ground, she tried to stand, her body swinging back and forth on the cold concrete like the pendulum of a clock. Something brushed against her trainers. It quickly gripped onto her leg and scurried up to her waist.

'Get off me.' Another one landed on her trainer, nibbling at her laces. Kicking hard, she felt them drop to the ground and run away. But for how long? 'Let me out of here.'

The door opened. It creaked like a drawbridge raising above a moat. Solid, secure. There was no escape.

Although the light from the hallway caused her discomfort, and it disappeared as the door was pushed closed, she craved the feeling of being able to see what was going on. It was a relief from the bleakness.

What's that noise? Liv thought as a faint, high-pitched hum reverberated through the darkness. Then suddenly she knew. The captor had night-vision goggles – another way to torture them, keeping them trapped in the dark.

Across the basement, the sound of a key opening a lock echoed around the room as a cell door opened. A person was whimpering, sniffing hard. Liv could only make out shadows.

The door slammed shut, locking automatically. Someone else had been trapped in the cell next to her.

Liv could sense it. The feeling of being watched. Then she heard a thud of heavy boots on the ground. Her captor was standing outside the cell.

'Let me out of here. You're sick! You won't get away with it.' Yelling at the top of her voice, she said, 'Answer me, you freak!'

Twice this monster, disguised with a sack over their head, had dragged her up the stairs, taking pictures of her and sending them to Connor. Would the next photo be her lying mutilated on the cold ground? Again, she pulled at the chain which held her arm.

The squeals of the rats were closing in on her. Would she have the strength to defend herself? *How humiliating,* she thought. *No one knows where I am. My body will never be found. Eaten alive by those—* Liv couldn't say the word.

From where she stood, she could smell her captor's warm, rancid breath. It was like death. Like digging up a rotten corpse and kissing them on the lips.

It made her gag, as though this freak was infecting her insides.

Suddenly charging at the cell door, Liv placed her hand out, fingers spread, and desperate to grab her captor. The chain snapped tight, and the pain in her wrist was severe. Collapsing to the ground, she crawled back to her corner and wept, listening as the captor walked out of the basement and locked the door.

The squealing was close.

The rats were getting braver.

34

E *arly Monday Morning*

'Is everyone alright?' Connor felt the car's frame pushing against the side of his body. Reaching across, the pain tolerable in his right shoulder, he undid his and Ella's seatbelts and helped with the passenger door.

Liam was sitting behind her and managed to avoid injury.

'I can't get the bloody driver's door open.' Tugging the handle, Connor barged against it, hearing a crunch as it gave way, and got out. 'He was waiting there. I saw lights earlier as we pulled into the petrol station,' confirmed Connor. 'The fucker was following us. It was a trap.' Stepping back, he assessed the car. 'Shit! Look at the damage.'

'It's never going to stop.' Rushing to the main road, Ella looked up and down for lights, but there was only a blanket of darkness on either side. The Transit van had long gone, and she felt relief and sudden guilt for Connor and Liv at its absence. Was he ever going to find her?

'You didn't think to tell us!' Liam spat, his tone sharp.

'I didn't want to freak you out for no reason.' Lowering his voice, Connor said, 'You know what Ella's just gone through. If I was wrong, you'd tell me to stop being paranoid.'

A voice chirped behind them.

Connor and Liam spun around.

'Are you hurt? I can't believe they drove off. Probably a drunk driver,' the shop attendant clarified. 'Or drugs. Shit houses. They're the lowest, doing that. The police are on their way.'

'What?' asked Connor, feeling like his mind had snapped. 'You called the police?'

'Yeah. They'll be here soon.'

'No sign of them,' Ella confirmed as she rejoined her friends on the forecourt.

We have to get out of here, thought Connor. The police had already been suspicious earlier when they'd called to his flat. Now this. He didn't need the hassle, and besides, he knew what would happen to Liv. Gazing at the fields across the road, he wondered if anyone was watching. 'No. We got to go. We're fine. Thanks for your concern.'

'Are you mad?' asked the attendant. 'Don't let that idiot get away with it. You want to throw the book at them. They'll only do it again. The next time, someone might die.'

'Yeah,' Connor said, thinking of his girlfriend, 'that's why we have to go.'

'What do you mean?' asked the attendant.

'Don't worry about it.' He climbed into the driver's seat, Liam and Ella following him. Connor shouted, 'Thanks for your concern. It's an old car. It doesn't bother me too much.'

'What do I tell the police?'

'You'll think of something,' Connor assured him, before pulling out of the forecourt.

Connor decided it was safer for the three of them to stay together. After stopping at Liam's house to feed the cat and ensure everything was locked, they headed to Connor's flat. He needed to be there in case there was news on Liv.

'I'm sorry, I need to turn in,' Ella confirmed as she stood in the hallway. 'Where can I sleep?'

'You can top and tail with Liam and me, or there's a mattress in the spare room. We can drag it in here. It's not much, but it's better than the hard floor.'

'I'll take the mattress.' Placing her arms around Connor, she pulled him close and kissed his cheek. 'Thanks for this. For looking out for us with everything you're going through. I can't imagine how you're dealing with it. We will find her, you know.'

'I don't think we will,' answered Connor, forcing the tears back. He needed to be optimistic, but hope was dying with every second that passed.

He and Liam dragged the mattress into the main bedroom. Once Ella had undressed and got under the covers, the lads jumped into bed.

'Don't try anything on,' Connor ordered. 'Keep your hands to yourself.'

'You'd be lucky,' Liam answered. 'There's loads of women who'd love to be in your position.'

'Yeah, mate,' scoffed Ella. 'In your dreams!'

Turning off the side light, Connor lay on his back, his eyes adjusting as he stared at the ceiling. The lump in his throat had returned, and this time, he wasn't strong enough to force it back. The tears spilled down his cheeks as he silently wept. As he closed his eyes, the loud crunch from the Transit van hitting them ran constantly in his mind.

Through the bedroom curtain, the light was harsh on Connor's face. Springing up, he saw Liam at the end of the bed, turned on his side and snoring. Ella was on the floor, her body half off the mattress. For a moment, he'd forgotten his friends were staying with him. He wanted to lie back down, cover his body with the blankets, and never get up. He missed Liv – her hoarse voice first thing in the morning, kissing his cheek, and the two of them cuddling. They'd plan their day, discussing ways to be a success together with the hope of owning their own gallery and displaying her paintings. Now, it seemed a million miles away. Reaching over to the bedside table, the anticipation already working through his veins, Connor checked his phone for any messages. Struggling to keep the phone still, his eyes hazy, he checked social media and WhatsApp. There was nothing. The relief dropped like a rock into water, but was it a good sign? Maybe the radio silence meant bad news.

He curled his fists tight, then scratched his wrist to relieve the strain. He pushed the blanket back, dressed, and went into the kitchen.

In the fridge, he found food to make a fry up. Tipping oil in the pan, he began cooking eggs, bacon, and sausages and filled the kettle with water.

Ella's voice startled him. For a split second, he'd thought it was Liv.

'Bloody hell. Don't do that!'

Yawning, she stretched her arms in the air and smirked. 'Do what?'

'You frightened me.'

Grabbing a glass of water from the sink, she turned. 'How did you sleep?'

'I didn't, really. I woke up so many times. And Christ, can Liam snore?'

'Yeah. Unreal. I didn't sleep well. I couldn't shut my brain off.' Stepping to Connor, she placed her arms on his shoulders. 'Are you alright? I know you're strong, but don't be afraid to express your feelings. You need to talk to us.'

He turned the food over in the pan, the smell enticing, then placed the spatula down. 'Where do I start? It haunts me. I've never been so frightened as when I saw someone behind Liv on that FaceTime call. And then her disappearing. It doesn't stop. The image. Like, it plays in my head all the time. If something happens to her, I'll never forgive myself.'

'Connor. Listen to me! It's not your fault. You didn't know Liv was in danger.'

'But if I hadn't gone to meet the artist. If only I'd stayed home, I could have protected her.'

'Hindsight is a wonderful thing. Don't beat yourself up.' Kissing him on the cheek, she stepped back. 'It isn't your fault! We need to get out of here, just for a while. We need fresh air and to clear our minds.' Ella walked to the cupboard, grabbed three mugs and teabags, and made tea. 'Let's go to the beach. Maybe we could hand out flyers. Do you have a recent photo of Liv?'

'I thought of that. But say someone calls the police. You know what will happen.'

Okay.' Ella puffed hard, looking defeated. 'Then let's go

to the beach and clear our minds. Just for a while. It will do us good.'

'I can't. What if... if someone calls?'

'You have your phone. I don't think anyone will come here unless they're trying to—' She stopped sharply, recalling the events last night at her house and quickly trying to put them out of her head. 'It will help you think straight. Come on. I'll go wake Liam. We'll eat and have some time together. We all need it.'

'Will I get stopped by the police?' Connor drove out towards the beach, the car feeling like it was ready to collapse. The dents would have to be fixed, but he had more important things on his mind. He shifted in the driver's seat, feeling a sharp piece of metal digging into his ribs.

From the back seat, Liam leaned forward. 'They'd be doing you a favour towing this shit heap away. Aren't you embarrassed?'

'Piss off. You can walk if you like. Meet me and Ella there!'

'I feel like the bottom will come away, and we'll have to run like the cartoon!' Liam started singing. '*Flintstones, meet the Flintstones.*'

'You're such a wind-up merchant,' Connor smirked. 'Keep going, and I'll dent your face to match!'

The sky was a bright blue colour, and wisps of thin cloud clung desperately to the air. Connor had his window cracked open, managing to force it with his fingers, the warm breeze invigorating. Although guilty for taking time out, he'd never appreciated his friends more than now. He just hoped they could pull him through if anything happened to Liv.

The car park was already bustling. A queue of vehicles packed with couples, families, and groups of friends sat patiently waiting to get a spot.

Ahead, a young girl waved from the backseat. Next to her, a dog had its head out the window and was barking excitedly.

Once they'd found a space, they got out, Connor paid, and they walked up the steep sand dunes, down the other side and onto the soft sand.

The tide was out, and people resembling specks on the horizon were already swimming in the clear blue sea. The water rolled over itself, creating small waves, and the aroma of fish and chips, seaweed, and the sweet smell of candy floss wafted in the air. Seagulls squawked as they dipped, looking for something to steal.

'Here's a good spot,' Ella confirmed as she dropped her carrier bag and spread one of Connor's towels she'd taken from the airing cupboard. Connor and Liam joined her, choosing to sit on the sand.

'How are you feeling now?' she asked, screwing her eyes against the bright sunshine.

'Better!' Looking between his friends, Connor thanked them both. The fresh air began to clear his head, and the warm breeze, although salty, calmed his body. But inside, he felt dead.

'Hey,' Liam piped up, 'remember Todd Simpson from school?'

'Oh yeah,' answered Connor. 'Geeky kid. Curly hair and glasses.'

'That's him. Well, he's running the local pub where I

moved to. He's sound. Give's the odd lock-in as well.' Liam lay back on the sand, pushing his hands into it.

'Wasn't his dad arrested? I'm sure I remember that!' Ella quizzed.

'That's him. He used to deliver groceries for one of those online stores. Customers were only getting half their orders, and when the police got a warrant to search his house, the outside shed was like a supermarket.'

'What a clown,' mused Connor. 'Talk about shitting on your own back doorstep. Christ! Some people. Why did you bail out?'

'Huh?' asked Liam gormlessly.

'You know what I mean!'

Stirring his left hand in the sand, Liam sat up, his right hand over his face, blocking the sun. 'I was paranoid. I didn't want to stay in Rye. Jesus, everywhere I went, bumping into old school friends, it was tough. It kept bringing back horrific memories. I felt like I was losing it. So... I... I had to break away – a fresh start.'

'You left us to deal with it, Liam. When we needed you the most. Do you know how many times Ella and I tried to contact you? Why did you never return our calls?'

'Shit, mate. I was dealing with my own mental health issues. Mum and Dad knew something was wrong. I couldn't sleep. I couldn't eat. I woke in the night with cold sweats, screaming from the nightmares. I saw Nathan burning to death in the store room. The smell of flesh, the cries for help. The guilt was too much, and I contemplated suicide.'

'What? You didn't tell us you were that low!' Ella said.

'Mum had antidepressant tablets. One evening, when I came back from work, my head ached so badly with remorse. I couldn't get Nathan out of my head. Fuck, it was a prank. We didn't know Fred would burn the school down. No matter how hard I tried to reason with myself, nothing worked. So, I grabbed my mum's pills, took a bottle of whisky from the drinks cabinet, and sat in the living room. I stared at the alcohol for ages. I started popping the pills. I think I got through four or five, opened the whiskey, and I stopped.' Pausing for a moment to gather his thoughts, Liam continued. 'It's weird. I don't know what happened.' He looked up, seeing Ella and Connor almost staring through him. 'I heard a voice. It was Nathan. I know it sounds stupid, But it said, I forgive you.'

Ella reached out and held Liam's hand. 'I think it was a sign. Liam, we tried. We were terrified. Mrs Franklin and her threats put paid to us confessing. But we wanted to come clean. We all did. What she said in the classroom and how it would ruin our lives, how it would drop us further into the shit. We had no choice.'

'I guess this is our punishment. Living forever with the guilt,' confirmed Liam.

'Ella's right. Mrs Franklin had her own agenda.' Looking at the clear sky, the warm air invigorating, Connor lay back on the sand. 'If only she knew how keeping her dirty secret from coming out ruined our lives.'

On the way home, Ella asked if they could pop into town and get some fresh bread, ham, and cold soft drinks. Her stomach was rumbling, and the fresh air had given her an appetite.

Connor pulled into a spot on Rye High Street. As they got out of the car, the paranoia hit hard, and he scanned the area, wondering if they were being monitored. He didn't want to worry the others. The morning at Camber Sands beach has been beautiful. Ella was right. It had lifted his mood, even if it was just for a while.

Inside the bakery, the smell of dough and coffee was intoxicating. Fresh bread, sandwiches, and rolls filled with everything you'd want were displayed in glass cabinets. The coffee machine whirred, the rich aroma from the beans filling the shop.

Connor treated them. He and Liam went for a tuna baguette, while Ella chose a pastry sausage roll and a ham sandwich. Although they'd only eaten hours ago, it felt like their bellies were empty.

Standing at the counter, Connor removed his phone, tapped it against the card reader, and grabbed the food. Outside, he could hear a commotion. People were gathering on the pavement across the road. Someone was screaming while others were filming on their phones.

'What's happening over there?' Liam asked as he stood at the front door.

Connor and Ella joined him.

A car was stopped in the middle of the road, and its young driver was pressing his hand to his head. 'Someone pushed him. I didn't have enough time to stop. It wasn't my fault.'

It dawned on Connor that maybe this was another ploy in this wicked game. If you could call it that. 'Quick,' ordered Connor. 'In the car. Go!'

From the passenger seat, Ella grabbed her phone and went on Rye News. A video had been posted a few seconds ago. 'Uh oh! This isn't good.' She held her phone up, the others watching as she clicked play.

A woman stood on the side of the road, holding a mobile phone and filming herself. She wore dark glasses, her long blonde hair tied back. Next to her was a male figure, also wearing dark glasses, with cropped black hair and heavy stubble. Suddenly, the woman flipped the camera, holding the phone at arm's length.

In the car, the atmosphere was one of dismay as Connor, Ella and Liam watched the recording.

The camera flicked along the street and then flipped back to the couple, making sure they could be seen. Suddenly, it swerved to a middle-aged man approaching them. A vehicle was driving along the high street, music blaring and the bass distorted. The camera jumped, unfocused for a second, but you could clearly see the woman pushing the midde-aged man in front of the car.

Connor took the phone. Scanning the Facebook page, he felt a knot in his stomach. Struggling to catch a breath, his heart throbbing, he looked at the recent posts.

Darren Simmons:

What is Ella McKenzie doing? Has she lost her mind? And I think that's Connor Murphy with her.

Shaz Dormer.

It's Ella. Always liked her at school. It must be drugs, kids. That's what they do to you. I'm calling the police.

Clare Smith.

It's definitely Connor and Ella. He works in a gallery. I'll never step foot in there again. Attempted murder is serious.

He dropped the phone to his lap. Ella had got out of the car, and stood on the road, gasping for breath.

A voice bellowed from across the street.

'That's her. Quick, get her!'

Slumping back into the passenger seat, her voice flat and demoralised, she instructed, 'You need to drive. Quick. Get out of here.'

As Connor pulled onto the road, people rushed over, kicking and thumping the back of the car.

35

Two Months Ago

'I'm going to miss you. I hate being away.' Lucas Dubois kissed his wife hard on the lips, and she reached down, trying to undo his belt and fiddling with the buckle. 'Whoa, I'm going to miss the train. We can't.'

'Come on, you've got time,' Jocelyn pushed.

'I don't know if that's a compliment or not,' he laughed. 'I have a couple of minutes until I have to leave.'

'Fine. Your loss. You're away for a week. I thought it would be a nice send-off.'

Their daughter rushed into the kitchen and wrapped her arms around Lucas. 'I love you, Daddy. I'm going to miss you.'

Crouching, Lucas brushed a hand through his daughter's short black hair. Her eyes were swollen with sleep, and she'd dropped the teddy bear on the kitchen floor that she slept with.

'Look after the teddy until I come back. Have you got school today?'

'Uh-huh. I hate going. Can't I come with you, Daddy?'

'Oh, sweetheart, I wish you could. But I have boring meetings in stuffy boardrooms. You won't like it.'

'Will you call us every night?' she asked.

'I will. I promise.' Standing, he clapped his hands together. 'Right, I have to go. I'll see you both at the weekend.' He kissed his wife and daughter, then grabbed his suitcase and left their Paris flat to catch the train.

He and Jocelyn had met in England. But after a work opportunity that was too good to turn down, they'd moved to France a few years ago and had Olivia. Jocelyn was pregnant with their second child, and they loved living in Paris.

Although the journey from Paris Gare de Lyon to Barcelona Sants station was a direct route with no changes, it took almost seven hours, and Lucas disliked travelling alone. The company he worked for sold stationery and was one of the market leaders. Luckily, he only met clients every so often and usually worked from their Paris office.

He killed time by working on his laptop, calling his wife, and staring out the window at the beautiful landscape.

Once he'd checked in to his hotel, Lucas dumped his briefcase and studied the time. It was almost 6 pm, and after talking with his wife and daughter, he decided to go to the bar for a drink.

Taking the lift to the ground floor, he found the hotel bar and grabbed a stool by the counter.

'Can I get a large gin and tonic, please?' he asked the barman, hoping he spoke English.

'Certainly,' came the reply.

The decor was modern, with an oak bar and exposed brick walls. The lighting was warm and intoxicating, intimating comfort.

A fridge displayed local beers, and pictures of the Barcelona football team hung on the walls.

The barman placed the drink on the counter, took Lucas's payment, and attended to a woman who ordered a sangria.

'Mind if I join you?' she asked Lucas, picking up her drink.

Please don't tell me everyone is this forward, Lucas thought. 'By all means,' was his reply, not wanting to be rude. He watched as she sipped the drink through a straw. 'That looks like it was needed.'

'Oh, you don't know how much.' The woman flicked her auburn hair off her shoulders and stretched her neck. 'So, I didn't catch your name?'

Oh, no. Here goes. Can't you see I have a wedding ring on? 'Lucas. And you?' The memory of his daughter, clutching him in the kitchen, wrapping her arms around him and not wanting him to leave, punched through his head.

'Hillary Parsons. You're English too. Is that correct?' She pressed her thumbs together in front of her, pouting her lips.

'You would be correct. We moved to Paris a few years ago. I had a job offer too good to refuse.'

'*Too good to refuse,*' she repeated in an accent taken from The Godfather. 'I love that film. Sorry.' She laughed.

'No. It's a good impression.'

'We?'

'Excuse me?' asked Lucas.

'You said we!'

'Oh, yes, my wife and child.' He watched the disappointment on her face as she tutted, the corner of her mouth curling down.

'That's too bad. But we're just talking. No harm in it.' As Lucas finished his drink, crunching on the ice, she voiced, 'Let me get you another!'

'Oh, I don't know. I've got an early start tomorrow. I need to keep a clear head.'

'One for the road. As they say back home. How about it?'

Flicking a look at his watch, he nodded, thanking her. 'I need the loo. Back in a minute.' Spanish guitar music was playing in the corridor to the toilets, and Lucas thought about how he'd love to learn as he opened the door to the gents.

Once he'd finished and dried his hands, something in his gut told him Hillary would be gone from the bar. He hadn't left a wallet or belongings on the counter, so if she had left, it would have been doing him a favour. *No such luck,* he pondered as he walked to his seat.

'Better?' The woman was leaning over the bar, her right elbow planted on the counter, holding her chin. 'You are handsome, aren't you?'

A blush worked to his cheeks, and he smiled through embarrassment.

'Don't be bashful.' Waving a hand in the air, she apologised.

'There's no need, really,' he replied. 'But thanks for the compliment.'

They spoke for another half hour, predominantly Hillary, who didn't seem to care that Lucas was married. She flirted, flicking her hair and eyelashes and pouting as though she was an animal, licking her lips and salivating.

The bar became blurred. Lucas could feel a sharp pain in his head, and he suddenly felt weak. Placing his hands on the counter, he coughed and sniffed hard, trying to clear his mind.

'What's wrong? Are you okay?' the woman asked, touching his arm.

'I don't... Ooh, I've come over all funny. I don't feel so good.'

'Here. Let me help you to your room. Do you remember the number?'

Placing his hand in his trouser pocket, Lucas removed the key card. Unable to focus on the number, he tossed the key card on the counter.

'Room 9. I've got you,' she insisted. 'Come on. Let's get you upstairs.'

Staggering, it felt as though his legs had lost all power; he was unable to go where his brain ordered him, and the woman had to help him to the lift.

On the second floor, he fell against the hallway wall, banging his head.

'My, you're not used to alcohol, are you?'

He went to speak, but it was one huge slur, as if his tongue was stuck to the roof of his mouth.

'Here. Let me tap the door. You'll be in bed in a minute. That's it, you got it. Take another step. That's it. There we are.'

Lucas slumped on the bed, and the woman walked to the front door, locked it, and walked back in, standing by the bed.

Removing his shoes, socks, trousers, and underwear, she climbed on top of him and began taking photos. Then she lay beside him in the bed, arms around him, and completely naked herself. Lucas had nothing on from the waist down as she took more pictures with her phone.

The following morning, Lucas woke with the mother of all headaches. It felt like the veins in his head had bulged, and they banged with his heart like a beat in an Ibiza club. It hurt to move. It hurt to think. It was as though he'd died and woken years later in a coffin in the soil. He tried to stir, lifting his body from the wet, soiled blanket. *Oh shit!* he thought, getting out of bed and stripping the mattress. *What happened? How did I get so drunk?* Slumping back into bed, he battled to stop his body from shaking. The mobile phone next to the bed pinged, and he looked at the screen, seeing a long list of missed calls. Unable to talk to his wife with the pain in his body, he closed his eyes and fell into a deep sleep.

It was gone 1 pm when he stirred again. Everything was dry and washed out. His lips were chapped, his mouth felt like the bottom of a birdcage, and his skin felt like it was being clawed from the inside. It was as if he'd swallowed a bottle of bleach.

Grabbing the phone, he saw more missed calls. The guilt ate at him as he dialled his wife's number, listening to her frustrated voice.

'Bloody hell, Lucas! I've been so worried. Why are you not answering the phone? Is everything alright?'

'Yes. I passed out,' he answered, gripping his short black hair.

'Passed out? Did I hear you correctly?'

'It's not what you think. I... I had a weird turn. It feels like I've got a brain tumour. Every muscle in my body aches.'

Jocelyn's voice softened. 'Oh no. Have you got any tablets?'

'No. I'm going to sleep. I'm so tired. I missed the meetings today, but I don't have the strength to call anyone. Look, I think I'm going to come home. I need rest. Can I call you later?'

'Of course. Rest up. If you're not well, don't worry about work. Do you want me to come down? I can be back with you on the train. I'll get someone to look after Olivia.'

'There's no need. I'll ring you tonight. I love you.'

'I love you too, Lucas.'

It was late afternoon when he finally stirred again. For a moment, he struggled to think where he was. The room was unfamiliar. Lucas sat on the edge of the bed, fighting the feeling of depression. He was so far from his family and all he wanted was to hold them tight and be in his own apartment.

He recalled the woman he'd met at the bar. They'd chatted for a good half hour. Small talk was what he'd call it. She'd insisted on buying him a drink.

Then, blank. He couldn't remember anything else.

As he noticed the soiled sheets which still lay on the floor, he was gripped with embarrassment. He hadn't done that since he was a child. *Was the drink that strong?* he considered. *Were the measures more than Paris? Surely not. And besides, I'd only had two large gin and tonics.* He was used to it.

Checking the timetable on his phone, he saw the next train to Paris left Barcelona at 5 pm. It was enough time. Just. But he had to be quick.

Lucas grabbed the sheets, stuffing them in a laundry basket. *Sorry to leave you this present. But it wasn't my fault. I hope you can forgive me.* After dressing in clean clothes, he grabbed his toiletries from the bathroom. Once he'd packed his razor, body spray, and toothbrush, he closed the door and took the lift to the ground floor, feeling optimistic about returning home so early. His job would understand, and besides, his family took precedence.

After checking out, he walked to the hotel bar and saw the same gentleman from last night behind the counter.

'Hi. I was here last night,' Lucas explained, watching as the barman reached for a glass above his head. 'I had a turn for the worse. Do you know what that means?'

'Er, sure,' the barman responded. 'Too much to drink. Not able to hold alcohol. How do you British say, a lightweight?'

'Ah,' Lucas chuckled. 'No, I don't know what happened, but it wasn't any of those things, I can assure you. Listen, the woman last night, do you know her?'

'The woman you left with?' He tilted the glass and began pouring a drink.

'Erm... I... No, I didn't leave with her. You misunderstand. I think... So, I went to the toilet. When I returned, I felt woozy, you know, dizzy, kind of. Anyway, do you know the woman? Have you seen her in here before?'

'No. I have never seen her. Is there a problem?' he asked, placing the drink on the counter. 'You want one?'

'I'm good,' Lucas responded, waving a hand. 'Only, this may sound crazy, but I think she spiked my drink.'

'Spiked? What do you mean? Poisoned it? Come on, you're watching too many films.'

The barman's reply irritated Lucas. He needed to be taken seriously. 'Look. Do you have cameras? CCTV? Anything that would have recorded her?'

'We are one of the best hotels in Barcelona. Our clientele is exceptional. I don't see a reason to set up cameras. And anyway, it invades people's privacy. So, no is the answer. But you could ask at the main desk.'

With a frustrated spat, Lucas pushed, 'It happened here.'

'I can't help you.'

Rushing to the main desk, Lucas gave a brief account of what had happened to him and a description of the woman he was looking for. 'Have you seen her? It's urgent. Please can you help?'

The woman behind the counter glared at him as though he was going mad.

'I wasn't working last night,' she informed him, 'but if you leave your details, I'll speak with the duty manager when she's back in the morning.'

'Could you call her now?'

'She doesn't like to be disturbed. As I stated, tomorrow!'

Lucas handed the woman a business card with his details, thinking it may be a while before he heard from her with her lacklustre response.

Spinning on his heels, Lucas walked out of the hotel hoping he'd still make the five o'clock train.

It was almost half past midnight when the train pulled into Paris. Lucas had slept for the majority of the journey. He felt better. The bug or whatever had happened had hopefully left his system. He'd take tomorrow off and rest with his family. Work could wait.

After leaving the station, he walked to the car park, seeing his wife standing by the driver's door of her car and his daughter rushing along the road towards him. Picking Olivia up, he swung her around and kissed her on the cheek, then he took her hand and hugged Jocelyn.

'You look better,' his wife remarked. 'I had to bring Olivia as I couldn't get anyone to watch over her. She'll be tired in the morning. How are you doing?'

'I'm okay. Still under the weather. I don't know what happened to me.'

'I think you should get checked out!' Jocelyn ordered with concern in her voice.

'Oh, let's just get home. I've missed you both so much.'

For the next two days, Lucas worked from home. He'd spoken to his boss, who sounded concerned and told him to rest. He didn't push himself too hard, working on the laptop, drinking loads of water, and taking breaks. He and Jocelyn also had early nights.

Although his wife suggested visiting a doctor, he felt much better and thought it was a waste of time.

Friday evening, Lucas tucked Olivia into bed, with her teddy bear beside her, and read a bedtime story. Before he'd finished, she was sound asleep. Kissing her on the cheek, he whispered, 'Love ya, baby,' into her ear and turned out the lights. He and Jocelyn ordered a takeaway and shared a bottle of wine.

In the kitchen, they cleared the plates together and stacked the dishwasher.

'I'm turning in,' Lucas announced.

'I'll be with you in ten minutes,' Jocelyn responded. 'See you up there.'

After undressing, he brushed his teeth, flossed, and washed his face. Staring in the mirror, he noticed his thick black stubble needed trimming, and his cropped black hair was growing out. He'd make an appointment with the barber on Saturday. As he lay down on the mattress, he thought how good his life was.

His mobile phone pinged.

Still in the horizontal position, he dabbed at the blankets, picked up the phone, and looked at the screen.

A WhatsApp message.

He didn't recognise the number, but he felt his jaw drop as he viewed the pictures it had sent. His heart was beating so fast he thought it would explode.

There were seven photos in total. Four with a woman lying on top of him. The other three showed her lying naked next to him.

Under the final photo, it read:

Arrive at this address no later than Saturday evening, or the pictures will be sent to your boss and then to your wife. Ignore this at your peril. You have been warned.

The Farmhouse, Raven Lane, Rye, United Kingdom.

'You look like you've seen a ghost?' Jocelyn undressed and climbed into bed.

Lucas had deleted the photos, fighting a pain in his gut. It felt like he'd been hit with a sledgehammer. A cold sweat appeared on his face, and he was certain he'd vomit. 'I don't feel well.' As Jocelyn pulled him close, he became aware of his body quivering, and he felt like a fish pulled from a lake.

'Honey,' his wife said, feeling his forehead with the back of her hand, 'we need to get you to a doctor. I'm worried. You may have a virus.'

Unable to answer, he turned away and stared at the wall, his head trying to process whether he'd slept with the woman at the bar under the influence of alcohol or she'd drugged him. Either way, it was too late to take a test. The drugs would have long since left his system.

He had to get to the address in England before his wife and boss found out.

'I have to leave this morning for England.' Lucas sprang it on his wife early Saturday morning as she strolled into the kitchen. Tucking his shirt into his trousers, he fiddled with the buttons, deciding to leave the top one undone. The sweat from his chest was already dampening the material.

'You can't be serious. Have they no mercy?' Jocelyn stood in front of him, her head slightly tilted and her eyes focused on him.

'The boss called. Said it was an emergency. There's a potential buyer who wants to meet. It could make the company an absolute fortune.'

'Tell them to send someone else!' She placed her hand on his face, rubbing his stubble. 'This is insane. You're recovering. Look how pale you are!'

'Leave it!' he yelled, instantly feeling guilty.

'Lucas. What's going on? You can tell me anything.'

Feeling his eyes glaze over, he pulled his wife close, holding her tight, aware his body was convulsing. 'I've booked on the first available flight. I have to go. I love you so very much.'

'When will you be back?'

Grabbing his coat from the hallway, he opened the front door. 'I don't know. Don't wake Olivia. Tell her I'm sorry that Daddy had to leave.' As he closed the door, Lucas could hear his wife calling after him.

He'd waited at the airport for a couple of hours and turned his mobile phone off. It was better that he didn't speak with Jocelyn; it was too difficult. He'd go to the address, see what the hell they wanted, and get home. His mind felt warped, unable to grasp why the photos had been taken. Desperate to retrace his steps, he went over every move. Each scene step by step. But Lucas couldn't remember whether it was drunken sex or something completely innocent. The more he thought about it, the more he believed he was being set up.

After a turbulent flight, he took a train to Rye and a taxi from the station, giving the driver the address and asking them to drop him a half mile from the property. Lucas didn't want to announce his arrival.

'Thanks. I appreciate it. Wait, here's a tip.' He watched through the window as the driver placed the coins in a compartment under the dashboard, and then made a U-turn.

The narrow road was ravaged by potholes, and grass pushed through the cracked tarmac. The fields were wild and rustic, and Lucas felt like the only person left on earth. The seclusion was eerie. *Who would ever live out here?* he pondered. As he scoped the area, his mind created an array of situations that might be waiting for him, but however hard he thought, Lucas couldn't find a single reason why anyone would have dragged him out here. As he walked, he thought about his school life, his job, and his workmates – the local pub he and his family frequented and restaurants where they ate. Any reason someone could be doing this to him. Nothing came to mind. Not a single person he'd encountered in thirty-eight years could be this cruel. Were they trying to frame the wrong person?

Lucas approached a farmhouse nestled in the bushes. It looked abandoned.

Surely, it's the wrong address? he thought as he looked through the broken ground-floor windows. Glancing over his shoulder, he examined the barren fields. A crow squawked as it hopped branches. Suddenly, more joined in. Their harsh tones were aggravating. It seemed they were warning him to run. To get as far away from the farmhouse as possible.

Debating whether or not to rap the front door with his knuckles, Lucas stepped through the bushes, feeling a nettle sting his hand. Anxiety made him fiddle with his collar, his face glistening with perspiration.

Click.

The front door seemed to swing back of its own accord.

Lucas approached it, keeping his body low, and crouched against the wall, anticipating an attack. The smell from inside the cottage was foul and damp, like soggy cardboard. He pinched his lips, counted to five, and moved to the front door, scanning the area inside. Across the living room, he could see a shadow. Someone was sitting in a chair, staring at him.

'Who the fuck are you?' Lucas called out, hearing his laboured breaths.

'Thank you for turning up. I knew you would!'

'I asked you who you were,' pushed Lucas, watching as the man stood.

'I'm Fred Kipler,' the low, deep voice responded. 'Although the name means nothing to you yet, it will!'

Eyeing the living room table, Lucas saw an empty glass bottle and rushed towards it, grabbing the stem tight in his right hand. 'Start talking, or I swear I'll smash this bottle and ram it in your throat,' Lucas warned.

With a calm, methodical voice, Fred responded, 'Have you met my mother?'

A woman appeared from the basement steps. 'It's ready. We have it all nice and cosy for your stay with us,' she said, her head jerking with a tic.

'You!' Pointing at the woman, Lucas dropped the glass bottle, hearing it smash on the floor. 'The bar. It was you. What did you do to me?' As he rushed at Fred, the woman produced a stun gun from behind her back.

36

M onday Afternoon

'There are loads of comments on the Facebook group. This is ridiculous.' Ella was forced against the passenger door as Connor swung hard around a bend. 'What now? We're fucked! We have to hide.' She scrolled down the page and saw more comments being added.

'Calm down. The worst thing we can do is panic,' said Connor. 'Let's think!'

'Calm down! Are you mad? We're going to get lynched. Half the town is probably looking for us by now.' Ella began banging her head against the glass of the passenger door.

'Stop!' shouted Connor. 'You're going to smash it.'

'Am I? That's rich. Look at the state of this shit heap.'

'Get a grip of yourself.' Ahead, a dog walked onto the road. The screeching sound was intense as Connor slammed the brakes. He looked at Ella as the dog reached the other side of the road. 'You need to take deep breaths.'

'Deep breaths! You're not seeing straight. I can't deal with this shit! Remember the witch trials? That's nothing when they get their hands on us. It looks like we tried to kill somebody. Then ran! They have it on video. Everyone thinks it was us.'

'Right,' Connor said, rubbing his stubble and pulling his bottom lip, 'we need to keep a low profile.'

'Hide, don't you mean?' Clearly worried they were being followed, Liam looked out the back window.

'Yes. Hide. Christ, this isn't happening. My flat isn't safe.' With a swift look at Ella, Connor declared, 'Neither is your place.' Over his shoulder, Connor said, 'Liam, we're bowling to your mum and dad's place.'

'Why there?'

'It was us that was caught on camera. Ella and me. At this moment, no one is looking for you. It's the safest place.'

Liam muttered something they couldn't hear.

'It's just until we work something out.' Steering down Mermaid Street, Connor pulled a left, and Ella saw him internally debating whether to park on the drive. It was risky; the police would be looking for his car. 'You two jump out. I'll park at the end of the road and be back in a few minutes. Once inside, make sure all the doors are locked!'

As Ella followed Liam to the front door, she thought, *We're well and truly up to our necks in shit!*

Once Connor had parked, he walked back along the road, checking Rye News on Facebook. Dozens of people had posted, many naming him and Ella. It was too much for his brain to process, so he placed the phone back in his pocket. It seemed everyone was looking for them, and some of the locals in town may have been just as dangerous as Fred Kipler.

After Connor knocked, Liam opened the door, and they sat in the kitchen with the curtains closed.

'Great list. I hope you're following the rules.' Ella pointed at the paper on the fridge door, grinning.

'Have you been left instructions?' Liam tapped his feet so fast on the floor it looked like he was dancing a jig.

'No. I just get things done!'

'What do you think our parents are doing now?' asked Liam, his voice fatigued and gravelly. 'If they only knew the trouble we're in. How everything can change so quickly.'

The cat brushing up against Ella's legs startled her. 'Jesus, thanks for that!' Leaning off the chair, she stroked the cat's back and watched it jump onto the table. 'Oh, probably drinking Margaritas and sunning themselves.' A gurgling sound emitted from her voice. 'Oh, God. Are they on Rye News?'

'I don't think so. Mum came off Facebook a few years ago. She got sick of the ads. And I don't think Dad has ever been on Facebook. What about yours?' asked Liam, directing the question at both of them.

'Same,' Ella replied. 'Dad doesn't like social media. Says it's intrusive. Mum was on it, but I think she deleted her account.'

Connor weighed up the question. 'I haven't a clue if Mum's on it.' His phone began ringing. It felt awkward in his hands, as if he were holding a sharp rock. 'We'll soon find out. It's her. Keep silent, and don't say a word.' Inhaling slowly, he answered. 'Hi, Mum. How are you?'

'Fine. It feels like I haven't spoken to you for ages. Are you well?'

'I'm well,' he answered, careful not to show his friends on the screen. He smiled, trying to put his mum at ease. 'So what you have been up to?'

For the next five minutes, his mother told him about their neighbour and how he was locked out. A dog shitting in the front garden. The car dumped up the street and accumulating parking tickets. Her hairdresser's cat being rushed to the vet. Connor registered nothing. His mind was too addled to grasp what she said.

'How's Liv?'

It felt as though he'd been sleepwalking and was standing on the edge of a cliff. He watched both Liam and Ella drop their heads in unison. 'Oh, good. Yeah, she's terrific.'

'Put her on a second. I don't want her thinking I'm neglecting her.'

'She's in the bedroom, Mum.'

'Well, bring the phone into her.'

'She's asleep,' lied Connor, feeling guilty.

'You two haven't had a row, have you?'

'What? No, nothing like that. I told you she's asleep. Hello? Mum, I can't hear you.' Ending the call, he placed the phone in his pocket, wishing he could hug her and tell her everything would be okay.

~

A short while after, Ella's phone pinged. She checked the message from an old school friend she hadn't seen for a while.

What is going on? I saw the video on Facebook. Have you lost your mind? Hand yourself in. You need help!

Sliding her finger along the screen, she deleted the message.

'Who was that?' Liam asked, standing with his hands pressed together as though praying.

'Tilly. I wouldn't mind, but I haven't spoken to her for years.'

'"Tilly Keane, she's lean, mean, and fancies Dean?" Christ, there were rhymes for everyone,' Liam quipped.

'"Nathan Kipler trapped in the fire, burning to a crisp, and about to expire. Freaky Fred tried to save his double, but the fire got him, and now he's in trouble."' As Ella recited the words, her arms were covered in goosebumps.

Again, her phone pinged. Another message. This time from a boy she'd dated after school. Rory Brown.

You're disgusting. I saw the video. You should be ashamed of yourself. What's wrong with you, Ella?

Turning the phone off, she slammed it on the floor.

'Er, guys! Guys!' Connor was checking his phone.

'What is it?' snapped Ella.

He turned the phone, showing a live video from his Ring doorbell of police at his flat, banging on the front door.

They watched with open mouths, struck speechless.

Moving his head closer to the screen, Liam asked, 'Are you going to say anything?'

'Like what?' snapped Connor. 'Oh, hey officers. I hope you're delivering a parcel or food. If not, I ain't answering the door, but if you call back next week, I can squeeze you in?'

'There's no need to be sarcastic!' Liam walked to the back door, peering out at the garden. Spinning around and facing his friends, he ordered, 'We have to run!'

'Run? Where?' Connor questioned.

Rushing across the kitchen, Liam was agitated, rubbing his face, turning one way and another. 'The police are at your door. Next, they'll try Ella's place. It won't be long until they put two and two together. We have to hide. Half the fucking town are on our backs. Fred Kipler is trying to kill us. The police are right on our tails. We need to act right now!'

'He's right,' Ella whispered. 'If we're taken in, you may never see Liv again.'

Connor looked as if he was struggling to breath, like he was drowning. He spasmed, closing his eyes tight. 'What do you both suggest?'

'Okay.' Grabbing a chair, Liam dragged it close to his friend. 'We can't drive for long. People know us. We're public enemy number one.'

That's an understatement!' Ella cut in.

'I don't know how it works, but we can't give details to hotels, Airbnb, Travelodges. And we certainly can't pay with cash. I think they'll know if we take money out of a cashpoint.'

'Christ, it's like we're Bonnie and Clyde,' said Ella.

'Who? Anyway, here's a plan,' Liam continued. 'It might just work. Keep us hidden until we can work out a way to resolve this.'

Connor stared directly into Liam's eyes, looking like he was pinning all his hopes on him. 'I'm all ears.'

'Mum and Dad are the... the Bear Grylls of Rye. Christ, they're sailing this week, rock climbing in a couple of months.'

'And?' pushed Connor.

'They have a tent. Like this... this huge monstrosity. It can sleep four or five people. We camp out in a field by the abandoned farmhouse where Fred used to live. It's a derelict area. Plus, we can keep hidden.'

'He's right,' Ella said. 'It's a great idea.'

'Hang on! It's private land!' said Connor.

'Yes, and Fred's family must still own it. No one will bother us,' pushed Liam. 'It's the perfect way to stay under the radar!'

37

Two Months Ago

'Sugar pie, come look.' Angela stood in the basement, watching Lucas Dubois squirming in the corner of his cell. She'd replaced the broken light bulb, but not with one of those energy-saving gadgets that were about as useful as a candle without a wick.

After she'd hit him with the stun gun, Lucas had slumped on the floor. Fred had covered his mouth with a rag dosed in chloroform, and they'd dragged him down to the basement.

Now, Angela listened to her son's awkward steps as he descended the stairs.

'Isn't he perfect,' she announced, clapping her hands together. 'The pieces of the jigsaw are fitting together. His hair and stubble. Although we'll need to give him a trim. The height, weight, and frame. He's simply perfect.'

'What if someone comes?' Fred asked, watching Lucas lying on the hard ground, his hand cuffed, the arm held out as he lay on the ground.

'Wait. Good question, Frederick.'

'I told you not to call me that!'

'I want you to scream at the top of your voice. As loud as possible.'

Her son did as he was asked.

'Not now, you idiot. I'll close the door and walk up to the kitchen. Give me a couple of minutes.' Angela left, closing the door, and climbed the steps, before slamming the hatch shut and waiting. *Not a peep*, she thought, as she walked across the kitchen floor and into the living room. On her knees, she placed her ear to the floor and, after a few minutes, returned to Fred.

She could see his rosy cheeks, the sweat dropping off his fat, grubby chin.

'Did you hear me?' asked Fred.

'Not a murmur.' She grabbed his cheeks, pinching them and seeing the irritation in Fred's face.

The chain rustled from the cell as Lucas turned sideways. 'You're sick. What are you? A sadistic team? Norman fucking Bates and his mother? I have a family. A wife and daughter. What the fuck is your problem? Let me go, and I promise I won't say anything.'

'Joycelyn and Olivia,' Angela stated. 'If you try to escape or disobey our orders, I promise we'll kill them both. Just try us!'

'You're deluded,' spat Lucas, spit dribbling from his mouth. With a raised voice, he yelled, 'You can't keep me here like a caged animal. People will be looking for me. Let me go. I'm begging you!'

Placing her hands on the cold, rough iron bars, Angela

watched as he tried to rip the chain from the wall, standing and yanking his arm.

'You'll do yourself an injury, silly man. We have a few tasks we need you to carry out. Once you've done them, we'll let you go. Is that a deal?'

'My daughter is six years old. She loves her daddy. I read her bedtime stories and she looks to me for protection. She's going to be upset and crying herself to sleep, knowing I'm gone. You have to understand. Christ, you have a son yourself.'

With a loud, boisterous voice, Angela replied, 'I had a lot more. They've taken everything from me. My husband killed himself because of what they did. Did you know I had twins?' she asked, again, jerking her head.

'How the hell would I know that? You mean another piece of shit like that fucker?'

'Oh, you really don't want to anger me, mister. It won't go well for you.'

Waiting for her body to calm, Angela remained silent for a minute. 'You say your daughter is six?'

'That's what I said. So please, let me go and see her.'

Angela reeled off Lucas's address, watching the stunned look on his face. 'If you fail to cooperate, I swear your daughter won't reach seven.'

The Wi-Fi was non-existent. There were no commodities. No fresh running water. Angela had a mobile phone she topped up when needed and could get reception by the front window and parts of the kitchen.

After discovering a website where you could upload a

picture and have it return almost perfect matches, she went to work on her plan. To wreak havoc and avenge the death of her son and husband by putting the people responsible through living hell before a death worse than anything they could imagine.

'This is a good picture,' she said as she held up her phone. Fred was standing behind her, his stale breath causing the hairs to stand up on her neck. 'Is this clear enough? Ella McKenzie. Her profile picture on Facebook is of her smiling into the camera. A recent selfie without a care in the world. That will very soon change. Christ, it lists her height, weight, hobbies, and the town where she lives.'

'It's clear. Have you found a match?' asked Fred, leaning forward and viewing the screen.

'Not yet. But I will. Can you hear him downstairs, in the basement?'

Straightening his body, Fred stepped away from his mother. 'No.'

'Exactly, young Frederico. I told you. It's insulated to within an inch of its life. There, what about her? Lina Janssens. She lives in Belgium. Height, five feet eight inches.'

'Too tall,' Fred suggested.

'Shame. She looks so much like her.'

'Why are you going to all this trouble?' Fred asked, picking at a spot on his chin.

Angela kicked the chair back and pushed her face into Fred's, her nose touching his brow. 'If you have to ask me that, you haven't really lost anyone.'

'Not true. I loved Dad. I loved Nathan.'

'Well, then, get a grip of yourself! Your father locked himself in the barn and suffocated himself with car fumes.' She began yelling. 'They locked my son in the store room and let him fucking burn to death.' Angela flipped a table and grabbed a chair, smashing it against the wall until all four legs fell off. Exhausted, she dropped to her knees, pulled her hair, and screamed until her throat was raw.

Fred Kipler didn't put his arms around her. He didn't hold her and tell his mother it would be alright. He just watched with a smirk on his face until she collapsed into a broken mess.

That evening, Angela went to the local shops and grabbed a takeaway from the chip shop. Two minced beef and onion pies and large chips. They'd be cold by the time she reached home, and they didn't have a cooker or microwave to heat them up.

While they ate, Angela jumped up from the kitchen floor. 'Oh, my goodness. Look at this. Fred, you must look.'

'I am looking. What?'

'Marie Toohey. Height: five feet four inches. Hair: long and blonde. Eye colour: dark brown. Build: slim. Look, Fred. What do you think?'

'Wow. It's... It's her. It's Ella. She's perfect.'

'Oh, Fred. It's as though the stars are aligning. And she's in Britain. Exeter. I'll leave first thing in the morning. It's all coming together, Fred.'

The front door slammed. Upstairs, Fred lay on a cold mattress covered with a thin sheet. The stench of piss was excruciating. His mother had left for Exeter, shuffling around downstairs and singing to herself like a princess from a Disney film. He'd imagined colourful birds swarming around her head while she stood with arms outstretched, palms up, kissing their beaks.

Although she'd nursed him back to health, he blamed his mother for breaking up the family. She'd walked out when they'd needed her the most.

The bouts of depression were severe, and his mother's behaviour was always unpredictable. Fred recalled often seeing her guzzling tablets like she was popping sweets in her mouth. It was as though she had split personalities, and he and Nathan had heard her many times confessing to their father that she'd heard voices in her head. Finally, she'd cracked, walking out and leaving the stress behind for someone else to sweep up.

He'd often go into his father's office, see him weep. But Fred never once consoled him, instead watching him slump further into depression.

When he'd learned of his father's death, it didn't surprise him. He'd been hanging by a thread, and Nathan's death had driven him over the edge.

Pushing the sheet off his body, Fred stood on his pale legs and threw on the same tee-shirt and jeans he'd been wearing for days. They, too, smelled of urine, but he hated washing. Running his tongue over his teeth, he could feel a layer of grime. He breathed on his hand and winced. Cabbage or sprouts. *Who cares*, he thought. He had no inclination to freshen up. His arms were scarred, and patches of his hair had fallen out. Sometimes, he wished his mother had let him die in the facility. But like lots of stories, love was blind.

'Mum,' he called from the stairs as he descended, avoiding the gaping holes in the rotten wood. Fred knew she'd gone but wanted to clarify for his own sanity. Judging by last night and her violent behaviour, he knew she was broken. The tragic events had again snapped something in her mind. Oh, he'd help her. After all, blood was thicker than water. Fred wanted revenge as much as his mother did, but he was worried about how far she'd go and whether she'd bring a spotlight on them. He was happy simply playing out the wicked thoughts in his head. Her plan was becoming too risky.

Lifting the hatch in the kitchen, Fred climbed down the ladder, opened the door to the basement, turned on the light, and walked to Lucas's cell.

He was lying on his back on the cold floor, his cuffed arm extended and a piss stain beside his head.

The hope he felt at seeing Fred was evident. Awkwardly scrambling to his feet, he tried to reach the cell door, yelping in agony. 'Please, I want to go home. What's your name?'

Fred stepped closer, able to smell his sweat. With a blank expression, he stared.

'I'm Lucas. I have a family. You'd love my daughter. I can show you a picture if you'd like. She's six years old. My God, she's incredible – the most beautiful girl in the world.'

As Fred fiddled with the lock, he heard Lucas thanking him.

'You won't regret it. Thank you for helping me.'

Fred entered the cell. The anticipation on Lucas's face as he approached was palpable. His lips curled up at each end, and creases formed by his eyes as he smiled.

With one swift movement, Fred kicked the guy's legs from under him, seeing his body dangling in the air as the chain around his wrist snapped taut.

'You bastard. I think you've dislocated my arm.'

As Fred walked out of the basement, Lucas's frantic pleas clawed at his ears.

Once Angela arrived in Exeter, she took a taxi to the address of a place she'd booked on Airbnb. It was a quaint English cottage on the outskirts of town. The landlady was away in Spain, and the key was in a lockbox in the outside shed.

Angela pulled back the warped wooden door, the creak as it opened sharp in her ears. The shed smelled of damp grass and petrol. There was an array of tools, a couple of lawnmowers, and shelves stacked with old paint cans and cartons containing bolts and screws. An old punchbag hung from a rafter, the stuffing spilling out, and empty pallets were stacked in the far corner.

Once she'd obtained the key, she opened the front door of the cottage and unpacked in a bedroom at the far end of the building.

In the kitchen, an envelope rested on the table with instructions for using the boiler, setting the heating, and the Wi-Fi password, as well as a reminder of the code for the key box.

A bottle of white wine and two single red roses in a vase were perched on the table.

This place is so clean. It's heaven, Angela thought, basking in the fresh, clean smell. There were no cobwebs, soiled mattresses, or the stench of drains. *I might never leave here.*

It was time to put the next part of her plan into action. Marie Toohey worked in a local Italian restaurant. A recent Facebook post had her confirming a late shift tonight. It was perfect.

After spending the day unwinding and getting her thoughts together, Angela took a taxi to Roselli's Fine Dining.

As she stepped out of the vehicle, the sudden, vibrant atmosphere of the city centre filled her with dread. Her legs seemed to tangle, and she stumbled back, leaning against the wall.

You have this. No harm will come. Just relax. With the deep breaths comes strength.

Angela walked along the street, paranoid people were staring. The voices in her mind became louder, and she was convinced she saw groups of people nudging each other, mocking her, and whispering.

She eased the front door back, and was greeted by a handsome young man with too much hair gel.

'Table for two?' asked the staff member.

'Er, one.'

'Madame, you are too beautiful to be eating alone,' he quipped.

Feeling a flush rise to her face, she smiled and followed him to a table next to the window.

The smell of garlic, onions, and dough made her stomach rumble.

'Drink, madame?' the same waiter asked, barely giving her time to settle.

'Just water. Sparkling,' was her reply. She needed to keep a clear head. Nothing could go wrong tonight. 'And a glass with ice.'

'Very good!'

She watched the chefs cooking in the kitchen, flames rising from the grills, pizzas being removed from ovens, and smoke wafting through the window to outside.

A woman caught her eye. She was holding a tray of drinks, heading to a table opposite. Her blonde hair was tight in a bun, and her puny frame looked almost too weak to hold the heavy tray.

'Excuse me!' Angela spoke authoritatively. 'I asked for sparkling water.'

'I'm sorry,' the young woman stated, stepping to the table. 'Let me find out where it is for you.'

There she was. The name badge confirmed the woman's name: Marie Toohey.

Nodding, Angela watched the waiter who'd taken her order return, apologising, and place the drink on the table.

'Okay,' Marie said, 'all sorted.' To the waiter, she instructed, 'That table over there needs clearing. I don't know how many times I have to tell you before it sinks in. Go and do it now!'

Angela watched Marie walk back to the kitchen, collecting more orders. *So she has authority. Interesting!* After ordering garlic bread and a bowl of pasta, Angela watched Marie like a hawk. The way she rushed about, clearly nervous that anyone would be left unattended, and ordered the staff around. It felt like observing someone desperate to impress the boss.

Passing the kitchen on her way to the toilet, she saw Marie standing with a middle-aged man wearing a sharp suit. The staff were loading the dishwasher and wiping down worktops. Waiting at the door, she peered in the hallway mirror at the reflection of the kitchen, seeing the man in the suit grabbing Marie's buttocks, certain no one could see.

'Shall I wait behind?' asked Marie.

Suit guy whispered something Angela couldn't hear. Whatever it was, it gave her scope to find their dirty secret.

After paying the bill and leaving a generous tip, Angela again headed to the toilet, and once finished, found a cleaning store cupboard under the hallway stairs. Making sure not to be seen, she knelt and climbed into the small space.

The plan was to stay in Exeter for as long as it took. She'd booked the Airbnb for a few nights, intending to shadow the young girl wherever she went. She felt like a private investigator armed with the task of unravelling someone's life without them knowing. There had to be something she could find on Marie. And if there wasn't, as with Lucas, she'd force something.

Reaching for her phone, she shone the torch over a couple of boxes with the word "Receipts" written in black felt pen. Angela crawled to the back of the store cupboard and lay down. After an internet search, she found the name of the owner. Roberto Morelli. Seeing his picture, she knew exactly who he was. But wanting to delve deeper, she again searched Marie's profile on Facebook. Her father's name was John Toohey. His profile and pictures were set to public for everyone to see.

Roberto Morelli and John Toohey were friends since childhood.

As Angela waited, listening to the toilet doors swing back and forth, the hand dryer humming every few seconds, and pans clattering in the kitchen, she hoped it wasn't a waste of time. As each footstep echoed beyond the store cupboard, she feared someone would find her or lock the door.

Then came the time.

The staff were saying goodnight to each other. One of them whistled the tune of a recent love song, opened the back door, and left. Behind them, feet dragged along the floor, and someone asked if they had their coat.

The back door slammed again. Then a third and a fourth time.

Is that it? Has everyone left? She crawled to the cupboard door and pushed it open, clenching her teeth, and stood, waiting quietly in the hallway. The lights were off in the restaurant.

There was no piercing alarm, usually set by the last person to leave. Above her head, a security camera pointed along the hall, but there was no red light indicating it was working. She was sure it had had one earlier.

Suddenly, a plate smashed in the distance. Angela panicked, debating whether to hide. Laughter came from the kitchen, and voices whispered.

As she stepped closer, she could hear what they were saying.

'Sod it,' a male voice said, 'don't worry about it. The staff can deal with it in the morning.'

'You drive me wild,' the woman said between wet, sloppy kisses.

The sudden sexual groans from both parties didn't need explaining.

It got louder. The gasps became heavier and more intense.

Angela tapped the video mode on her mobile and began recording, creeping to the kitchen.

The owner was standing with his back to her, naked apart for his black socks. Marie was perched on the worktop, her legs wrapped around his waist.

As Angela zoomed in, filming everything, someone pounded at the back door. She jumped so hard the phone shuffled between her hands and almost dropped to the floor.

Urgent voices resonated from the kitchen as Roberto pulled on his clothes.

'Quick,' he ordered. 'They're early.'

Marie leaped off the unit. 'No. I think I've broken a heel!'

Again, a fist pounded the back door.

Angela gasped, turning one way and another, feeling sandwiched in. At the last second, she darted into the women's toilet and hid in the darkness. Through the outside window, she could see a small truck. A large, muscle-bound man in a tee-shirt and jeans stood by the passenger door. Another equally sizeable guy stepped from the back door with his phone to his ear.

Who the heck are these people? Have they seen me? She wanted to check the phone footage to ensure the video had been recorded. What a waste of time and money if it hadn't.

Crouching, she lay on her stomach with her ear to the toilet door.

She heard the abrupt sound of the back door opening, and Roberto telling the men to be more patient. Then he called for Marie to help.

As Marie's wonky footsteps clattered along the hall, Angela carefully stood and peered through the window, keeping low and watching. Again she switched on video mode and recorded what was happening.

She saw the two men walk to the back of the truck, undoing the thick, clear wrapping stretched taut like industrial-strength cling film, and tearing it away from the pallets. Tightly packed, square-shaped bundles were handed to Roberto and Marie: drugs, Angela realised, seeing the weight of the cocaine pressing into their palms.

What the actual fuck, thought Angela, as she filmed them

through the toilet window, walking back and forth from the van. Once they'd taken around ten bundles in total, Roberto grabbed a massive wad of cash, handed it over, and hugged both men.

The truck pulled away, and both Roberto and Marie walked back into the restaurant.

As they resumed their love-making position in the kitchen, Angela fled through the back door.

38

M *onday Evening*

It was chaotic. While Liam emptied the cupboard under the stairs, pulling out the tent and a bag with the poles and robust pegs, Ella and Connor dashed around the kitchen, getting in each other's way as they grabbed cups, teabags, and frozen food from the freezer.

'There's a few of those small barbecues in the outside shed,' Liam instructed. 'The ready-to-light, disposable ones. Grab those, will you?'

While Connor rushed out to the shed, Ella grabbed a carrier bag from a drawer and filled it with food. 'Christ! This stuff will go off in a day. I think we should bring the microwave meals in the fridge!'

'Oh yeah, because we can plug it into the soil!' Liam dragged the tent and bag to the front door, hearing Ella call him an arsehole. 'I'll load the camping gear in the boot.' He opened the door, half expecting someone to be standing there. Sighing with relief, he dumped everything in the car and came back inside. Ella was in the kitchen, placing microwave food into a bag. 'You're really going to bring those?'

'Are you that dim?' she fired back. 'We empty the contents, chicken, beef, whatever, and cook it. Just because it says the word microwave, doesn't mean it's gospel. For goodness' sake, Liam, no wonder your mum left instructions. I bet there's a partner out there that can't wait for the day they meet you.'

He grinned, her sarcasm embarrassing him. 'I think we're ready,' Liam said as he watched Connor come in from the shed with the small barbecue sets. 'Excellent. They'll do.' He opened a drawer under the kitchen unit, grabbed a couple of lighters, and looked at the cat curling around his legs. 'Hey, I'll be back soon. I'll leave enough food for now. You know how to come in and out. I'm sorry, puss.' As they closed the front door behind them, the feeling of dread gripped his body, almost suffocating him.

'I thought you said you know how to pitch this thing?' Connor was reading the tent instructions, the paper creased and stained with coffee.

'It can't be that difficult. I think we attach it to the pegs and hammer them into the ground.' Picking one up, Liam placed it in the hard soil. 'Now we drive it in and attach the loops of the tent. The poles are the frame that holds it all together. Simple.'

Shaking his head, Connor jested, 'You don't say?'

'You know what?' said Liam, 'I forgot the hammer.'

'We could use your head! Jesus, Liam. Wait!' Looking at the car, Connor had an idea. 'The spare tyre in the boot. There's a bolt spanner. We can use that.' Rushing to the rear of the car, Connor pulled the tyre out, grabbed the spanner, and handed it to Liam. 'I'm going to have to hide the car. It's the first thing anyone will see if they're passing.'

The area was secluded. It looked like the end of the world – wild, overgrown, and barren. The fields spread as far as he could see, and the damp grass and earthy smell assaulted his lungs. It was a clear evening; although sunny, the wind carried a chill with just the odd wisp of clouds in the deep blue sky. In the distance at the end of the track, Connor could make out the shape of the Kiplers' abandoned farmhouse.

Back on the road, Connor jumped into the car while Liam and Ella removed large pieces of stones from a ditch.

'You're going to have to hit it at speed to get over it,' instructed Liam. 'The ditch is about half a foot high. Steer hard, hit the accelerator, and you're good to go!'

'Got ya!' Connor eyed the ditch and the brush beyond, braced himself, and slammed his foot on the pedal. The front left tyre hit the ditch, but the car bounced back.

'You didn't go fast enough! Try again,' Liam shouted, looking for damage to the tyre. 'Wait. Don't do nothing yet.' He searched the fields and found some wood, lying it across the ditch. 'This should help as a makeshift ramp. Hit it hard.'

Again, Connor reversed, this time further along the road to give himself time to get the speed up. Composing himself, he slammed his foot on the accelerator, the stones crunching beneath the wheels and dust thick in the air. The tyres hit the wood, snapping it, and the bumper smashed into the ditch. 'For fuck's sake. This is insane.'

Looking along the narrow path, Ella pointed. 'Or you could just drive in there. There's a gap.'

The men were speechless through shame. Shaking his head, Connor backed away from the ditch and edged the car towards the gap Ella had spotted, where he could drive straight into the brush.

It felt like the front wheels were buckled, and a vibrating noise resounded when the tyres turned. Where Ella had pointed him to, a gate hung on its side, leaving a gap wide enough for his vehicle. Once through, he got out, glancing through the long grass and into the horizon. 'I'll pull it down there,' he said to Ella as she joined him. Liam was a few feet behind. 'Tell me if you can see it.'

A few minutes later, he walked back towards Ella, who watched from the top of the road.

'It's fine,' shouted Ella. 'Only the top of the car is visible. I think if anyone passes, they'll assume it was dumped there.'

Traipsing through the grass, Connor joined her, looking down the valley. 'Excellent. It's perfect.'

The inside of the tent smelled of stale socks and sweat. There were a couple of large gashes as though the material had been ripped with a knife. It reminded Connor of a circus tent, though much smaller: ideal if a performer misbehaved, cast to this contraption as punishment. Connor hated being confined. But he had to admit, it was the perfect hideaway until they took charge of the escalating situation.

The idea Liam had come up with was genius. Would anyone approach a tent and ask who was inside? He doubted it.

'It's roomier than I thought.' Ella was placing the throw-away barbecues in the corner.

'I'll have to charge rent then!' laughed Liam. 'It's alright though, isn't it?'

'Apart from the foul smell. I hope your parents haven't, you know, in here,' she chuckled.

'Really? Bloody hell, Ella! It's not something I want to think about.'

Lying back on the rough ground, Connor placed his hands behind his head. Directing the question to Ella, he asked, 'Have you had any more messages?'

'I... I don't know. I've turned my phone off. People I haven't seen in years are coming out of the woodwork with accusations. I don't want to read them. It's too upsetting.' She lay down between her friends. 'Do you think we're safe here?'

'We have no other choice,' answered Connor, hoping they'd hear if anyone approached the tent and realising there'd be nowhere to run.

The sun was beginning to set, and the temperature had dropped inside the tent. They'd spent the evening resting and talking about the school days.

In the distance, a siren rang out. The three of them locked eyes and Connor pushed through the tent door, keeping low. The siren was getting closer. He tensed, clenching his fists, and tried to work out the best route for them to escape. Then his body loosened as the siren disappeared. 'It's gone.' The blood seemed to plunge down through his body as he calmed. 'I wonder if they're looking for us?'

'Let's start the barbecues. I'm starving.' Ella pushed her way out of the tent. 'We can't freak out every time we hear a siren. We'll have no bloody nerves left. No one will bother us out here. Look around you.'

'Ella, families walk through the countryside. You know that,' urged Connor. 'Rye is full of tourists. Dog walkers. Cyclists, photographers, bird watchers, ramblers.'

'You've made your point. You're rambling yourself.' With an outstretched arm, she placed her hand on his shoulder. 'Stop worrying. Let's eat.'

Liam lit the barbecues, though they worried the smoke would draw attention. The food had defrosted, and they cut up pork chops, chicken, and sausages, warming them on the flames. The rice was cold, but it was edible.

The three of them sat outside the tent, lying on the grass and listening for any sounds in the distance.

Connor's food dripped down his lips, and he wiped it with the sleeve of his tee-shirt. 'We should start a fire and sing songs.'

'Yeah, that's a great way to remain hidden. That reminds me. Mrs Adams. Remember her?' asked Ella. 'The music teacher. I was in the school choir for a while. You were too, Liam.'

'Er, I can't remember,' he answered awkwardly. 'Anyway, what about her?'

'Wait! You were in the school choir!' Connor grinned as he dropped a piece of chicken on the grass. 'Five-second rule! I didn't know you could sing.'

'He couldn't,' added Ella. 'If I remember correctly, she kicked you out.'

Visibly irritated, Liam asked, 'What's the point you're making?'

'My point is, I saw her on one of those reality TV shows a while ago. She retired from school, and she coaches people to be better singers. She's doing really well. One of her groups was picked to sing at Westminster Abbey.'

'She can't be that good,' joked Connor. 'Liam hasn't got a note in his head. How's the food?'

Both his friends nodded as they pulled the meat off the chops.

'It's going to be dark soon.' Throwing the remains of her chop in a carrier bag they were using as a bin, Ella looked around. 'It's beautiful out here. How's all this going to end?'

The palpable silence drifted over them like a dark cloud, clawing at their skin.

None of them knew how it would end, but at this moment, they just had to hide and keep hiding.

Connor settled down to sleep in one corner of the tent, Liam in the other, and Ella chose to rest in the middle.

The sleeping bags were worn and stained, and the zips broken, but they kept them warm.

'I hope there aren't any snakes or spiders out here.' Grabbing a small torch Liam had given her, Ella shone it along the ground of the tent.

'Are you for real?' Sitting up, Connor watched as Ella searched the tent. 'This is England!'

'I know. But you hear stories. Recently, I read that a crate of snakes brought over on a plane escaped.'

'Yeah,' Liam jested. 'How did they get through customs?'

'Oh, go to sleep,' Ella snapped. 'Smart arse.'

'Did they have passsssssssssssss-ports?' joked Connor.
'I'm not talking to you both. Sod off!'

It was almost two in the morning. Ella was lying on her side when something woke her. Slowly, she sat up, grabbed the torch, and shone it over her friends. Both Connor and Liam were lying on their backs under their sleeping bags and snoring.

After shining the torch around the tent and finding nothing out of place, she lay back down, closed her eyes, and tried to sleep. Again, it felt like a flash of light flared on her face. Not wanting to wake the others, she placed her fists against the hard ground and pushed her body up.

The light was gone.

She worked her way out of the sleeping bag – after struggling with the zip – crept to the opening of the tent, and pushed her head out. The cold air was sharp, and the stars above glowed brilliantly in the clear sky. She listened hard for anything approaching the tent and scanned the nearby fields for light in the dense shadows. Breathing deeply, steadying her racing heart, she forced herself to relax and climbed back into the tent.

'Connor,' she whispered, waiting for an answer. 'Liam, can you hear me?' *Maybe we should take turns*, she deliberated. *One could keep watch while the others slept.* Then she wondered if she was overreacting.

Lying back down, Ella thought about the previous night. The phone calls, the lights going out, and the knocks at the door. If it hadn't been for Connor and Liam arriving when they had, she knew she may not be here. But what if the same person who'd got into her house was now outside the tent? What if they'd been watching as they set it up, hid Connor's car in the brush, and ate dinner? Someone could have been watching as they'd sat on the grass, the smoke from the barbecue drifting in the air, as they chatted and laughed together.

Maybe the same person who broke into my house is about to enter the tent, she thought.

A twig snapped right outside the tent. Ella gripped the sleeping bag, her body trembling as she waited for another sound. Holding her breath, letting it out in controlled spurts, she closed her eyes tight. Something sharp in the grass dug into her back. Ella shifted across the ground. Her friends were still sleeping, and she didn't want to wake them unless it was absolutely necessary. But maybe it was. She was sure someone was outside the tent.

Another snapping sound, almost in stereo, came from the other side of the tent. Unable to move her body from fear now, she lay there, almost paralysed, biting the corner of her lip, and digging her fingernails into the palms of her hand.

It felt as though she'd been awake for ages. The tent was dark, and her ears rang with the stillness.

If anyone was outside, guessed Ella, *surely they're gone now.*

Then, right in line with her head, a light shone straight through the side of the tent.

39

E *arly Tuesday Morning*

'Are you sure it was a light?' Connor had sprung up from his sleeping bag, confused about where he was. Ella had shaken him so hard he'd felt his bones rattle.

'What's going on?' Liam asked, on his hands and knees, exiting the tent behind them.

'Ella thinks she saw a light.'

'I don't think it. I know it,' she whispered. 'A twig snapped. Someone was out here. I was lying between you two. Oh, by the way, some protection you both are snoring your heads off. They could have reached in and dragged me out, and you both would be none the wiser. I feel so secure knowing you're both there beside me. A light shone over the tent. I'm telling you, someone was here.'

'Hello,' screamed Liam at the top of his voice.

'Are you mad?' snapped Ella. 'Why did you do that? Let's all draw attention to where we are! Honestly, I wonder about you, Liam. Just when I think there's a tad of maturity creeping in, you go and do—'

Another twig snapped just a few metres from where they stood. The half moon above them cast only a faint light. The sky was black as if it were a void waiting to suck them through. A light mist curved in the air, and the smell of smoke could be detected.

'Who would light a fire this time of night?' Connor turned, looking into the valley, seeing only shadows.

Another snap, right beside them, louder this time. It sounded like someone had broken a plank of wood over their knee.

'Who the fuck is there?' yelled Connor, feeling Ella's hand in his. Her skin was freezing, and her hands were shaking.

'Maybe it's an animal.' Liam rushed to the tent, grabbed his phone, and shone the torch along the grass, scanning the light around them.

Something screeched in the distance. Although faint, it was clear enough for them to hear it.

'I say we get back in the tent.' Gripping Ella's hand, Connor could feel her angst as she dug her fingers into his.

Then they saw it. Around fifty yards from the tent and low on the ground: a torchlight, flickering, darting left and right.

Connor's hand slipped from Ella's as he rushed towards it. Liam followed, trying to hold his phone still and provide enough light for them to see.

Ella waited by the tent, the torch shaking in her hand, her arms clutched around her body, stepping from one leg to the other. 'Be careful!'

'It's moving away. Quick, shine the torch. What is it?' Connor got close enough to see before the animal scurried away, the light fading into darkness. 'A fox.'

'What?' asked Liam as he reached his friend, bending over to catch his breath.

'It... It looked like one of those small head torches. You know, the type miners use. Someone strapped it to the fox.'

Inside the tent, the three of them lay on the ground, wrapped in their sleeping bags, eyes staring ahead and listening for sounds to indicate someone was outside.

Playing with the zip of his sleeping bag, Connor said, 'Someone did it.'

'But no one knows we're here!' said Liam. 'How could they?'

'Well,' said Ella, 'they obviously do know!'

'It's a ploy. Another way to freak us out, to punish us before they—' Connor's voice trailed off as he thought about Liv. It was as though he hadn't made the slightest progress. He wanted to ask his friends about the likelihood of seeing her again. But he didn't need their pity. They were no more sure than he was, and besides, if he ever wanted to see his girlfriend again, the focus had to be on getting out alive.

'Shall we take turns?' asked Ella. 'Just until the morning. We can do an hour each. One sits up and listens, and then we swap.'

'Sounds good to me,' Liam quipped. 'I don't think I can sleep anyway.'

Connor and Ella closed their eyes, drifting in and out of sleep, steadying themselves for anything Liam may hear.

The intense light was uncomfortable. Connor was lying on his side, his body cold and sore from the rough grass. He blinked, focusing on his surroundings. Sitting up, he saw Ella beside him, mumbling something in her sleep.

Liam's body was stretched out on his stomach.

'Oi. Liam! Are you for real? Liam!'

'What?' he asked as he sat up. 'It's early. Why are you disturbing me?'

'You were supposed to keep watch!'

'Huh?' he said as he lay back down.

'Great. Remind me to go camping with you again. Did you hear anything for the minute or two you were awake?'

'Nothing. Sorry, mate. I don't know what happened.'

'You're such a dick!' joked Connor. 'How have your parents left you looking after the house?' He leaned his arm through the tent opening, grabbed a handful of grass, rolled it in his hands, and fired it at Liam.

'Are you still there? I thought you'd have breakfast done. Shout me when it's ready,' ordered Liam. 'Good lad.'

'I can try, but I don't know if the food has gone off. Ella, are you hungry?'

'I could eat,' she replied in a sleepy, husky voice.

As Connor placed his sleeping bag back in the corner of the tent, he crawled through the gap on his hands and knees, struggling to focus in the intense sunlight. 'It's a glorious day. Oh, fuck. Guys! Guys!' As he stood outside the tent, he saw two slim wooden poles planted into the soil with a thick rope stretched across between them. Tied to the rope were two rats, cooked almost to a crisp, their paws intertwined.

Liam and Ella joined him, covering their mouths in unison.

'It's a sign,' Connor exclaimed as Ella rushed away and vomited. 'The burnt rats. It's a re-creation of the fire. And the two of them are identical, almost like twins. Fred Kipler knows we're here!'

~

'We need to get out of here!' Feeling the isolation, Connor scanned the area. Since they'd been here, they hadn't seen anyone else. But it was obvious their hiding spot had been compromised.

'We can't move again,' urged Liam. 'The upheaval, moving everything, it's too risky. We'll be seen. We just have to be vigilant.'

The mist had cleared, and thin strands of cloud adhered to the bluest sky. In the valley, Connor could just see the roof of his car, and although it was suspicious, who'd be bothered to report an abandoned vehicle in a field? He glanced along the single track leading to the Kiplers' abandoned farmhouse, feeling a pulse rush through his body.

'Should we get rid of them? I can't stay here with those hanging like that?' With a shaky hand, Ella reached for the burnt rats. Liam grabbed her, laughing at how she jumped. 'Is there something wrong with you? What a dick!'

'At least we won't go hungry,' joked Liam.

'Yuk,' Ella grimaced. 'If you're hungry, be my guest. I'm spooked enough being out here without you trying to scare me. Grow up!'

Dragging his eyes away from the farmhouse, Connor went inside the tent. 'I don't think this food is safe to eat.'

Bringing chicken wings to his nose, he winced. 'It doesn't smell great. I'm not going to chance it.'

Back outside, he could feel his stomach rumbling. It felt like the three of them were on a reality show, slowly trying to suppress their hunger and survive. 'Do you think it's safe to drive to the shops?'

'You are kidding, aren't you? You know how many people messaged yesterday. Everyone is looking for us. We're... We're bloody fugitives. I don't know how much longer I can take this. I'm hungry, and I need a shower and clean clothes.' Connor saw Ella's eyes water, but seeming determined not to crumble, she wiped them and sighed deeply.

'I think we should play I Spy,' Liam suggested. 'It will kill some time and take our minds off food.'

'Go on then, fields and trees. That's the choices we have,' sniped Ella. 'Game over!'

Eyeing Connor, Liam shifted his eyes up and smirked. 'Wait. I have the drone. My father loves those things. Let me get it out.' Liam grabbed it from inside the tent and began setting it up.

'Do you know how to use it?' asked Ella enthusiastically. 'I've never seen one but always wanted to have a go.'

'It's pretty simple. This is the controller, and you steer it with these joysticks. One controls altitude and rotation, while the other is for direction and speed. It returns to the take-off point automatically when the battery gets low. It's good fun.'

'What if someone sees it?' Connor didn't feel good about it, but he didn't want to dampen the mood any further. It might draw unnecessary attention, but on the other hand, pinpointing the pilot's exact location wouldn't be easy. He had to loosen up, if only for a while.

'Okay, let's do it.' Powering it up, Liam launched it into

the air. The buzzing sound was grating as it drifted up. He let Ella take the controls, showing her how to operate it. With his help, she soon had the hang of it, watching as it skimmed through the sky.

'This is so cool.' she stated, sounding giddy. 'How far can it go?'

'The range on this one is around five miles. I like to keep it local, though.'

Ella passed it to Connor and he took the controls.

'Wow, it's amazing how this thing stays up. Does your father fly it much?' Connor watched the drone dip, feeling an adrenaline rush.

'He used to. Me and dad would go to the fields the odd weekend and fly it. I think he lost interest, though. He'd rather be flying himself than the drone, you know. He's a proper adrenaline junkie.'

'Well, definitely a junkie,' joked Connor.

'Sod you! He's never done a drug in his life, hence the extreme sports. Whoa, don't let it go too far.'

Handing the controller back to Liam, Connor stood, watching the drone, mesmerised at how easy Liam made it look as he brought the drone back and landed it.

They spent the rest of the day sitting outside the tent in the long grass, talking about school, who they'd seen since leaving, and what they hoped the future would bring. Connor broke down several times as he reminisced about Liv – their plans to open a gallery and the emptiness he felt without her. His voice often slipped into the past tense, referring to her as though she were already gone, despite his hope that they'd be together again. Ella and

Liam gently corrected him, assuring him she'd be back soon.

'I can't deal with this hunger.' Thumping her stomach, Ella tried to think about something else. It was almost twenty-four hours since they'd eaten, and at this moment, she was starting to wonder what her friends tasted like. 'If I don't eat, I'm going to go all zombie on you.'

'Remember the story, *Alive*? The plane crashed, and all the survivors started eating each other. Such a harrowing story,' Liam reflected.

'I don't think our situation is that dire just yet. We're in Rye – a couple of miles from a shop,' pointed out Connor.

Liam's face lit up at the thought of food. 'Should we chance it?'

'I don't think so,' responded Connor. 'Let's see how we are in the morning. If we can't bear it any longer, one of us can make the trek. Use your hoodie to disguise yourself.'

'So,' Liam answered, 'you've already nominated me?'

'Well,' replied Ella, 'you are the one with the least memorable face.'

'Thanks for the insult. I'm going inside the tent. It's a bit nippy.'

'Yeah, I was thinking that.' Following him, Ella again sat on the grass beside her sleeping bag, and Connor joined them.

'Did you know it could do this?' Grabbing the drone, Liam removed the microSD card and plugged it into his phone. Connor and Ella moved closer.

'Oh, what?' said Ella as she watched the footage the drone had recorded from the air. 'I didn't know it could film. That's wicked.'

'Yeah,' stated Liam. 'They've been able to do that for years. People use them as spyware to watch neighbours, or if they're just nosey and want to see what's going on around them without having to leave their back garden.'

'It's a wonder they're legal,' stated Connor as he watched the footage.

The video showed a view from above the fields, their tent, and the long, winding, narrow path leading to the abandoned farmhouse. 'That's where Fred Kipler and his family used to live?'

'That old, dilapidated place?' asked Ella. 'It's so... eerie.'

'Yeah, that's where Liam and I went. It's in a right state.'

It had gotten dark quickly, and the chilly breeze coming through the gaps in the tent was biting. They were tired, hungry, and nervous about staying another night in the wilderness.

As they continued watching the recording, a raucous wail bellowed in the distance. It sounded like a banshee.

'What was that?' asked Ella as she linked her arm with Liam's.

'I... I think maybe a fox or something.'

'That didn't sound like a fox,' Connor retorted.

'Fuck! I don't want to stay another night out here!' Ella pulled the sleeping bag around her, zipping the side up to her neck.

'I have to get out of here. You guys stay. Keep hidden. I'm no closer to finding Liv and I can't stay out here wasting time. I have to do something.' Panic clutched at Conner's throat as the desperation seeped into his skin.

'If you're leaving,' Ella stated, 'we're coming with you.'

'Stop!' he shouted, crouching and looking at the recording.

Both his friends turned, staring at him.

'What?' Liam asked with a concerned tone.

'Go back. The recording. Rewind it a little.'

Doing as he was instructed, Liam went back, seeing the drone over the valley. He estimated it was around half a mile from where the tent was set up. 'What is it?'

'Keep going. More. Yeah, a bit more. There!'

As Liam zoomed in, Ella pushed her body closer.

The footage showed four people standing in the field with what looked like sacks over their heads.

It appeared as though they were looking towards the tent.

40

E*arlier Tuesday Evening*

'I'm going to make a run for it today.' Lucas knew he'd lost weight. His already thin frame was ebbing away, the fleshy areas reduced to skin and bone. The mother and son fed them nothing but rice and water. There was no set time. Often, they came in the morning, unlocking the cell and dropping a bowl on the ground like they were animals – in which case, Lucas would have to make it last the whole day. Sometimes they came at lunchtime, which was perfect as it broke up the day – a balance on either side and not as long to wait. The cramps were severe at first, and he powered through by punching his stomach. It was amazing how quickly the body adapted.

'They have a rifle trained on us,' Marie said, chained in the cell opposite. 'Don't be stupid. They'll think nothing about shooting you and burying you on the farm. You want to see your wife and daughter again, right?'

'Yes, but I'm weak. It feels as though my body is infected. I used to count the days at first, filled with hope, but now I can't remember. One day bleeds into the next. I'm so dehydrated that if I cried, there'd be no tears left.'

A soft, gentle voice came from the cell next to Lucas.

'Hey,' Liv's voice said, 'don't stop fighting. I know I haven't been here as long as you two, but you can't give up. There'll be a time for us to run. We just have to be patient and plan it right. Lucas, are you listening?'

Sniffing hard, Lucas answered, 'I have to make my move today!'

'They'll kill you. Christ, you want to see you're family again. Then—' Liv's voice trailed off as a lock began clunking open. 'Keep silent. I think they're back.'

Fred Kipler and his mother entered the basement and passed each cell as though wardens from hell, smirking at their captees.

'It's time to move in,' Angela instructed. 'We know where they are. This is going to end today.'

'And what happens to us?' Lucas was slumped on the floor, lying on his side and facing the cell door with his arm out, chained to the wall.

'Well,' Angela began, 'when it's over, you're free to go.'

He knew that would never happen, not after everything they'd seen. Lucas recalled how he'd stood in Frank Dawson's living room, filming everything while Fred Kipler mutilated his face and body with a pen. He'd never seen anything so disgusting in his life. It would stay with him forever. He felt he'd changed after that. They say experience often transforms people and makes them think differently, but Lucas had never seen anything so evil in his life. Fred was often quiet, taking instructions from his mother, but while committing these vile, sick acts, his facial expressions remained almost numb and blank. Lucas couldn't believe people like this existed and walked among everyone else. After what they'd seen, he knew Angela was lying. There was no way they were walking out of here.

'Fred, the cells.' Pointing the rifle at Lucas and Marie, Angela told him to open both doors.

With the widest grin, Fred did as he was told, unlocking both cell doors, his eyes alight with excitement.

'May I remind you both,' Angela raised her voice as though on a stage in a theatre, 'what we have on you. One phone call or email will ruin both of your lives. Don't try me.'

The four of them left the basement, leaving Liv alone, lying on the cold ground.

As Lucas walked silently with the others along the field, he thought about the mother and son's deluded games and how, most recently, he and Marie had been instructed to push someone onto the road, knowing there'd be witnesses. It was just one of their twisted ideas to torment these young people before they were killed. Lucas had no doubt that's what would happen. He'd filmed the death of Mrs Franklin, a poor, defensive old lady. Fred had mutilated her much the same way as he had Frank. The squelch as he gorged her eyes out would stay with him forever. He knew it was only a matter of time before they got to the others they were looking for. He couldn't stomach anything else. Lucas had to make a run for it.

Stopping suddenly, Angela pointed in the distance. 'See over there,' she said, directing her words at all three of them.

'What are we looking for?' Fred chuckled, hopping on the spot with excitement.

'You don't see it?' Angela's voice was irritated and stern. 'Look harder, sugar pie.'

'I don't see it!'

Grabbing his hair, she turned his head in the direction she wanted him to look. 'There. The tent.'

'Oh,' came his gormless response.

'The three of them are in the tent. I left a little present for them this morning to keep them on their toes. I mean, does it get any easier than that?' Angela stated. 'They've been delivered on a plate.'

'What's the plan, Mother?'

With a hand on her hip, she answered, 'We wait. When it's dark, we move in. No one will care about gunfire out here!'

They sat on the grass a few metres from the abandoned farmhouse. To any layperson, it looked like a group of friends relaxing or about to have a picnic.

Marie eyed Lucas, shaking her head as if to warn him not to run. But he'd already made up his mind. He missed his wife and daughter. It was painful every time he thought of them. If Angela did email the pictures, he'd have to explain what had happened. That he'd been drugged and the photos were staged. The only problem was he didn't have any proof.

Their captors watched over them. Angela flitted in and

out of the farmhouse, handing the rifle to Fred and instructing him to shoot if they tried anything.

'I need to pee,' Marie said. 'I can't hold it.'

'Go over there.' Fred pointed to a tree a few yards from where they sat.

'Can't you let me have the slightest bit of dignity?'

'Over there, I said.'

As Marie stood, she mumbled something under her breath. Fred didn't even register it.

'Okay.' The eagerness was obvious in Angela's eyes as she came out of the farmhouse holding a handful of brown sacks, the type used to feed horses. 'Put these on. We can't risk being seen.' She threw the first one to Fred. 'I've cut holes so you can see and breathe. We can't have any of you passing out.'

As Fred burst into laughter, Lucas clenched his jaw, his hatred for these two becoming difficult to bear.

'Right!' said Angela enthusiastically, handing the other sacks to Lucas and Marie, who had returned from peeing under the tree, 'we move in slowly. The key is patience. When it gets dark, Fred and I will do the rest. When it's over, you two can walk!'

Yeah, thought Lucas, *as easy as that. A handshake, a thank you for everything you've done. Bringing our wickedness and acts of retribution to life. Making it real and being a part of the sick, depraved game. Have a nice rest of your life, young Lucas. Make sure to visit sometime. There's always a bed here for you and your family. So long now. Farewell.*

As they stood and walked along the field, the tent in sight in the distance, a drone flew overhead.

'Oh, shit. Quick,' instructed Angela, 'everyone place the sacks on. Damn it, we can't be seen. It will ruin everything.'

Above their heads, the drone buzzed, gliding through the sky, and disappeared over the trees.

Once the drone had disappeared Angela instructed them to remove the sacks, and she took them back, folded them, and placed them in a shoulder bag. 'Right,' she commanded, 'I can see the tent in the distance. Lucas, you're going to draw them out.'

Listening but unresponsive, Lucas glared at his surroundings. Below in the valley, tall trees bunched together, providing the perfect hiding spot, but it was risky. There was no doubt Angela would fire off a couple of rounds, and Fred would give chase. His heart sped fast in his chest, and panic consumed every fibre in his body.

'Am I making myself clear?' asked Angela. 'You'll enter the tent, draw them out. Got it?'

'How do you propose I do that?' asked Lucas, eyeing his escape route.

'Simple. Push your fucking face through the gap. Once they see you, they'll come out. As you run, I'll slaughter each one of them. Fred has already dug four shallow graves beyond the farmhouse. We can't forget about our friend in the basement. We'll need to hide the bodies. No one will ever know they're buried here.'

Fred has dug four shallow graves. The words repeated in Lucas's mind. *Don't you mean six?* He knew his and Marie's graves were already waiting.

'Ready? Let's do it! You have your instructions. It's time to finish this.'

Suddenly Lucas rushed at her, jumping with his right leg extended and kicking her in the face. She hit the ground hard, banging the back of her head and holding her face.

'You bastard,' she yelled, reaching for the rifle. 'I think you've broken my nose.'

As Fred raced towards him, Lucas wrestled the weapon from her hands, turned, and with the butt of the gun, hit Fred full whack on the side of his temple. He dropped, writhing in agony as blood seeped from his head.

'Quick,' shouted Lucas. 'Run!' Seeing Marie's stunned eyes, wild and empty, he grabbed her hand, and the two of them raced away from the farmhouse.

'Are they behind us?' Lucas focused on the tent, desperate to get to the others and warn them. Angela blackmailing him, taking photos with the threat of sending them to his wife and work colleagues, seemed insignificant at this moment. He was fighting for his life and the lives of five others.

'I don't think so?' Marie glimpsed over her shoulder, fearful of seeing Angela and Fred on their trail. 'I'm so fucking scared. If they catch us, we're dead.'

'We can't let that happen,' Lucas said, breathless. Stopping abruptly, he inhaled, gulping air to calm himself. He turned, half expecting one of them to grab him. The farmhouse was distant but not far enough. The long grass made it impossible to see if they were still lying on the ground. Dusk had settled, the sun dipping below the horizon, and soon, darkness would consume their surroundings.

'Where are we going?' Marie was still holding Lucas's hand as they reached the trees. The smell of bark and damp wood was detectable; leaves crunched under their footwear. Thick deformed-looking branches hung around them, resembling witches' claws, as they raced deeper into the woods, hoping to remain hidden.

Turning, Lucas glanced back across the field, ensuring they weren't being followed. 'We have to get to the tent and warn them. Fred and his crazy mother are going up there to kill them. We can't let that happen. I'd never live with myself. That poor woman is still locked in the basement. We have to help!' Looking through the trees, Lucas saw a gap that he hoped led to the road. 'Let's go in that direction. We can keep hidden and approach the tent from the side. You ready?'

Nodding, Marie squeezed his hand, and they continued running.

Their lungs burned, pins and needles sharp on their skin, their calves and legs ached, and although they were dehydrated, both sweated profusely. They gasped in unison, aware they could be heard, but the focus was on the tent and getting the others to safety.

They could see the silhouette of it through the trees.

Lucas stopped and listened to his surroundings. Apart from the wheezing from their chests playing in his ears, there was only deathly silence.

Composing himself, he wiped the sweat from his brow before they charged across the field. Reaching the tent, Lucas looked at Marie. 'Okay. Let's do this!'

41

*T*uesday Evening

Connor was still looking at the video recording from the drone. He'd rewound it so many times, paused it, and zoomed in. The three of them knew the game was up. They had to leave the tent immediately and keep running. The feeling of deflation was nauseating. It felt like there was nowhere to turn. Right now, Connor wanted the ground to open up, so he could fall into a hole and keep falling. It was pointless. Hope drained from his body as if there were a hose rammed into his mouth. He felt shrivelled, like a dried prune left in the heat.

As they gathered their belongings, a face pushed through the tent's door.

'What the hell?' Eyeing Liam, Connor jumped to his feet, his head hitting the top of the tent. The guy standing beside him had black hair. The crop had grown out, and the stubble was much heavier. The black glasses were missing, but he knew who it was.

Ella gasped, crawling backwards on the ground to the edge of the tent. Liam was dumbstruck, not believing what was happening.

'You son of a bitch.' Shoving the guy hard, Connor punched him on the side of the temple, wrestled him to the ground, and placed his hands around his throat. His face went bright red as he tried to say something, but his words were just a muffled sound.

Liam joined his friend, booting the guy hard in the stomach.

'No. Stop! You don't understand.' A woman charged at them, trying to pull Connor's arms from around Lucas's throat.

'I don't understand. Are you for real? This... This fucker kidnapped my girlfriend.' Directing his words back at the man, Connor yelled, 'What have you done with her?'

'Please!' screamed the woman. 'They're coming. We're here to help. I promise. Let him go!'

Tightening his hands on the man's throat, Connor shouted, 'Why should I believe you?'

'It's true. I'm begging you. Let go. Stop! You're going to kill him.'

Releasing his grip, Connor rolled over and sat on the ground. 'This better be good. Where's Liv?'

'She's at the farmhouse,' the man said, coughing like a tractor as he rolled onto his side.

'The farmhouse. What farmhouse?' Connor got to his feet, brushing himself down. He was paranoid that it was a trap, and any minute, Fred Kipler would come rushing through the darkness.

The man's voice was broken, and he struggled to clear

his throat. 'There.' Getting to his feet, he pointed his arm to the end of the track. 'Liv is down there.'

'You're kidding, right?' pushed Connor. 'We were there. It's abandoned. No one lives down there.'

'They have this... this hatch in the kitchen floor. Right at the back. You go down the stairs, and there's a metal door. Behind that, they have cells. It's a makeshift prison and as scary as fuck. It's insulated, so no one can hear you down there.'

'It's horrible,' added the woman. 'I never want to go down there again.'

Ella joined them, looking at her. The likeness was astonishing. 'You're the person who's been mimicking me? Stealing clothes from the boutique and dumping them outside my house. Following me along the street? Pushing that person in front of a car? Fuck, they could have picked someone prettier.' Connor could see she felt bad for the sarcastic remark, but it was her way of releasing the tension. It was clear from their faces what they'd endured.

Then the man, who called himself Lucas, explained everything. From the time he was blackmailed, the photos being taken, him being summoned to the farmhouse, and the threat of his family being murdered if he didn't do exactly as Fred and his mother had ordered. He broke down several times. Connor realised it was a genuine story and actually felt sorry for him.

'His mother?' Connor asked, astonished. 'She's involved as well?'

'Yes. She's the main instigator.'

Then the woman, Marie, revealed her story and how Fred's mother, Angela, had pursued her, blackmailing her with photos of her having sex with her father's best friend, and of her taking delivery of copious amounts of drugs at the restaurant, which Angela had sent to her on social media.

The hush that fell around the tent was oppressive. For a short while, no one said anything. There were so many questions, but the shock seemed like poison gas, heavy in the air and striking them mute.

'You came into my flat,' recalled Connor. 'You grabbed my girlfriend while we spoke on FaceTime. You... You kidnapped her.' Fighting the urge to pound Lucas again, he restrained himself, balling his fists and swallowing hard. 'She's there now? In the basement of the abandoned farmhouse?'

'Yes,' Lucas answered, 'we saw her this morning.'

'And' – Connor tried to choose the correct words – 'she's still alive?'

'Yes. She's fine. I mean, shook up, you know, but she's alive.'

'I have to go to her. I have to go now.'

'Mate,' Liam urged, 'they're not going to let you waltz in there and get her. They'll be waiting. We need to think of something.'

Connor pulled at his lips, his mind racing. 'I'm going down there now. Nothing is going to stop me! If what this guy says is right, and Liv is in the basement, I'm going over there.'

'Liam's right,' added Ella. 'They'll be waiting. Think about it; they won't let you walk in there, brazen as anything, and get Liv. It's a stupid idea. Look at everything they've thought up. Look at the lengths they've gone to fuck with our brains, to ruin our lives before our imminent deaths. We are one up now. For the first time in this sick, depraved game of theirs, we have the upper hand. We know where they are keeping Liv.'

Pacing back and forth, Connor wrestled with his thoughts. There had to be a way to get in there. Then it hit him. He turned to Lucas. 'You've been locked up for how long?'

'Erm, a couple of months. I don't know how long exactly. Can I ask a favour? Can I borrow one of your phones? I want to ring my wife and let her know I'm safe.'

'On one condition,' Connor pushed. 'Take off your clothes.'

'Excuse me?'

'You heard. I'm going to flip the game. Now, I'm going to imitate you!'

42

Tuesday Evening

'They fit fine!' Connor pulled up the black jeans and buttoned them up. Next, he slipped on the thin black jumper, pushing his arm into its long sleeves. Removing his trainers, he placed his feet into the boots and tied the laces. As he came out of the tent, he saw Lucas, wearing his clothes and walking around the field, desperate to get reception.

'It's no good. It won't connect.' He handed the mobile back to Connor and stood next to him. 'I hope they fall for it. We're the same height and shape. It's dark down there. They keep the lights off to remain hidden. Just make sure you stay in the shadows.'

'Anything else I need to be aware of?' Connor was filled with apprehension. Although he tried to put on a brave face, he was utterly petrified. So much could go wrong, and if they suspected anything, it wasn't only his life in danger: he was risking Liv's, too.

'Er, you know where the key is?' asked Lucas.

'Yes. As you go down the stairs, it's hanging on a rack by the metal door.'

'The hatch! You know where that is?'

'It's er... at the back of the kitchen in the far corner. Oh, you say you were locked in cells. What about those keys?'

Marie interrupted. 'That's a problem!'

'How so?' Connor felt his heart skip a beat. There couldn't be any mistakes. It had to go smoothly, in and out, with no problems.

'Well, I never saw where they hid the bunch of keys. The main one, yes, as Lucas explained, by the metal door. It's a single key hanging on the wall. But the keys to the cell, it's anyone's guess. They lock automatically, but the mother, she has keys.'

That is a major spanner in the works, thought Connor. If he couldn't find those, there was no way to get Liv out. 'What else? Guns?'

'Fred's mother has a rifle and isn't afraid to use it. She's threatened us enough, and I believe she'll pull the trigger as quick as look at you. She's one evil bitch,' confirmed Marie.

Liam eyed the two strangers, clearly still suspicious of them and wondering if they were leading Connor into a trap. 'Why don't you both go with him? You know the layout of the farmhouse.' He could see the sudden change in their faces. The fear was genuine.

'No!' urged Connor. 'They'll slow me down. The more people down there, the more chance of being seen. I'm going alone. But do not let these two out of your sight.' Looking between Lucas and Marie, he warned, 'If you run,

I'll make sure we find you. We leave here together, or not at all. Do you understand?'

The two strangers nodded as though they were exhausted. They'd been through so much. Another hour or two wouldn't make much difference.

'Right,' Connor said, drenched with uncertainty, 'I won't be long!' After hugging Ella and Liam, he turned, raising his eyebrows at Lucas and Marie. 'See you all soon.' Peering into the distance, he began walking through the tall grass towards the farmhouse.

It felt like his boots were filled with concrete, and he struggled to put one leg in front of the other. *How the hell did Lucas run in these?* Although it was dark and the temperature had dropped, his skin felt hot and blotchy. He scratched his wrists and wiped the perspiration from the sides of his face and forehead. His hair felt clammy, and the grit in his eyes was irritating. He needed to sleep, but he pushed his body to keep going. The tent was far behind him, and Connor was completely alone.

As he approached the farmhouse, he pictured the inside and contemplated how anyone could live there. It seemed as though someone had picked it up, rattled it, and turned it on its arse.

We were so close. How did we miss it? he questioned. *Liv was in the basement while Liam and I searched the place. She was a stone's throw away. This time, I won't leave without her.*

The song ran over and over in his mind.

Nathan Kipler trapped in the fire, burning to a crisp, and about to expire. Freaky Fred tried to save his double, but the fire got him, and now he's in trouble.

The anger festered inside him, and it felt like a firework about to explode.

So many scenarios played out. So many cards these sick bastards could play. They always seemed a step ahead. Always knowing where they were and how to hit them where it hurt. Liam had made a stupid mistake by locking Nathan in the store room. Connor and Ella were ordered to keep quiet about it. If only they'd known the consequences at the time. It was as though they'd been through hell and back to pay for their sins. It was time to put a stop to it.

The farmhouse stood in solitude. A wicked, evil building that held so much horror. So much torment. Shining his phone torch on a cracked window, he placed his face to the glass and peered into the blackness. There were no shadows standing waiting for him, and there was no sign of Liv.

Remembering the door at the back of the farmhouse, Connor crept along the path, hearing his boots drag along the ground.

A snapping noise came from behind him.

Shit! Leaning against the wall, he waited, listening hard, ready if someone approached. *Did the bush move?* He shone the torch across the narrow path and scanned the area. After waiting in silence for what felt like hours, he stood and made his way to the back door. Again, he shone the torch into the kitchen, seeing it in the same shitty state as it had been when he and Liam had been here. Reaching inside through the cracked window, he shoved the handle down and pushed the door open. Lucas had said the hatch was in the corner of the kitchen.

The smell was worse than he remembered. Mouldy cheese, socks, and vomit. That's how he'd describe it, all blended together and boiled in a pan. He felt his stomach twist as though about to puke and fought to keep it down.

Outside, he heard the sharp rustle of grass caught in the
wind as it swept one way and another. Then a clunk, as
though a gate was banging against a post.

Clunk.

Clunk.

In the corner, Connor pulled the lino back, shone the
torch at the floor, and found the hatch Lucas and Marie had
talked about.

Taking a long, deep, lungful of air, he dropped to his
knees and lifted it.

He shone the torch over the stairs, revealing wood that
was bulging and warped. There were cracks in each step,
and dry rot was evident. As he descended, the steps bowed
under his weight, each one groaning like a rusty nail being
pried from timber. Reaching the bottom step, he collected
his thoughts, steadying himself and shining the torch on the
wall. *Excellent. The key is where they said.* With a shaky hand,
he lifted it off the hook – it was heavier than he imagined –
and placed it in the lock. Twisting it slowly, aware the noise
could attract attention, Connor unlocked the metal door
and pulled it back.

He stepped into the basement, reminiscent of a
dungeon, and could almost smell evil in the air. It was stuffy,
thick, and suffocating, as though tainted with depravity.

Closing the door behind him, he reached for a light,
flicked the switch, and gasped.

Each of the cell doors was open and every cell was
empty.

Bastards, he said to himself. He walked around, imagining
how Liv must have felt while locked up. The panic, fear, and

everything else she must have experienced while caged up like a wild animal. He could almost sense it, the desperation clinging to the walls. Each cell had a chain attached to the wall with a leather strap. *How did she cope?* he wondered. As he moved closer, angst gripping him like a vice and the smell of urine and excrement overbearing, he choked up. The floor was stained with piss and blood from where the captives lay and had tried to pull away from the chains that held them. Connor imagined them night after night, staring into the darkness and held behind the iron bars.

It all became too much for him. Suddenly he snapped out of the trance, his mind so occupied with the horror that he'd forgotten Liv had been taken out of the farmhouse.

Quickly, he turned and opened the metal door, closing it again behind him, and rushed up the stairs.

Racing to the living room window, he looked out across the fields, seeing only a dark blanket over the horizon.

Where are you? What have these evil fuc—? Footsteps rushed behind him. Connor felt his legs turn to jelly. He stumbled as the sound was right upon him. Then, the footsteps ceased.

'Lucas. What is wrong with you? Where did you go? Mother's going to be so very cross!'

At the last second, Connor grabbed a broken brass ornament from the window sill, turned, and cracked Fred Kipler across the face. He slumped to the floor, banging the back of his head, and whined in pain.

As Connor booted him in the face, Fred grabbed his leg, knocking him backwards. He jumped up and rugby-tackled Connor, the two of them landing head-first over the rickety sofa. The legs collapsed, and Fred tried to reach for one of them to use as a weapon.

For the next few seconds, they wrestled each other,

Connor whacking him in the face several times while Fred shoved him against the wall.

'Where is Liv?' screamed Connor as he spun Fred's body and wrapped an arm around his throat. 'You freak! What have you done to her?'

'She's dead. You'll never beat us,' insisted Fred, his throat croaky from the lack of oxygen. 'Do you hear? I will always come after you. That's a promise.'

Grabbing his top, Connor launched Fred across the living room floor and rushed at him. Fred only laughed hysterically, wiping the blood from his lip as he stood.

'You'll never beat me! You don't have the fucking balls.'

As he gasped, watching Fred race into the kitchen, Connor followed, ducked and rammed him head first, using the weight of his body.

Stumbling backwards, Fred tried to grab something to support him and fell through the hatch and down the stairs.

Connor hurried down after him. Seeing Fred almost unconscious, he dragged him into the basement and hauled him into a cell. As Fred managed to climb to his feet, Connor quickly closed the door, hearing it automatically lock.

'You stupid prick. You won't get out of here,' spouted Fred. 'Open the door. Connor! Open the door.'

'Let's see how you like it,' Connor said as he shut the basement door. Then he left the farmhouse.

She's dead. She's dead. Connor struggled with the threat Fred Kipler had made. *Please, God, don't let it be true.*

He shone his phone torch, walking across the narrow road and into the rugged fields, hoping he'd see a light or hear a shuffle in the darkness. Anything to show that Liv was out here. Lucas and Marie had claimed Fred's mother was part of it. So where the heck was she?'

The farmhouse was far behind him now, and the rough ground and heavy boots made it awkward to walk. Fred's threat wouldn't leave his head. It felt like a tune you'd hear first thing in the morning, only to have it play over and over in your head all day.

She's dead.

As he approached the trees, a deafening crack rang out around him. He was certain it was gunfire. 'No. No, No. Please, not Liv.'

There was no sign or warning. It was silent until something rammed into the back of his neck.

'Hands where I can see them!'

'Angela, you don't have to do this,' begged Connor.

'You!' she howled. 'Connor Murphy. Even better!'

Wondering for the briefest of moments what she was talking about, Connor suddenly realised she'd initially thought he was Lucas.

'Please,' he said, trying to turn around, 'it doesn't have to end like this.'

'No? Don't tell me what I should and shouldn't do! You want to know how long I've waited for this moment? It's all I think about. The first thought in the morning and last at night. While I sleep, I can smell the fear. I've counted the days until I get to watch you all squirm.'

'I don't doubt it's excited you. But Angela, you have to listen to me. It was a mistake. Christ, we didn't mean for Nathan to die.' His arms were getting tired, and it felt like his body was closing down from fear.

'You took everything from me. Everything,' she screamed, raising the rifle from his neck to Connor's head.

He thought about the time Mrs Franklin had ordered them into the classroom, threatening them with what would happen if they said anything. It was no good trying to reason with this psycho. She wouldn't listen. But he had to try. The words almost blurted from his mouth. That he and Ella pleaded with Liam to leave Nathan out of it. If they'd only known how it would turn out, maybe they could have done more. But Liam was determined. Nothing could stop him and his silly prank. Taking a deep breath, Connor said, 'We were kids. Christ, can't you see that? Liam, Ella, and me, don't you think we're tormented enough how the prank turned out? It's something that will never leave us. A noose around our necks. I think about it all the time. We all do.'

'It's not enough! An eye for an eye, don't they say? My boy is dead! My husband committed suicide because of what you all did. Look at Fred! Nothing more than a freak. You've taken everything from me. You've ruined my life. Now it's my turn.'

As Angela squeezed the trigger, about to pump Connor with a bullet, someone came charging over, knocking her to the ground. The gun went off, firing the bullet in the air.

'Run, Connor!' Liv grabbed his hand, and they sprinted through the dark fields.

Once they'd gained enough distance from Angela and the farmhouse, they stopped and turned to each other. Connor gently pulled Liv into his arms, holding his face against hers, feeling wet tears roll down her cheeks. Her short hair was dry and messy, and the bags were pronounced under her eyes. Her lips were chapped, and she had bruises on her face.

'I thought I'd never see you again. I can't believe it's you.'

Liv's body shook in his arms. She was dehydrated, her clothes were stained, and she stank, but she'd made it out alive. 'I'd like to go home now.'

'Oh, that might be a little tricky,' Connor laughed.

'Why?'

'Well, half the town is after us.'

'Huh?' Liv asked.

'It's a long story. Once we get reception, we'll call the police. It's a heck of a story. I just hope they believe us.'

'Wait! Lucas and Marie. Have you found them?'

'They're safe and up by the tent.'

'Tent?' Liv's eyebrows dropped with the confusion.

'Again, a long story. Let's get to the others.'

As they rushed hand in hand towards the car, Liv joked, 'Don't ever leave me again. If someone wants to exhibit their art, put the phone down.'

'It's a great hiding place, right?' Connor opened the passenger door, helping Liv into the seat. He thought it was a dream, and any second, he'd wake up and find her gone.

'It's genius,' she joked. 'Jesus, you can see the roof. Whose wise idea was it?'

'We're hardly spoilt for choice! We need to be quick. Let's drive up to the tent and grab the others.' Placing the key in the ignition, Connor tapped the clutch and glanced at Liv.

'Look at the state of the car! Let me guess. Long story. What's up?' she asked, placing her seatbelt on.

'I think the battery is dead. I left the lights on.'

'Oh, shit, Connor. She's going to find us.'

Opening the door, he rushed to the boot, constantly checking around for Angela. She'd fallen hard, but it wouldn't be long until she got back up.

Connor grabbed the portable jump-starter, and powered the device up.

'How long does it take?' Liv asked with desperation in her tone.

'I don't know. A few minutes, I'm guessing.'

'Oh, Connor, please be quick!' He could see that the trauma was beginning to take shape. Fred Kipler, his mother, and being locked in a hellhole thinking she was going to die. Her body looked drenched in anxiety, and she rocked back and forth in the passenger seat, as if desperate to blank out the noise in her mind. She pulled at her hair, small clumps coming out in her hands, and shuffled in the seat.

'Liv, we're getting out of here. Another minute, and we'll be on our way. Please hold it together. I'm here, and I won't let anything happen to you again. Listen to my voice. Are you doing that?'

'Yes,' she answered, 'but please hurry!' Scrambling back to the driver's seat, Connor placed his foot back on the clutch and turned the key. 'Yes, you beauty!'

Liv sighed hard. 'Thank God!'

Connor ripped the leads off the battery, closed the bonnet and got back in the car. He dumped the device in the footwell, released the handbrake, and jabbed the accelerator. At the same moment, a shadow bolted in front of him.

'You fuckers aren't going anywhere.' Angela had the rifle trained on the front windscreen, steering it back and forth between Connor and Liv.

'Do something!' roared Liv.

'You wanna bet?' Slamming his foot hard on the accelerator, the vehicle surged forward, hitting Angela and knocking her back. Then Connor reversed, carrying out a three-point turn, and drove towards the tent.

An almighty crack rang out as the rear glass shattered. Connor lost control, almost hitting a tree. 'Get down!' he ordered, gaining control of the car. 'The bitch is shooting at us. She's relentless.'

Another crack echoed over the valley as a bullet tore into the back bumper.

In the rearview mirror, Connor could see Angela hurl the rifle to the ground.

～

'It's just here. We've been hiding in the tent for a couple of days.' Connor could see his girlfriend's confused stare. 'Don't worry, I'll explain later.'

They saw Ella first. She rushed over to the passenger seat, hugging Liv as hard as she could.

'We heard gunfire,' Ella said. 'Are any of you hit?'

'We're good. But it was a close call,' responded Liv. 'We need to get going. It won't be long before she's up here. Are you ready?'

'You bet. I never thought I'd hate camping so much,' Ella quipped.

Liam joined them, again darting to Liv and giving her a hug. 'Don't ever do this to us again,' he ordered, jumping into the back.

'Oh' – Liv pointed to Lucas and Marie – 'can we give them a lift? They kept me going.'

Yeah, thought Connor. *They kept us on our toes as well.*

～

Angela reached the farmhouse and went in the back door. 'Fred. Are you here? Sugar pie, it's Momma.' After searching the farmhouse, she lifted the hatch and descended the stairs into the basement. Her mouth opened in shock, and she giggled at seeing her son locked in a cell. 'Now, why are you so very stupid, sugar pie? Wait there. I'll be back in a minute.'

Fred didn't answer her as she walked up the stairs.

Under the sofa, Angela found the set of keys for each cell bunched together. She made a stop in the kitchen before returning to the basement. Walking over to Fred, she placed the key in the lock.

Her son grabbed the iron bars, squeezing them in his fists with frustration.

Suddenly, she dropped the keys on the floor.

'What are you doing?' asked Fred. 'Hurry! I have to get out of here.'

'Is that right?' quipped Angela, kicking the keys across the floor.

'Mother, what's going on?'

Placing her face against the cold iron bars, she spouted, 'What's going on? I'll tell you exactly what's going on. Why do you think I nursed you back to health? It was you, sugar pie. All of it was your fault.'

'This isn't a fucking joke. Grab the keys and let me out of here. Now!'

'Oh,' Angela said, 'you'd like that, wouldn't you? You drove me out of the house once, but not this time. You're the one going now.'

'Going where? Open the door,' Fred roared.

'You set fire to the school. I wish it had been you instead of Nathan. I fucking hate you with every fibre of my body. You killed your father, and you killed my son. How did you not realise you were part of the plan? How stupid are you, Fred Kipler?'

'Please don't do this,' begged Fred.

'They say twins are in tune with one another. Well, now you'll feel exactly what Nathan felt. I hope you burn in hell.'

Angela emptied the can of petrol, dousing her son in it. Then, she doused a rag in the fuel, lit it, and threw it into Fred's cell.

His desperate screams for help bellowed as she climbed the stairs and left the farmhouse.

43

Tuesday Night

Leaving the farmhouse and tent behind, Connor pulled away from the narrow track and onto the A259. He'd never felt more relief, and with Liv sitting next to him in the passenger seat, he had hope. They were going to build a life together, live out their dreams, and grab every opportunity to be a success. He needed to give Liv time to cope with the terrible trauma of being locked in Fred Kipler's basement and to hold her, reassure her, and be her rock with every trauma she faced. He'd get her the help needed, no matter what the cost. It felt like he was in the presence of a celebrity as Liam and Ella fired questions at her, but Connor needed to give her headspace.

'Guys,' Connor remarked, 'give her a chance to adapt. Enough with the interrogation already.'

Placing a rough, dry hand on Connor's lap, she whispered, 'It's fine.'

Connor did everything to restrain himself. Lucas and Marie had put them through hell, and if it hadn't been for Liv, he would have left them behind in the field. He had to understand that they, too, were kidnapped and ordered to participate in the twisted games. Whatever beef he had with them went out the window as Lucas asked if he could borrow a phone again.

Connor reached behind him to hand his over. 'Knock yourself out.'

Dialling the number, Lucas accidentally put it on the loudspeaker. A woman answered, and you could hear the pain in her voice. 'Hello?'

'Jocelyn. It's me. It's... Lucas.'

The ache in her voice was unmistakable. She howled, gasping for breath as she tried to speak, but the heavy gasps and choking noises made it difficult.

'I'll take it, Mummy,' a young voice said, sounding like an angel. 'Daddy, is it you?'

'It's me, sweetheart. I've missed you so very much.'

'I've missed you too. Are you coming home now?'

Unable to control his grief, Lucas desperately tried to speak through the sobs. 'I'm coming home now, sweetheart.'

'Daddy, you've been on the news. I see your face all the time. Mummy has been crying a lot, but she'll be happy now. Everyone at school keeps asking me how I am. Even the horrible teacher, Mr Edwards.'

'Has he, darling? Look, I'm going to get myself together and catch a flight as soon as I can. I love you both so very much.'

'We love you too, Daddy. Hurry up and get home. I'll make your favourite pancakes. Love you.'

'Love you too, darling.'

On the drive back to Rye, they decided to go to the flat. The
first thing Liv wanted was a hot shower and a change of
clothes. As did Lucas and Marie. One after the other, they
drenched their tired, stressed bodies under the hot water.
Connor let Lucas keep the clothes he'd worn after they'd
swapped outside the tent, and Liv found a clean pair of
black leggings and a jumper for Marie. The latter hadn't
called her family yet. The embarrassment was too much,
and she didn't quite know what to say to her parents. The
drugs were going to be a problem. She'd have to find a way
to deal with it and hope Angela didn't honour the threat of
sending the photos.

After Connor had showered and put on a clean tee-shirt
and jeans, he dialled 999, briefly telling the story of how Liv
had been kidnapped and Angela Bennett was still on the
loose in Rye.

The call handler instructed them to wait at the property
and that officers would be there soon.

When the officers arrived, they checked over the flat to
make sure it was secure and took separate statements from
all six of them.

'And you say this woman, Angela Bennett, and her son,
Fred Kipler, kept you locked in the basement?' Officer Willis
asked, jotting down notes.

'Yes. I was home alone on Saturday. Connor, my
boyfriend, went to meet a potential client. While we Face-
Timed' – Liv pointed at Lucas – 'he broke in with Fred and
abducted me.'

'He did? This man here?' the officer confirmed, with a confused stare.

'Yes. But you don't understand. Lucas was taken as well, from his home in Paris. Oh, and Marie.'

'Officer,' Lucas intervened, 'it's er... complicated. You see, Angela and her son Fred were hellbent on revenge. Something that happened at school. It's beside the point. While they held us captive, I heard their twisted plans. They were so excited, plotting and talking for hours about what they'd do. It was sick. Marie, this lady here,' confirmed Lucas, 'and I were forced to do things.'

'What type of things?' Officer Denham asked.

'Fuck with all our heads – excuse my language,' Marie stated. 'Psychological torture! They threatened to ruin our lives and kill our families if we didn't obey their instructions.'

'You're telling us' – Officer Denham's voice was stern – 'you were forced to take part in these crimes?' To Connor, she asked, 'Why didn't you call for help sooner?'

Connor was sitting on a chair, holding Liv's hand and unable to take his eyes off her. To the officers, he answered, 'They said they'd kill her. As soon as I contacted the police, it would seal her fate. How scared do you think we all were?' Watching the police take notes, he shouted, 'Angela! She's still out there. You need to find her.'

Officer Willis left the room to call in the emergency, asking for officers to attend the farmhouse and check over the area.

Connor showed Officer Denham the photos that had been sent via WhatsApp showing a knife held at Liv's throat. 'See. This is the reason I didn't call the police. I was terrified.' He described the video footage that had been emailed of Frank Dawson being mutilated, the clothes with the warning tags delivered to Ella, and the Facebook page, Rye News, showing the recording of Lucas and Marie pushing someone onto the road in front of a moving vehicle. Luckily, the man hadn't been badly injured and was recovering in hospital with broken ribs. They gave the names of the priest, the young woman, Jennifer, who worked at the cafe, and the nurse at the facility to help verify their story.

Officer Willis walked back into the kitchen. 'Officers are on their way to the scene now. Someone has called in to report a fire. A farmhouse off the A259. The firefighters have it under control. We're actively investigating a suspect near the area.' Once the officers had taken statements from everyone, they eyed the room sceptically.

We'll need each of you to be available for follow-ups,' Officer Willis ordered. 'If you remember anything else, call us immediately. Until we locate Angela Bennett, we need to take precautions.'

∾

Angela Bennett was arrested just minutes after the police left Connor's flat.

An officer read Angela her rights, and told her she was being arrested under suspicion of kidnapping, false imprisonment, arson, and murder. Angela was taken into custody and transported to a police station for further questioning. At the station and while being quizzed, she confessed to everything, including starting the fire in the basement of the farmhouse.

Once it was safe, crime scene investigators moved in and went to work, discovering the charred remains of her son, Fred Kipler, in a basement cell.

It was four days before Lucas and Marie were allowed to

return home after lengthy follow-up statements and a full confession from Angela Bennett, claiming total responsibility. Given the trauma of captivity and forced participation in the crimes, they were encouraged to stay for debriefing, counselling, and psychological evaluation.

Both wanted to get as far away as possible from the memories of Fred Kipler, Angela Bennett and the prison under the farmhouse.

44

F*ive Days Later*

'It's Fred Kipler. The charred body in the basement. They've confirmed it.' Connor placed the tea and toast on the bedside table, seeing Liv stretch. 'I just heard it on the radio.'

'What time is it?' she asked, stretching her arms and yawning.

'Just gone eight. It's Sunday. We have the day off.'

'You're an arse! We've been off all week. Look, I don't want special treatment, you hear?' Liv rubbed her finger along Connor's smooth face. After seeing Lucas, who was a dead ringer for him, he'd shaved off the stubble and decided to let his hair grow out. When he looked in the mirror, all he could see was the image of Lucas on the FaceTime call.

'It's not special treatment, Liv. I told you, whatever it takes, I'm here for your recovery.'

Sipping her tea, she thanked him.

Connor's phone pinged. Every time it did, his body froze. 'Oh, it's a joint call with Ella and Liam. Hey, you guys. What's happening?'

'Pub! That's what's happening. You guys up for it?' asked Liam.

'Er.' He looked at his girlfriend, still unable to believe she was back in their bed, and watched her nodding enthusiastically. 'Sure,' answered Connor. 'Say lunchtime?'

'It's a plan,' Ella responded. 'See you all there.'

'Okay.' Placing the tray of drinks on the table, Liam listed them aloud. 'Two beers, a gin and tonic, and a large red wine. Get them down you.'

The barmaid looked over. 'I hope you're not going to spill them and make a mess like last time?'

A flush rose on Connor's face. 'No. I'm good.' He laughed, sipping the beer. 'It's mental to think that a few days ago we almost had a hit out on us. I never thought we'd see this town again. Shit! Did you hear about Fred Kipler? They found his body in the basement.'

Stirring her gin and tonic, Ella sucked it through the straw. 'How evil can someone be? I mean, when we escaped, she must have gone back into the farmhouse, down to the basement, and set her own son on fire. It's mental! What a sick bitch!'

'Mind you,' Liam piped up, 'if you had a son like Fred, wouldn't you set fire to him?'

'No, mate!' smirked Connor. 'Too soon. That's just too soon. You've lowered the tone, mate.'

'It's what we were all thinking!' said Ella. She turned to Liv. 'How are you doing hun?'

'Oh, good and bad days. I wake sometimes, thinking I'm still locked in the cell. I hear the bars clanging, and Fred's there with a baseball bat. It's a reoccurring dream. I manage to escape, and he chases me through the fields.' She jolted, as if an icy chill had driven through her body.

'It must have been horrendous. We're here. Anything you need. You know that, don't you?' Ella placed a hand in hers.

Liv's eyes blurred. 'I know. Right now, I just want to get pissed.'

Lifting his glass, Connor clunked his drink with the others'. 'Sounds like a plan.'

'I know you both had doppelgängers. Ella had Marie, and you had Lucas. What am I?' Liam remarked. 'Chopped liver?'

Liv spat her drink out. At least she could see the funny side of it. 'I've missed you guys so bloody much!'

'One thing I want to know?' Placing his drink on the table, Connor looked between the other three. 'If there were only two doppelgängers, who was Mrs Franklin's nephew?'

'Good point,' said Liam. 'She was certain it was him, only he's been dead for ten years.'

Leaning into the table, Ella widened her eyes. 'Maybe it was his ghost.'

'No.' Liv took another sip of her drink and placed the glass on the table. 'It was Fred. I heard him and his mother planning it while they were in the basement. They couldn't find anyone quick enough who looked like him. And they worried about having too many people locked down there. So Fred found a picture of him on the internet and made some kind of mask. He said he'd wear a hoodie so she could only see the face. Let's be real. If you glimpse at anything quickly enough, your mind can fool you.'

'Fucking freaks,' spat Ella. 'Have you heard from Lucas and Marie?'

'Yeah. Well, Lucas, anyway. Marie was going back to face so much shit. Angela took pictures of her with drugs,' Liv said, 'and I think she was having sex with her dad's best mate. They're going to find the proof on Angela's phone. Poor sod is really in for it when the police see the evidence. So I doubt she'll call.'

'Not from a prison cell anyway,' Liam said. 'Nathan Kipler trapped in the fire, burning to a crisp, and about to expire. Freaky Fred tried to save his double, but Mummy burned him, and now she's in trouble. Sorry, I know. I know. Too soon.'

45

The Past

Stirring in her bed, Greta Franklin felt an arm around her. 'Did I wake you?' Her husband's hand felt heavy on her body.

'Don't worry, love. You were tossing and turning. At one stage, you mentioned his name again. Fred. Look, it's only a job. Why not look for another one? If he's getting to you that much, it's not worth it.'

Greta got out of bed and dressed. 'I'm going to be late. Are you working from home today?'

'Yeah, I'll start in a while. Don't let him bully you. Do you hear?'

With a raised voice, she said, 'Albert. There's nothing I can do. Jesus. How long have I been there? Twelve, thirteen years. I've seen them all, and I've dealt with them. I've got through it.'

'I know you, Greta. I've never seen you this troubled before. The stress will end up giving you a stroke. You have to do something.'

'We can't afford for me to retire. I love it there. It's just—' Standing in front of the full-length mirror, she fixed her hair and grabbed a jacket from the wardrobe. 'He's evil. The way he speaks to me. I'm terrified of him.'

'Well, let me come to the school. I'll say something to him. It's not fair. Christ, there's always someone who'll spoil the party.'

Kissing Albert on the side of the face, Greta left the bedroom, knowing she didn't want her husband to turn up at the school. She had her reasons.

'You have to do something. I'm at my wit's end here.' Greta leaned over the table, fearing it would fall over. Mr Conway sat, staring at her through his thick glasses, wisps of his hair falling to the side.

'Leave it with me. I'll sort it,' he promised. 'Where is he now?'

'I don't know. He stormed out of the room. It's a complete disruption having him in my class. I can't cope anymore. The stress is making me ill.' She went to say something and hesitated briefly. 'I'm on tablets. Valium. You didn't know that, did you?'

'No, I didn't, Greta. Look, do you want time off? It would have to be unpaid, but I could get a stand in for a week, just to give you a break, let you destress.'

'I can't afford it,' said Greta. 'Albert and I are struggling to make ends meet. I'm begging you to do something about Fred Kipler.'

'And I said I will. I'll suspend him for a week.'

'Suspend him!' she said, her mouth agape. 'What the heck would that do? Like... Like a holiday. Oh yes, that will work.'

Fiddling with his tie, Mr Conway was clearly starting to get frustrated with Greta's tone. 'If, after the week, his behaviour hasn't changed, we'll call his father in and stress that Fred could be expelled.'

'Do it now!' urged Greta. 'Why wait?'

'Because these things take time. Trust me on this: the suspension will be in place as of now, and then, if needed, we'll take further steps.'

Unable to control the tears, Greta raced out of the office, her head spinning so hard she thought she'd collapse.

Her nerves took over. Greta feared she'd have a stroke. She fell against the wall, trying desperately to calm down. Dust seemed to dance across her eyes, and it felt as though her blood pressure was through the roof.

'Greta, goodness, are you alright?' Frank Dawson surged across the corridor, helping her up and bringing her into the staff toilet. 'Here, wet your face.' With his hands cupped, he turned on the taps and patted her skin down.

'I'm fine,' she insisted. 'I had a funny turn, that's all.'

'Do I need to ask who caused it?'

Greta didn't answer the question. Instead, she filled him in on her visit to Mr Conway's office.

'Well, that's a good thing. It's progress.'

'It's not. He'll get suspended. Maybe his parents will be called in. But Mr Conway doesn't believe in expelling a pupil. He'd rather work with them. He told me that before. He will never, ever expel Fred Kipler!'

Frank placed his strong arms around Greta, holding her face to his chest.

Pulling back, she looked into his eyes, and they kissed hard on the lips. It wasn't the first time.

Suddenly, a shadow appeared through the outside window.

Someone saw them.

~

The Next Morning.

'Hey. You three. What are you doing in the science lab unsupervised?' Frank's voice echoed from outside the door. 'No one is allowed in there without a teacher.'

Mrs Franklin came out of the staff toilet and joined them in the corridor, still fixing her hair. 'What's the racket?'

'I found these three in the science lab unattended.'

'What were you doing in there? Connor. Ella. Liam. Answer me!' Mrs Franklin waited, watching the gormless, blank expressions. 'Right, well, detention then. Starting now. Go and wait in Mr Conway's office.' To Frank, she said, 'I'll deal with them. They're good kids. I'm sure it was something innocent. I had more problems with Fred this morning. I bloody knew Mr Conway wouldn't suspend him. I'm at my wits end. What's wrong?' she asked.

'Can you smell that?' asked Frank.

Inhaling heavily, Mrs Franklin walked further along the corridor towards the science lab. 'Oh shit. A fire. Oh my God. There's a fire. Quick.'

With his mobile phone, Frank smashed the glass of an alarm. The piercing noise was almost deafening. Kids charged from classrooms as a small explosion came from the science lab.

The pupils were out at the far end of the playing fields. Most of them stood in disbelief. There was a muffled cry for help from the store room.

'Did you hear that?' Pointing across the room, Frank stated, 'I think someone's in there.' Looking desperate, he rushed to the store room, trying to reach the fire extinguishers. 'Who's down there?' he called at the top of his voice.

'Nathan... Nathan Kipler. They've tied me up. Help!'

Another explosion caused Frank to stumble backwards, the heat intense.

'It's Nathan,' he bellowed.

Grabbing Frank by the arm, Mrs Franklin ordered, 'Leave him. It's not worth risking your life.'

Frank grabbed her hand, but she pulled away, watching him rush out into the school yard. Behind her, Fred Kipler climbed in through the window. She watched as he worked his way across the room and opened the door to the store room. She wanted to call out and plead for him not to go down there. To run as fast as he could to safety. But she didn't. She couldn't. Instead, Greta walked to the store room. She saw Fred, his arm linked with his brother's, climbing the stairs.

'Are you alright?' Greta called out. 'Quick, as fast as you can.'

'No thanks to you,' Fred spat. 'You left the class unattended again.'

'What are you talking about? Hurry!'

'It's all your fault. Nathan could have died.' The brothers

were near the top of the stairs, coughing profusely and desperately trying to clear their throats.

'Come on. Only a few more steps,' ordered Greta.

'I saw you through the staff toilet window – you and Frank. Wait until everyone finds out. It will ruin you. I wonder what your husband and Mr Conway will say.'

As if temporarily insane, her mind snapped, Greta slammed the store room door and locked it.

Both Fred and Nathan pounded on the door, screaming for help.

After a couple of minutes, the stairs collapsed, and Nathan plunged to his death, burning alive.

Fred managed to break the lock and get the door open. In his struggle to get to the playground, his arms and legs caught fire, and the poisonous fumes were about to take effect.

46

O*ne Year Later*

'I can't believe it. It's really ours?' Liv looked like she was floating on air as she spun on the gallery floor. 'We did it, Connor. We really did it.'

'I told you we would,' stated Connor, his eyes filled with pride. 'Christ, Mr Humphries was so pleased when we got the business loan. At least he knows it's in safe hands.'

Let's go see it again.' Connor's fiancée linked her arm into his, her back straight, and they stepped out of the shop like they were walking along the yellow brick road. Looking above the gallery, they saw the name written in white, glowing against a neon backdrop.

Livonner's Gallery.

'It's perfect. Excited?' asked Connor, almost feeling the adrenaline surge through Liv's body.

'I couldn't be more happy. Thank you so, so much. We'll make this work. I promise.'

'I have no doubt. Oh, that's a great painting in the window,' stated Connor, seeing a ballerina balancing on her toes and her arms outstretched. 'Who's the artist?'

'Oh, her name is Liv Jenkins. Do you like it?' she laughed.

'I do. She's extremely talented.'

'Well, come inside, sir. I can sort you out with a small discount.'

Back inside, Liv began sifting through the art. 'I think this one would look better over here. What do you think?'

'Yeah, it's an eye-opener. Maybe above the counter?'

The phone rang. Liv answered and put it on speaker-phone. 'Livonner's gallery, Rye, how may I help?' It would take time to remember the new greeting, but they loved it. A play on both their names.

'Hi. I'd like to enquire about displaying some of my paintings. Could I speak with the owner?'

'Oh,' answered Liv, feeling her skin tingling with excite-ment, 'I'm one of the owners.'

'Great,' the woman said. 'Would it be possible to meet with you?'

Connor felt the memories come flooding back. Him on a train and the FaceTime call. Neither of them were ready to explore that avenue yet.

'I'm afraid you would have to come to us,' Liv said. 'I can give you the address. How about this Saturday?'

'That sounds great. Looking forward to it.'

Liv gave her the address and ended the call.

The bell chimed above the front door.

'Shut up, already. You're kidding me. It's awesome.' Ella

rushed over and hugged both Liv and Connor. 'You've done it. Shit! I'm so bloody pleased for you both.'

Liam bowled in a few seconds later. 'Come on. Livonner's Gallery. Yes, guys.'

'You know you'll have to take up art, Connor,' Ella instructed. 'She'll get rich and famous one day and leave you on your arse.'

'I am an artist. A piss artist,' joked Connor.

'Yeah,' laughed Liv. 'That would be right.'

Connor went to the coffee machine and made drinks while Liv showed them around. They'd just decorated the shop, but there was still so much to do.

'I love this one. Is it yours?' asked Ella.

'Yeah. Do you think it's too expensive?'

'No way. You're talented. Know your worth!'

Liam grabbed a coffee and took a slug. 'Have they found her yet?'

'No. It's been three days. I haven't slept since we heard. Christ, it never goes away.' Connor looked at Liv, annoyed that the bad news had put a dampener on the party.

'How's she holding up?' asked Liam.

'She's trying to put it out of her mind. But it's difficult.'

'How did they let Angela escape from the psychiatric ward?' asked Liam, sipping his coffee. 'It's beyond comprehension.'

'I don't think she'll come back here,' surmised Connor. 'It's too risky for her.'

'You think? She's batshit crazy. It wouldn't surprise me after what that psycho did.'

'Do me a favour,' whispered Connor. 'Don't mention it to Liv.'

'Understood!'

For the next couple of hours, the four friends chatted,

drinking copious amounts of coffee and laughing together. They never mentioned Angela's or Fred's names. It was as though they had never existed. The memories were too painful, and they had to deal with it in their own ways.

At just gone 7 pm, customers began flooding into the gallery. Connor and Liv held hands behind the counter, proud of what they'd achieved together. They'd spent the afternoon setting up tables with drinks and food to celebrate the official opening. The two of them, with the help of Ella and Liam, walked around with trays of champagne, handing glasses out. Even Jennifer, the waitress from the cafe, turned up to wish them congratulations and Liv spoke with her briefly, offering her a job. She was now studying art at uni and was overwhelmed with the offer of a position.

A reporter approached them, pushing through the crowds of people. 'Are you the owners?'

Having to think for a moment, Liv answered, 'Yes. How can we help?'

'A picture please for Rye News.'

'Oh, absolutely.' She grabbed Connor's hand, and they walked around the counter.

'Can we have these two in the photo as well?' asked Connor, beckoning Ella and Liam over.

'No problem. Okay, bunch a little closer. That's it. A wry smile, please. Ha ha, get it, "Rye" smile?' The photographer listened to the groans as he clicked the camera. 'Right you are. This will make the front page. Congratulations to you both.'

They all thanked him and tore into the champagne.

For the next hour, Liv and Connor observed everyone

chatting, laughing together, and admiring the paintings, many of them hers. They'd never felt happier, and whatever happened in the past was slowly becoming a distant memory.

'So,' Connor said, 'a successful day. Do you think you'll ever tire of it?'

'Never, we're living the dream,' Liv answered, with her arms wrapped around his neck. 'So, I was thinking, we could open a franchise. We could have galleries all over Britain. Then, Europe and America. The Far East.'

'Whoa! Steady there soldier. Rye is perfectly fine for now. Imagine the stress. And you'd be painting all the time, I'd never get to see you.'

'Don't start getting all possessive on me now, Connor Murphy.'

'As if! Anyway, I'm the boss. I tell you what and when you paint.'

'Er, I'm the boss and the one with the talent,' she jested.

'I can paint!'

'Yeah, go on then.' Placing a piece of paper on the counter, Liv handed him a pen. 'Draw your favourite thing. I'll mark it out of ten.'

'Okay, then.' Connor drew a stick man. 'How's that?'

'I give up!'

'Erm, art is subjective.'

'So, you're telling me if you drew this and put it in a frame, someone would buy it.'

'I think so,' Connor said sheepishly. 'I mean, look at the ballerina at the front. It looks like a frog.'

'Oh, really?'

'Yes.'

Fine,' she laughed, throwing a wet tea towel in his face.

Connor's phone rang. He grabbed it from the counter and saw it was a FaceTime call. They always made him dubious. Liv was locking up and turning off lights. They'd planned to meet Ella and Liam after the last of the well-wishers left the gallery.

'Hey, Mum. I was worried when I didn't hear from you. Is everything alright?'

'Yes. We're fine.' Connor's mother scanned the phone over the marina, showing the moored boats and dazzling lights from the bar area.

'It looks amazing. Are you enjoying Spain?'

'Stop worrying. It's great. The weather's glorious. We're all at the bar.'

'And Liam's parents aren't pushing you too hard?'

'No. They've been wonderful. We're going out on the boat again tomorrow. You want to see it. It's massive. I've been sunbathing most of the time. They've been scuba diving, and I think they want to go and explore caves tomorrow.' Laughing, she said, 'I'll leave them to it. I'm too old for all that now.'

'Well, be careful. Don't do anything you don't want to. Are Ella's parents enjoying themselves?'

'Yes. Stop worrying. We're all getting along fine. I know you were dubious about me going with them, but I've been taking it easy. Honestly, it's such a laugh.'

'I was only worried because they're adrenaline junkies. I'm much younger, and I couldn't keep up with them.'

'How is the gallery going?' his mother asked.

'Amazing. The launch was incredible. So many people turned up. Oh, and get this: we've made it to the front page of Rye News. We're just closing up. Liv is in her element. You want to see her.'

'I bet. She deserves all the success. Sorry,' she corrected herself, 'you both do! Especially after all you've been through.'

'Thanks,' Connor said. 'Enjoy the rest of the holiday.'

'Oh, tell Ella and Liam there was a break-in late last night. Someone got onto the boat and stole phones. I'm the only one who has a mobile left. Liam's dad woke up and scared them off. I've told them they can use my phone, but they're so busy with activities. They haven't touched one since they've been here.'

'That's worrying. Did Liam's dad get a look at the person?'

'No. It was so dark. I have to go. My battery is about to die.'

'Okay, Mum. Thanks for calling. I love you so much. Are you staying in the bar tonight?'

'Oh, I almost forgot to tell you. It's weird. There's a woman we got friendly with. She's on holiday from Poland. The scary thing is, she's the spit of Angela Bennett. It's her doppelgänger. Obviously, I know it's not her as she's locked up, but the resemblance is uncanny. Hang on, she's beside me. Let me show you.'

'No! Can you hear me, Mum? You have to listen! I have something to tell you about Angela!'

The mobile phone scanned to a woman with short, black hair and heavy bags under her eyes. She stared a sinister glare into the camera and grinned. 'Hello. It's good to meet you,' she said in a weird accent Connor couldn't place. 'I can't wait for them all to come over tonight. Don't worry, I'll take good care of them!' Then, her head began twitching as though she had a tic.

The reception cut in and out.

'Mum. Can you hear me?' screamed Connor. 'You need to listen.'

'The signal is breaking up. I have to go. She's invited us to her place for dinner. A beautiful cottage in the country-side she's booked through Airbnb. It's supposed to be spectacular. No one around for miles. I can't wait to see it. I think the taxis are here. Love you, son. Speak soon.'

'Mum. Don't go. It's her. Mum! Mum! Mum!'

The End

NEWSLETTER.

Sign up to my newsletter and receive a free short story called Seance.

You'll also be able to keep up to date with all my future plans and get an insight into my life as an author.

Here's the link.

https://dl.bookfunnel.com/es984sqtnz

ABOUT THE AUTHOR

Stuart James is an award-winning psychological thriller and horror author and all his novels have been Amazon best sellers.

His thriller, The House On Rectory Lane, recently won The International Book Award in horror fiction and he was shortlisted for TikTok breakthrough author of the year.

Make sure to click the link below and sign up to my newsletter to keep up to date with everything I'm working on.

https://dl.bookfunnel.com/9eeewtcu03

Books by Stuart James.

The House On Rectory Lane.
    Turn The Other Way.
    Apartment Six.
    Stranded.
    Selfie.
    Creeper.
    The Macabre.
    The App.
    The Footage.

ACKNOWLEDGMENTS

Firstly, I'd like to say a huge thank you to my family for your extreme patience and listening to my ideas constantly. I love you so much.

I feel you know my thrillers as well as I do.

Thank you to editor Abigail Fenton for your amazing work and recommendations. You are wonderful.

A huge thank you to everyone on my Facebook page who are the most supportive people I know and my arc group for your ongoing support. I can't thank you enough.

A special mention to these lovely people who always recommend my thriller novels.

Mark Fearn. Book Mark.

The lovely Debbie Schutt.

Susie at Prescription Books.

Also to the incredible book bloggers who have supported my journey so much and to all you wonderful readers.

Also massive thanks to author Lindsay Detwiler whose friendship is cherished.

You really are amazing and I can't thank you all enough.

Make sure to keep up to date with projects I'm working on and sign up to my mailing list at:

https://dl.bookfunnel.com/9eeewtcu03

Also, you can follow me on social media.
I love to hear from readers and will always respond.
Twitter: StuartJames73
Instagram: Stuart James Author
Facebook: Stuart James Author.
TikTok: Stuart James Author

That's it for now.
Once again, thank you so much for choosing,
Doppelgänger.
I've finished a chilling ghost story called Beneath The Fold
and it will be released soon.
Watch this space.
Love to you all and keep safe.
Stuart James.

Printed in Dunstable, United Kingdom